D0726026

Low Country Blood

A Vega & Middleton Mystery

Sue Hinkin

Literary Wanderlust | Denver, Colorado

Low Country Blood is a work of fiction. Names, characters, places, and incidents are the products of the author's imagination and have been used fictitiously. Any resemblance to actual events, locales, or persons, living or dead, is entirely coincidental.

Published in the United States by Literary Wanderlust LLC, Denver, Colorado. www.LiteraryWanderlust.com

ISBN print: 978-1-942856-33-7
ISBN digital: 978-1-942856-37-5

Cover design: Ruth M'Gonigle

Printed in the United States of America

Acknowledgment

Deep gratitude to the Rocky Mountain Fiction Writers (RMFW) and my amazing Thursday night critique group at Tattered Cover in Littleton, especially Mindy McIntyre, Michael Hope aka Michael Arches, Kevin Wolf, Mary Ann Kersten, Michele Winkler, Natasha Christensen, Wendy Howard, Charlie McNamara, and Kathy Reynolds. All amazing writers, teachers and friends.

Sincere gratitude to Susie Brooks, publisher at Literary Wanderlust. It's a privilege to be part of this great indie team.

Props to my husband, Alan Klein, who's been patiently watching me disappear into reading and writing for years, and to my amazing beta readers Lacey Klein, Marlene Simon, and Allicia A. Pickett-Byrden.

And last but definitely not least, thank you my dear Savannah friends and to the City of Savannah where I made my home for five fascinating years.

1

When Marcus "Muhammed" Trotter heard the boy play, he knew without a doubt the kid was the real deal. At fifteen, Jayden Middleton had the voice of a young Stevie Wonder. On his fiddle, he tore up "The Devil Went Down to Georgia" like Charlie Daniels on speed. His chops at the organ would make Bach rise from the grave and shake his old dried-up booty.

Tonight, at Forsyth Park in Savannah, Georgia, half the city had shown up for the Arts Academy High School summer concert, where Middleton's budding genius was on display.

In the darkened wings, Muhammed, former Special Ops, and Blackwater mercenary, now full-time bodyguard to the most important man in the Afghan heroin trade, was to keep a leash on Emad Al Alequi, the boss man's worthless son. With his fist pumpin' and skinny ass bumpin,' Emad was totally into the music scene. As the band let it rip, he edged closer to the musicians. A moth to the formidable flame of Jayden Middleton's electric talent, Emad was in complete thrall.

Muhammed knew there were only two ways to break this kind of spell: crush the moth or put out the seductive fire.

I'm watching you, boy," Muhammed called. He knew he could barely be heard above the sound system, but Emad, who now called himself "Evan Doobius," turned and flashed Marcus the bird. Then he moved even closer to the action. Practically onstage, his hair flared as red as blood in the spotlights.

Muhammed only had to glance at Emad to know what the dude was thinking. He was deciding to give up his lucrative stake in the family business and dedicate his life to taking Middleton's career into the stratosphere. Although Emad's skills were not musical, he had a head for commerce, and managing a rock and roll band was almost as hot as being lead guitar.

This dangerous fantasy had to be nipped in the bud. It could blow their whole operation. The family would have to take a decisive stand on Emad's looming defection. The funky aviator-style shades, the torn T-shirt with the logo of some obscure band, the black nail polish said it all. And if the boy was hiding any tattoos, when his old man found out he would have 'em sliced off with a dull knife.

Tall and lean, with a face and figure as sculpted as an underwear model, Muhammed reached for his own ear and felt the minute dimpled rows of scarred-over piercings. He understood rebellion. The piercings were the least of it. With both parents long gone, his oldest brother had given him an ultimatum: enlist or die. It was a tough decision, but at eighteen years old Muhammed had joined the Special Ops, then later become an operative for Blackwater where he was labeled highly effective but a loose cannon. A decade later, he had found the true religion—the heroin trade. He was not about to let Emad put all this at risk.

Ӿ

The next evening, Muhammed met with Emad's father, Farouk, in the company's worn, dark-paneled office trailer. They sat on sagging folding chairs at a chipped yellow linoleum table. The scent of caffeine and cardamom hung warm and humid in the air. A decrepit window-mounted air conditioner vainly struggled to pump in cool air.

"I reminded Emad for the hundredth time, his only life is with the family business," Muhammed was saying. "Afghani sons respect their fathers and honor their families before themselves. Always." He bowed his head for an instant to show deference. He fucking hated being the boy's handler. He'd rather blow the asshole's brains out and put an end to him once and for all.

"And his response?" Farouk rattled ice cubes in an otherwise empty coffee cup.

"He told me to fuck off and then left with the band. You've asked me to try and guide him, sir, but he's out of control. He shames the family with every word and action." Muhammed's fingers danced like nervous spiders on the table. He clutched his hands together and pressed them to his lap.

Farouk groaned and pulled at his thin, graying hair. A sheen of sweat dampened his thick neck, staining the collar of his brown cotton tunic. Half-frame reading glasses slid off his long nose and fell onto the floor with a clank.

Muhammed suppressed a flicker of satisfaction at Farouk's discomfort as he retrieved the glasses. A repressed piece of him would do anything to replace the asswipe Emad as Farouk's only son. "With all due respect, sir, you never should've sent him to the University of Miami for that accounting degree. Should've done it online, or back in-country."

"Yes," Farouk said, "I admit it was a mistake. That is why, for the honor of our family, this music must stop. The Middleton boy must disappear."

Muhammed shifted in his seat. The metal chair groaned.

"Middleton." Muhammed went still then let out a gasp. He covered his mouth, feigning a cough. How had he missed it? A connection was being made like a finger in a live socket. Synapses fired and hummed as his brain struggled to arrange names, impressions, and old memories. Middleton was not an uncommon name in the area but if this Jayden dog was kin to that bitch Beatrice Middleton—*shee-it*. His hand went to a silvery scar on his jaw that looked like a cat claw had got him good.

Perspiration beaded on his lower lip and he scratched at the stubble on his toast-brown chin. He wasn't supposed to touch the heroin the Al Alequi cartel pumped into the Western economy to destroy the infidels, so instead, he snorted a line of coke once in a while. Even his skin fucking hummed. What could be wrong with an occasional toot? No harm, no foul. It's not like he was a junkie.

"You know of this Middleton boy, personally?" Farouk asked, eyes narrowing.

"Naw, but it just hit me that the dude could be related to someone I used to, uh, hang with when I was at Savannah High School." Muhammed's fingertips drummed the table. "Like a million years ago."

Farouk paused for a moment then filled their cups from a pitcher of iced coffee so strong it made Red Bull feel like weak tea. "We need a plan. Something fast and final."

"Grandfather Parsa won't approve a hit," Muhammed said. Adrenaline pumped hot in his chest, arousal warmed his groin. *Could the kid be related to her?* An opportunity to pull the trigger on one of the bitch's own was a fuckin' gift. He downed the drink and gritted his teeth, ran his tongue over the gold half-moon that'd been incised into a lower canine.

"Grandfather Parsa need not know." Farouk folded his arms across his chest, his face grim. "And stop sampling the wares, Muhammed. Quality control is not your assignment. You hear me?"

"You misjudge me, sir."

"I do not." Farouk's moist, brown lips thinned to a wet slit. Tight, airless silence gripped the dank office.

Muhammed mentally kicked himself in the head. Farouk could smell a lie a continent away. Should have known better than to get reckless with the old man's friendship. Muhammed was like family, but he was not family, no matter how much he wanted to be. He needed to remember his place. Not doing so would get him killed.

Muhammed lowered his eyes, bowed obediently, and broke the standoff. "Forgive me, sir. It is my honor and duty to obey your wishes. I will take care of the Middleton problem." His voice was humble and his eyes still averted. "*Allahu Akbar.*"

"*Allahu Akbar,*" Farouk responded. They raised their drinks.

2

I used to know exactly where I was in life, but last Friday my psychic GPS was shattered like a windshield in a car wreck.

Late afternoon just before change of shift, the officious, clipboard carrying vice president of human resources at KLAK-TV News in Los Angeles, poked her head into my office, carefully avoiding eye contact.

"Meeting, Beatrice, right now."

Behind her, the news director hustled toward the conference room where the staff was gathering. I rose to follow.

"What's up?" My throat tightened. A terrorist attack? A school shooting? I hated that my mind always leaped to those scenarios. Probably just the staff parking lot rates doubling again.

The VP disappeared without a response.

It was over in minutes.

No terrorist attack, no parking rate bump.

Our jobs were history.

I'd had a week at the top as the new evening news director, then *wham—gone*.

After almost two decades of paying my dues, I'd just moved into a prestigious corner office high above Sunset Strip in all its disheveled glitz and grime. I can still see my reflection in the two-inch thick, supposedly earthquake-safe, floor-to-ceiling glass in my new digs. The yellow linen designer dress I wore did nice things for my dark complexion. *Goodbye Ross Dress for Less, bonjour Dior*.

Today, I was back to *hello, Walmart*.

Upper management invited me to stay at the newly reorganized station at half the salary. No, thanks—a despicable offer. Others had little choice but to accept the shit doled out by the new management. Among my closest friends at work, sound recorder and field producer Ray Truckee had four kids to put through college. He'd recently been declared permanently disabled from injuries in a cartel-related attack that had left him partially paralyzed, which also left me with a bullet in my shoulder. Ernie Vargas, our producer, had to suck it up and stay—he just had a new baby and his wife had quit a full-time job to go freelance.

And then there was Lucy Vega, my closest friend. She'd just inherited a Malibu ranch worth millions, so when she heard about the pay cuts and the rapacious *nouveaux* station owners, she walked out the door and never looked back. She said she'd give it all back in a heartbeat if the uncle who'd left it to her could be brought back to life.

I prayed for the safety and health of my friends and family and mopped my eyes. Life was too short to hang somewhere in misery and resentment. I took the option of a flimsy parachute of six months' pay and said a big *adios*. I hoped it wouldn't turn out to be the stupidest decision of my life.

※

Now, alone on a cross-county road trip that had long been on my bucket list, my head spun with both disorientation and excitement. Nothing like a personal crisis to launch you on a new path. With the roof open, I drove way too fast down the dark, empty highway in east Texas. The dusty smell of a soft August evening was otherworldly. Lightning sparked the distant cloud banks like lanterns shorting out on a faulty wire. The night was as dark and the stars as bountiful and beautiful as the sublime nights of my childhood in south Georgia's Low Country.

My family and friends had been "quite concerned," as my momma had put it, when I announced that I would be driving cross-country from Santa Monica to my hometown of Savannah, Georgia, by myself. Before I hit the highway, my big brother Luther, a sheriff in rural Shellman County, Georgia, texted me a message: "*keep a heads-up, baby sis—hot black woman in hot silver Beemer, all by herself in the middle of nowhere. Keep that kick-ass Glock I sent you for your birthday under the front seat.*"

He left a smiley face with a bullet emoticon next to it.

In my job, my former job—I'd seen some serious

action. Los Angeles was made up of many worlds, some of which were always at war.

I was not afraid of much, but right now, firearms scared me. I fingered the puckered scar on my shoulder. I'd seen what bullets could do, up close. I was a damn good shot and my old Smith & Wesson had once saved my life. But still, I'd chosen to leave the gun at home in a lockbox. Someday I'd take it out again, but my trip home was about family and forging some personal peace with that crazy bunch.

Racing on from those thoughts, I pushed the gas pedal farther down than I'd ever pushed it before. Whoa, had it hit the floor? Sweet Jesus, what a rush. In my years commuting in Los Angeles, I don't think I'd ever been able to go faster than sixty-five, and that was probably in the middle of the night on a Tuesday. I felt like a wild woman as the car raced ahead like a fast, sleek panther.

Licking my lips, I sought the briny tang of the Pacific, but it was gone. Other flavors were on the rise. I took a long swig of water. I was good. A little anxious, but good. For better or worse, I was heading home. Mine was not an easy family but my mother had been ill and I had been avoiding a visit for far too long. Now unemployed with time on my hands, I had no excuse for staying away.

I cranked up "Midnight Train to Georgia," part of a mix of classic Southern music my two teenagers, Alyssa and Dexter, had downloaded for me. I belted it out, like a contestant on *The Voice*, desperate for a save. Out across the plains, lights of some small community twinkled on the horizon. Overwhelmed with a deep sense of spirituality in the face of this vast emptiness—I had forgotten that such places existed—I pulled my car off the road and sat in the darkness gazing at the heavens through the open roof, soaking up this rare transcendent moment. A gentle night wind whispered through the rolled-down windows. The call of a coyote sounded in the distance. It was answered by another, closer by, and then the pack began their song. Family. What a concept.

My cell phone joined the chorus. I was surprised I had any reception out here at all. I checked the number. It was my brother calling. He never called, he texted.

I hit the Bluetooth icon on my steering wheel to connect. "Hey, big bro, I'm on my way, in the middle of the Lone Star state. I've been speeding. Thirty-five over the limit. No cops anywhere. Yee-haw."

"Beazy…"

He didn't join in the banter.

Silence hung between us. My stomach tightened. "Everything okay?"

It took me a less than a nanosecond to know it wasn't.

He cleared his throat. "Slow down, baby girl. Way down. I have bad news."

"What're you talking about?"

"Our baby cousin, Jayden Leroy Junior, is dead."

"What?"

I felt like I had been hit in the stomach by an exploding airbag. Jayden was only fifteen, my son Dexter's age. No, no, no. I had to have heard it wrong. So wrong. I jammed on the brakes even though I was already stopped at the side of the road.

"Our boy was shot. Murdered. Outside of Savannah Central High School."

"Murdered?"

Shot dead at fifteen? At the same school where my

mother had been the principal for twenty years.

Bang. Gone.

The news hit like sand thrown into a piston. My brain started to grind and seize up. Jayden's mother, my aunt Honey, was responsible and kind, a terrific mom. She was the organist and choir director at the All Glory and Mercy Baptist Church. Her husband, my dad's youngest brother, was killed in Kabul. Jayden was her life.

"They had Momma identify the body, Aunt Honey couldn't handle it. You need to get here. STAT," he said.

"This is insane." I was beginning to get light-headed. I'd reported on more senseless killings of children in Los Angeles than I could count. But none of them had been mine. My family. My nephew. My blood.

The phone began to buzz with another incoming call.

"Luther, let me get back with you. Momma's on the other line." We disconnected.

"Momma?"

"Beatrice, you heard?" Her voice was small and distant.

"I just talked with Luther. This is unbelievable."

"You almost here, daughter? I had to go to the morgue. His face was so sweet and beautiful like he was sleeping." She uttered a thin, terrifying keen.

Then my rock of a mother started to sob.

My mother didn't sob.

Ever.

"I'll grab a plane out of Dallas, Momma. It's not too far from here. Leave my car in the lot." To hell with my road trip bucket list.

"We need you, Beatrice. I need you. Your aunt

Honey's falling apart. I can't help her. My sisters are blaming me because I encouraged Jayden to come up to Savannah for the Arts Academy High School this year. Such a talent, a musical prodigy. Needed more than tiny Shellman County could provide." Tears resumed and then she began to sniff and cough. "I reminded them of Matthew 5:15—neither do men light a candle, and put it under a bushel but let it glorify the Lord."

I heard a tissue crinkling in the background and deep, hiccoughing breaths. I visualized Momma sitting in her rocking chair next to the painting of my father's Baptist church with her hand clutching our worn, leather-bound, family Bible.

"But now Jayden's dead. His light's extinguished and the universe is so dark without him. I can't handle this alone, Bea. We all need you to help us through this."

I hadn't seen my aunt Honey since Jayden was five. He and my Dexter fought over a tricycle.

"Beatrice?" Momma's voice was fading.

"I'm going to call the airlines right now." I fumbled madly with the GPS trying to figure out just where I was. "Airport's not too far." *I hoped that was true.*

A caravan of semis rumbled by. My car trembled in the backdraft. I pulled out after them, sucked into their slipstream.

"Oh, Beatrice, my heart is racing and my arm is going numb."

"Oh, God. Momma. Hang up right now and call the EMS."

I could only make out a mewling sound. "Momma?"

Not good at all. Panic wrenched my diaphragm. I could barely breathe.

"Mother, did you hear me? Hang up and call 9–1-1."

"Yes, okay," she said, wheezing. The line went dead.

I punched Emergency on my cell phone and waited anxiously for a dispatcher to pick up. They could contact Savannah in case my mother couldn't. Dead zone.

Nothing.

No connection.

It took almost ten minutes for my call to go through. It felt like a year.

My fingers were damp and skidded off the phone's buttons. I dialed the Savannah Memorial Hospital ER. The call went through. The attendant said the EMS had just radioed ahead. Mrs. Middleton, my momma, was in route. They didn't want to give me any information but I played the "my brother, the sheriff" card.

Likely a myocardial infarction. A heart attack. Oh, my God. I couldn't lose her. Please Lord, no.

The guilt I'd always worked hard at avoiding about my long absence from Savannah, gripped hard. My mother would come to Los Angeles to visit like she had this past winter, but I imagined myself too busy to reciprocate. In reality, my Savannah family suffocated me with their judgment and small-town attitudes, so I stayed away. But now it was like they knew I was coming home and their collective need was splitting open like an overripe watermelon.

No job, a dead nephew, and my mother struggling for her life. Beatrice handled things—that was the family lore. In their limited eyesight, I was strong, rich, famous—a lottery winner. My family needed me to take care of them. I felt the weight of their grief and resentment at my long absence as I rushed toward

Savannah. Who the hell was responsible for all this? I was on my way to find out. The gas pedal found the floor.

3

I abandoned my car in long-term parking and booked a direct flight out of Dallas-Ft. Worth to Atlanta. Cost me a ton but it would get me there fast. The flight was tooth-rattling with turbulence but the plane touched down in Atlanta a couple hours later, on time.

I sprinted through Atlanta-Hartsfield airport, past the Arrival-Departure signs, the restaurants, and souvenir shops on my way to the boarding gate for Savannah. I texted my kids, who were ensconced with their respective dads, my two exes, just to say, "I love you." Then I dialed my brother. An answering message droned.

"Call me, Luther. I'm waiting on a commuter flight. What the hell is going on with everything? Jayden dead, Momma in cardiac arrest. Call me."

At the gate, I paced the floor for another two hours,

waiting for a bad storm to clear out of the area. No news from Savannah. Then there was a rogue alligator that had to be wrangled from the runway. Another forty-five minutes crawled. My vision began to glimmer, the precursor to an ocular migraine. I took a pill.

As I thought about my children, a stab of fear raised bumps on my skin. Dexter's father is a newly retired Los Angeles Lakers point guard with a good heart, bad knees, and an emotional maturity level just south of junior high. He'd be able to keep our fifteen-year-old entertained for a couple weeks before the responsibility of real-life child-rearing proved too overwhelming. His lifetime of being an entitled elite athlete turned out not to be a good thing for any of us, but he would at least keep Dexter safe.

My baby girl, Alyssa, studious and anxious from the day she left the womb, was already ordering college catalogs. She was with her dad for the month, my former news producer. He, his new psychiatrist wife (who I think is responsible for the college fixation), their new baby girl, and Alyssa were off to Maui. I'd accept no more whining from my poor daughter saying that she never gets to do anything fun. At twelve, she was a blooming peach, and that scared the hell out of me.

A garbled loudspeaker announced boarding for the flight from Atlanta to Savannah. I pushed concern for my children away. For now.

As I stood in line with the other travelers, cloying humidity leached in from the open jet-way doors. Ah, Georgia. My hair was already frizzing up. As I dragged my carry-on down the ramp, high anxiety hummed through my chest like electricity through a transformer.

At last, a call came through from my brother.

"Luther, sweet Jesus. Is Momma okay? What's going on?"

I struggled into the plane; found my seat then hoisted my bag into the overhead bin, dropping my phone in the process. I fished it from between the seats as another passenger crawled over me. Then I told Luther to continue.

"She's gonna be fine," he said. "It was mild but it was a heart attack."

I could hear his police radio in the background, squawking and angry as the plane pulled back from the gate.

"When are you arriving, baby girl?"

"Plane's on the runway. I think we're next to go. Should be there in forty-five minutes."

The engines began to roar their readiness to ascend. The flight attendant instructed me to turn off my phone. I bid my brother goodbye, switched my phone to airplane mode, and prayed for my mother.

XX

Our little jet came into Savannah Hilton Head International Airport fifteen minutes early. We had one heck of a tailwind and enough turbulence to loosen my teeth. Upon exiting, I practiced deep breathing to keep myself from rudely pushing past the passengers ahead of me. They all seemed to be swimming in slow motion.

Glancing around at the familiar terminal, I felt like Dorothy returning to Kansas after an extended time in the Land of Oz. I rushed past the welcoming rocking chairs in the lobby, grabbed my baggage off the carousel, and proceeded toward the taxi queue just outside.

The lack of sleep was sapping my endurance. I barely got to the curb before a small, wiry, black man with a grizzled gray beard slipped out from behind the steering wheel of a bright green cab. He held up a boldly lettered piece of notebook paper with my name on it.

"You Miz Honey's niece? Miz Beatrice? That you, ma'am?"

"Yes, sir," I said, moving into Southern formality as easily as tired feet into an old worn pair of slippers.

"I'm Mr. Winn Crawford, here to getcha, take ya over to the hospital."

We shook hands. His skin felt like sun on paper.

"I'm in the choir wit' Miz Honey, at church. Bad, bad bidness, wit' Miz Honey's baby boy. I hear about yo' momma, too. Our Savannah sure is a purty one, but she one nasty bitch sometimes, one nasty bitch. 'Scuse my cursin' Miz Beatrice." He shook his head in dismay.

"No problem, Mr. Crawford. I couldn't agree with you more."

Despite its genteel appearance, some might say Savannah could give South Central Los Angeles a run for its money in the poverty and resultant crime department. You won't find that in the tourist brochures. I still loved it though. Always would.

He took my bags and hoisted them into the trunk. Slammed it shut and Winn's Winning Taxi Service was headed toward Savannah Memorial.

My big brother met me at the door to the hospital lobby. Luther looked strained, rumpled, and entirely wonderful. I threw myself into his arms and held on for dear life. His whiskers were rough and he smelled lightly of coffee and sweat.

Leaning back, he checked me out then shook his head. "You're a sight for sore eyes, Beazy. I have so missed you. We all have."

My eyes welled with tears. I was the family crier.

"And I can't even begin to describe how good it is to see you," I said. "Too long. Way, way, too long." Had my last visit really been almost ten years ago?

Luther's cell phone buzzed. "Sorry, baby girl. Gotta grab this. It's the detective in charge of Jayden's murder investigation. O'Hanlon—she's this red-haired Irish gal. Came here from the LAPD. You might know her."

I hadn't heard of her, but it was a huge police department.

He took a few steps away from me and listened. He said "shit" a couple times and ran his hand distractedly over his short-cropped hair. It was starting to gray just a bit at the sideburns. Even though I knew we weren't kids anymore, the obvious seemed shocking at this moment. Where did the time go?

He thanked the detective then disconnected. I could see Luther's jaw clench and unclench, a nervous habit he had adopted in childhood when things were stressful.

"So, fill me in, big bro. What is the story on Jayden?"

"Wish I had something solid to tell you. It'll be a couple weeks before final tox results are in but his early screen came back negative."

"That's good news," I said, hopefully.

"But here's the bad news. Completely off the record, okay? I want to fill you in before we see the family."

"Of course."

"Initial thought before the medical examiner checked

things out, was that Jayden'd been shot multiple times. The cops on the scene drew that conclusion 'cause the boy's head was pretty much gone. Turns out there were only two shots. Probably came at him from a moving car. Our boy was struck once in the head, directly above and behind his ear. A shot so perfect that you'd have to be a professional sniper to land that kind of hit."

"My God," I said, shaking my head in disbelief. I wanted to throw up.

"The second shot was to his violin. Went right through the body of the instrument. Kept on going. Took out part of the goddamned sidewalk.

"And one more thing," Luther took a deep breath again, letting the air out slowly. "Jayden had over a thousand bucks in his pocket when they found him."

The migraine that had been lurking behind my eyes hit full force. My eyesight shattered into pixels. *What the hell had that child been up to?*

4

From the hallway of Savannah Memorial, I could see that Momma's hospital room was a double. The second bed was unoccupied by a patient. Aunts Freddie May and Hattie sat together atop the mattress like a couple of giant penguins on a white ice flow.

Hattie wore a black velour designer sweatsuit, her inch-long nails painted in rainbows. She and her daughters owned the beauty salon in Midberry. Freddie May wore a funereal gray dress with enough material to cover an SUV. I chewed at the peeling polish on my thumbnail, dreading our meeting. They'd never forgiven me for "abandoning the family" and moving to the West Coast. Hell, I'd been awarded a full basketball scholarship to the University of Southern California, but as far as they were concerned, there was only one true USC, and that was in South Carolina.

My big brother Luther moved to the foot of Momma's bed. In his dark blue Shellman County sheriff's uniform, he was in-shape, tall, and handsome. A star football player at Georgia Southern, he was still somewhat of a local sports hero. He hugged me again; his embrace was as hard as a warm cement post contrasted against my aunt's pillowy squeezes.

Aunt Honey, my father's baby sister, was in her mid-forties, and more a cousin to me than an aunt. She was asleep, crumpled into an uncomfortable-looking chair next to the bed, bleached hair in a fluffy bun on her head. Wearing a plain white blouse and tan trousers, she was reed thin like my mother. As I kissed Momma's cheek, my eyes welled with tears.

Momma, Florence Rose Middleton, the human terminus of an array of wires and tubes, was dozing too. Her hair was short and natural in style, her face a visage of polished dark leather, the kind used for expensive shoes. Her fine bone structure gave her an elegance, even as sick as she was. I put my cheek next to hers; saw a smile flicker on her lips. Her eyes opened.

She smelled medicinal, slightly sour, with the barest hint of the Herbal Essences shampoo she loved to use still clinging to her hair. She did not smell like death. The knot in my chest began to loosen. I took a deep breath and joined the family.

The aunts behaved themselves and didn't grill me about what they used to disparagingly refer to as my "Hollywood" lifestyle. They'd nail me with that later. After more crying and catching up, ordering chicken fingers, mac and cheese, collard greens, sweet tea, and sweet potato pie from a local eatery, the nursing staff finally threw us all out so Momma could get some rest. I couldn't help but linger by the door. Momma, remarkably lucid during our time together, had finally nodded off again. Her soft snore was reassuring.

Walking into the hall just beyond the busy nurse's station, I peered out a broad window. Across the parking lot beneath a streetlight haloed in dense mist, Hattie and Freddie May wedged their ample bodies into the front seat of Freddie May's ancient baby-blue Ford Fairlane. Honey was in the backseat, small and alone. The car pulled out, heading back to Midberry where they would begin planning Jayden's funeral. In my work in TV news I had attended funerals for murdered children, other people's children. They were nightmares. All kid's funerals were.

I was relieved to see the women finally leave because I was looking forward to having a moment with my brother. Luther soon joined me in the lobby. It was freshly painted a creamy yellow, almost cheery, with nice photographs of low-country creeks, marshes, and wildlife. We grabbed a couple drinks from a vending machine.

I watched my smart, handsome sibling as he returned several phone calls and growled orders into a chattering radio. He graduated college with a major in business and then enrolled in the police academy where he had excelled. He'd wanted to be a cop from as far back as I could remember. Luther served seven years in Atlanta before he returned to Shellman County as a young assistant chief. Finally, he ran for county sheriff and took it on as successfully as when he ran for student council way back when. Shellman was a small, rural, mostly black county and they were glad to have one of their own in charge.

"I've missed you, Luther," I said, taking his hand. I had a feeling I'd be saying that a lot this week.

"Bring it here, girl," He put his arm around me and gave my shoulders a squeeze. Tears welled in my eyes again. I quickly dried them with the back of my damp, mascara-stained sleeve.

I was anxious to get my brother's take on Jayden's murder. It was clear he didn't want to talk about it in front of Momma, Honey, and the aunts. They were all convinced that it was a hideous act of random gang violence. Plenty of that in Savannah but Luther clearly believed that there was more to it.

"So, big bro,' what's going on with this thing?"

"Well, Beez," he said, "Detective O'Hanlon is keeping me in the loop even though I don't have any jurisdiction in Savannah."

"I didn't know her. LAPD wasn't usually my direct assignment. Nice to have a woman in that head detective job."

"Yeah, well things do change, even down here in *Deliverance* country," he said smiling, referring to the classic Southern swamp thriller film. "And she's been very generous to me, very willing to share information because it's my family involved here."

"I'm surprised she didn't ask you to recuse yourself, precisely because it *is* your family."

"You forget where you are, little sister. Some things do change and some things never will."

I knew he was right, for better or for worse. Family trumped all. He gave my hand a tolerant pat. There was so much I had lost track of in my years away. For instance, who was Jayden, really? Despite our love and devotion, mothers, aunties, and grandmothers are not the best sources of information on their teenagers' extracurricular activities.

5

I settled back on the couch in the hospital lobby and sipped my soda, willing my growing headache away. "Jayden came up to Savannah to live with Momma so he could get into the Arts Academy High School, right?"

Luther shifted in his seat, adjusting all the tools on his cop belt for a bit of comfort. "Yup and Honey came into town every weekend to be with him. She was looking for a full-time job teaching music up here. I think she's had a couple interviews already."

I nodded. "So, he was clearly a true talent."

"No question. World class. Check him out on YouTube. That voice—just amazing. Think little Stevie Wonder at his best. And he could play anything—piano, violin, horn, was learning a mean guitar. He'd been raised on classical and church music but had just discovered everything that Honey had never let him listen to."

"Oh, my. I don't know how you keep kids away from anything anymore," I said, wondering what my own kids were up to.

"Yeah, well, you don't. And he knew he was late to the party so he really threw himself into it like he was making up for lost time."

"What kind of kid was he?"

"Shy, kind of geeky—except when he performed." Luther smiled, remembering. "He was skinny like his mom and Momma. Big black glasses."

"Big black glasses are all the rage," I said. Maybe the kid was hipper than he seemed.

"A local group invited him to sit in with them at a gig this past summer at Forsyth Park," Luther continued. "Lots of people saw him, heard him sing, play. Then he started performing regularly with a group of kids called the GratiFlyers."

"GratiFlyers?" I rolled my eyes. "You must be kidding."

"Nope, all very young, male, playing hormone-driven hip-hop with a rock and blues sound. He was drinking all that music in like from a fire hose. Momma and Honey tried to stop him from getting involved with all of them but Jayden had found his calling in life. Goodbye Sacred Child of Jesus Singers and handbell choir—hello, Jay-Z, and Biggie."

"Rock and roll and all its iterations," I said. "Powerful stuff, especially at that age. We've all succumbed at one time or another." I tried not to think about a guitar man I once knew early on in Los Angeles.

"Tell me about it." Luther rubbed an old tattoo

under his sleeve. It was a flaming heart with "Shaundra" inscribed in the middle. She was long gone but the moment of drunken, teenaged, post-hip-hop-concert impulsiveness still survived on his espresso-brown skin.

"Any witnesses to the shooting?" I asked.

"Not that we know of. He was riding his bike home from band practice at one of the kid's houses. Was around dusk. Happened right over near the gym entrance."

I pictured the scene in my mind. Savannah Central High School—mid-century brick, blocky architecture surrounded by a broad parking lot and magnolia trees with shiny dark green leaves along the sidewalks. Athletic fields rolled out behind the main building, off the street.

Luther's cell phone rang again. He pushed a button and checked caller ID.

"It's O'Hanlon. Maybe she's heard more from the medical examiner."

They spoke for a couple minutes. Luther mainly listened and shook his head. He sighed, then disconnected.

"What?" I asked, impatiently.

"Aw, man. This is bad. Bullets were 9mm hollow point, Teflon-tipped."

Sweat began to dampen my neck. "Cop-killers. We see them in Los Angeles. My God."

I tried to get my head around this news. "Doesn't make sense." I closed my eyes and rubbed my forehead. "Money still in his pocket? Expert kill? The gangbanger angle doesn't fit this story. At all. And they'd never leave a thousand dollars behind."

"It all points to drug involvement, despite what

Honey and the family wants to believe."

"Maybe the cash was payment for a gig," I said, ever the optimist. But it was way too much money. "Or maybe he wasn't using, just moving stuff. Or maybe he's being set up somehow."

"Yeah, could be any of those things, or something else."

"We're gonna figure it all out. The asshole who took Jayden's life can count on that."

Pixilated vision brought on by an impending migraine sparkled like shattered glass behind my eyelids. I had to get some sleep. Darkness. No stimulation. Momma, Jayden, murder—it was all too much.

"Where are my damn pills?" I rooted in my purse to no avail. Found a gas bill I hadn't paid and an earring I thought was gone for good.

Luther unhooked a car fob from his belt. He jingled it, distracted. "Let's get you back to the house, let you catch some rest."

He stood up and grabbed my suitcase. We headed toward the hospital exit, the roller wheels squeaked on the yellowing linoleum. A Shellman County squad car waited in front with *SHERIFF* emblazoned across the side. The heavy mist was beginning turn into light rain.

"I'm meeting O'Hanlon tomorrow midmorning. Getting updated on her interview plans with the band members," he said as he opened the car door for me.

"I'm coming with you."

"Sorry, baby. Not protocol."

Damned if I was going to be cut out of this. What would I do if this Detective O'Hanlon wouldn't include me? "What time are we meeting her?"

"Aw, Jesus. Y'always was a pain." Luther loaded my bag in next to me. "It's not like you to have just one suitcase. And so small. They lose some of your luggage? Like all the shoes?"

"Don't change the subject, Luther. What time? I'm in this, Lu. You hear? You have to make her understand that."

He sighed, rolled his eyes and smiled, at least a little.

"Okay, ten o'clock, Historic District station downtown. Not likely she'll talk to you though, Beazy. She's a by-the-book kind of gal."

"Except where family's involved..."

Okay," Luther said, "you got me there."

"Promise me you'll do your best to convince her because I'm going to be in on this, one way or another."

Luther gave me a look of disapproval.

"I'll do my best, but she runs the show. I think she's a good cop. Got big city kick-ass experience, knows what she's doing."

"Well, big brother, let me remind you, I got some big city kick-ass experience of my own."

6

Cornelia Chan crouched amid the overgrown lilac hedge that surrounded the front porch of a white clapboard house across the street from the Middleton residence. Pretty and petite with Asian features, she had long dark hair with bangs chopped in a straight line just above her eyebrows.

She puffed on a cigarette held delicately in her slim fingers. Hot pink nail polish alternated with silver. She checked her iPhone. The case was leopard print. She keyed in a few responses to texts.

Cornelia had been watching the Middleton home since Jayden was killed. She'd loved him from a distance since she first heard him play "The Devil Went Down Down to Georgia" on his fiddle in a school concert. She'd never heard the song before then. The boy was electric.

Cornelia took one last drag of the cigarette before

stubbing it out on the mossy ground. She wiped tears from her eyes as she envisioned Jayden's sweet, sexy face.

She was his number one fangirl. She had seen what happened to him. She had been there.

Hidden.

She wasn't exactly a stalker but she loved looking at him. Imagining things.

She was a watcher. Curious, always had been. She thought his family should know what happened. She wanted to tell them.

But she also wanted to live.

A door slammed above her somewhere inside the house. Three students from Savannah College of Art and Design, SCAD, lived there. Garrity, Jose, and Tim. She knew their names because she had checked their mail. Also overheard them talk the previous evening as they sat on the porch smoking dope.

Across the street, a Shellman County police car pulled up. Cornelia pushed herself tight against the old porch. Decades of peeling paint in many hues were rough against her skin.

The officer jumped from the vehicle. He moved fast and easy for such a large man. That was Jayden's cousin, or was it his uncle? Either way, he was kind of scary looking. He pulled a suitcase out of the car. An attractive woman, late 30s wearing skinny jeans and a gauzy white tunic, walked slowly up the steps to the Middleton residence. Was that the uncle's girlfriend?

So much more to figure out.

X

The atmosphere held its breath. Not a whisper of air rustled the leaves. Hoary Spanish moss hung in damp tendrils from the crepe myrtle trees on the parkway as I followed Luther and mounted the steps to the house I'd grown up in. Like every other place on the block, our home had been built in the early 1900s. It was still white-washed clapboard with black shutters and a haint blue porch ceiling to protect us from evil spirits. My African-Irish grandmother insisted on that color. My parents protested, swearing they were not superstitious, but the ceiling went blue, and still is. Chewing on my lip, it had been way too long since I'd climbed up these steps.

Inside the house, the walls were the color of key lime pie, the sofa looked new, but everything else seemed frozen in time. Family photos, sports trophies, books—lots of them, and needlepoint pillows of birds that Momma stitched were the artifacts of life in this home. Original pine floors shone warm, even in the dim streetlight that filtered anemically through the blinds.

Above, a fan spun lazily, suspended from a high, twelve-foot ceiling rimmed with elaborate crown molding. An oil painting of my father's Baptist church that the congregation had presented to my mother just after his death, hung over the fireplace mantel. Only fifty years old, he had suffered a brain aneurysm.

For years, I thought every headache was going to kill me.

They never did, so far at least, just made me miserable.

I finally found my migraine medication and swallowed a pill. Swore to myself I'd clean out the purse this week. It contained everything but a rusted car on cinder blocks.

Luther deposited my suitcase in what was now Momma's craft room and office. A daybed with a magnolia quilt, handmade by my great-grandmother, was lovely and inviting. Pale pink petals with forest-green leaves—it was comforting and calm, like Gran'nanna herself. All was prepared and ready for the coming guest. Prodigal me. What a different kind of reception we were all expecting. I shut the curtains.

Luther saw me settled then took off for Shellman County, anxious to get back to his office and finish up some time-sensitive paperwork for a couple of search warrants unrelated to Jayden's case. In parting, I reminded him I'd meet him in the Historic District at the police station in the morning. He pretended to ignore me and honed in on the intrusive radio conversations crackling on his shoulder.

7

It felt like minutes had passed, but it was eight in the morning eastern time when the distinctive sound of a Harley-Davidson reverberated through the subdued Henry Street neighborhood. Glass rattled in the window panes. I stretched across the cozy single bed and the quilt dropped to the floor. As usual, sleep had done wonders for my headache, but I needed more—hours more, a week more. I was still on West Coast time which made it about dawn back there. Definitely too early to get up.

I grabbed my phone to check texts and emails. Luther left a message saying Momma was already feeling better and he'd pick me up at 10:00 a.m. to meet with Detective O'Hanlon.

The Harley seemed to be pulling in front of our house. I always thought heavy-duty mufflers should be required on those things. I'd been told many times when gearhead bikers heard that obnoxious sound, it was practically orgasmic. Mercifully, the cycle coughed and belched to a stop. I pulled the quilt back on top of me and cuddled in.

The doorbell rang. I ignored it, but then thought if it was a friend wanting to leave something for my mother, I'd better check. I grabbed my robe, raked my fingers through my hair, and trudged down the stairs. Step number five still creaked loudly. We kids had learned to avoid that one when sneaking in late.

Looking out the peephole, I saw a huge man, shaved bald, about my age, dressed in black leather. A diamond glinted from each earlobe. A brain-pan helmet was tucked under his arm. Aviator sunglasses. Definitely the Harley owner. The machine shined at the curb, as black and imposing as he was. Didn't look like a casserole or flowers in his hand. Slowly, I opened the door, glad the screen was locked.

"Can I help you?" I asked, ready to slam the door if he made a move. I didn't need this. No casserole, no admittance. I pulled the pink robe tighter around my body.

He stared at me and then began to grin.

I gulped and hesitated for an instant. The grin was familiar... but. But, what?

"Beazly. Girl. You're all grown up. My Lord. Haven't seen you since you left for California. And you stole my Savannah Sand Gnats team jersey when you were walking out the door."

Between my headache, lack of sleep, and the fact that the man who once had a generous head of hair worn in a cotton-candy-sized Afro, was now completely bald, recognition was a bit slow in dawning but when it came it was completely joyous.

"Rio. Oh, my God. Come in." I unlocked the screen door and threw it open, almost knocking him off the porch.

"And I still hate it when you call me Beazley."

"You've been saying that forever."

"And you've been ignoring me forever."

We laughed out loud together. "Bring it here, little sister." He leaped across the threshold, scooped me up and swung me around. My slippers went flying. I'm not a small woman, but he lifted me off my feet effortlessly, unexpectedly. Left me rather breathless—and it was not just the bear hug. He was goddamned gorgeous.

"And about the Gnats jersey," he said, smirking and setting me down. "It's mine and I still want it. You finally gonna give it back?"

My energy picked up, or maybe it was the pheromones. "Let's get this straight about that Savannah Sand Gnats jersey," I said with feigned seriousness. "You gave it to me for telling Momma that those cigarettes of yours belonged to my girlfriend."

"I only smoked for a month."

"You're such a liar."

It all came rolling back like warm waves on the beach of my memory. Luther's best friend, Rio Deakins, had just bounded back into my life.

People always thought that Luther and Rio were twin brothers. He and Luther were in sixth grade and I was in third when we quasi-adopted him after his mother passed away. Officially, he went to live with his aunt who had eight other children but he spent more time with us. His dad was long-time MIA. Lu and Rio were my co-bodyguards, the two biggest pains in the rear end a girl could want.

Rio, named after the Savannah River which supposedly had some hazy linkage to his conception, played minor-league ball for the Sand Gnats the summer before he left for the University of Georgia. I coveted that Gnats jersey. White with green pinstripes, a "Gnate the Gnat" logo on the shoulder. It was a funny, sweet little piece of the city I needed to take with me to California. Maybe I needed to take a funny, sweet little piece of him, too.

"You'll be sad to know that the Gnats went to Columbus and now we're the Bananas."

My mouth dropped open. "What? The Savannah Bananas ball club. No way."

"Yes, way. Break out those yellow booty shorts." Rio stood back, his smile fading. He took a deep breath. "Bea, so great to see you, girl, but what an awful, tragic situation. Can't believe little Jayden is gone. Sang like an angel. I wanted to stop by this morning and tell Miss Momma I'm here for her, always. Got the call from Luther on my way over. He said you'd just arrived. It's hard to believe we almost lost her too."

"I can't imagine life without her."

"Got to treasure every moment, right? *Carpe diem.* Sometimes I can't believe that with all the shit that happens in life, I still take things for granted."

"Welcome to humanity, big guy," I said and punched him in the arm. It was like hitting granite.

We sat on the couch, drank sweet tea and ate the Fig Newtons that Momma liked. Always a fresh box in the cupboard. I filled him in on everything.

Time flew.

He glanced at his watch. "Oh, man. I gotta get back to Atlanta."

"The weather looks awful again. Maybe you should stay here tonight," I said, thinking that it would be nice to have him around a bit longer.

He stood up and collected his gear, smiled.

"Thanks for the offer, but I teach tomorrow morning at 8:00 a.m. sharp. Can't let the students down, right?"

"How often are you in Savannah?" I asked, wondering if I would see him again anytime soon. I wrapped the remaining Fig Newtons in a napkin and stuffed them in his pocket.

"I ride with a group of vets first Sunday of the month here in town. That was yesterday. We have barbeque out at Sand Fly; do some A.A. kind of stuff geared toward PTSD survivors. Been with them for quite a few years."

"Sounds like you're doing fine work, Rio. You were always a good man. Even when your behavior was marginal, which was often, as I recall. And you still look a bit wicked. But you're never getting that Sand Gnats shirt back. You totally gave it to me."

He laughed. "Maybe I did, just to get you off my back."

"No, it was to hide your nasty secret."

"Okay, okay, I confess to ulterior motives."

Rio had a core of happiness that I always envied. Despite a really screwed up early life, he graduated college, had a great Division I football career at UGA, was Special Ops in Iraq, and now taught school and worked with vets.

He also told me, or I guess I pried it out of him, that he had a serious relationship with a woman he highly admired. "Admired," sounded a little bloodless to me, but she was very fortunate, indeed.

"I hope our paths cross again before you head back West," he said as he reached for the door.

"Me, too. It was so great seeing you. I'll give Momma and everyone your love, of course. We'll stay in touch this time, okay? Love you, Rio."

"Always love you, baby girl. And Miss Momma and Lu—you're family."

He kissed me on the cheek then took off down the walk.

I couldn't help noticing those tight black jeans.

The Harley revved. The windows rattled. He flashed me that big smile and then disappeared around the corner as rain began to spatter.

Moments later, the sound of the heavens unfastening and the storm ripping loose hit the neighborhood with silvery sheets of rain. Jayden's blood on the sidewalk outside the high school would be washed away. And Rio, caught in the storm, would be on his bike down the highway toward Atlanta.

I closed the door and sat back on the couch, utterly exhausted. The empty bag of Fig Newtons was still in my hand.

It fell to the floor. That's the last thing I remember until Luther was pounding on the door.

8

Built in 1870, the old brick Savannah-Chatham Metro Police Station, located in the central Historic District, was still known as the "Barracks." Luther liked to point out that it's the oldest continually operating police headquarters in the nation.

On the rain-soaked sidewalk outside of the station were a couple of 1947 vintage cruisers, probably the two most photographed police cars in the US. A black one from the Savannah Police Department and a gold version from the Chatham County cops, stood as a remembrance of times past—both good times and really bad, particularly for the local African-American population. A city worker in a brown uniform hosed debris off the cars from the previous night's storm. A chamois hung from his back pocket. He was talking to someone on his Bluetooth.

Luther had been at the hospital earlier checking on our mother. Momma was weak, but her spirits were good. The doctor told him that if all went well, we could take her home in a day or two. She had begun the countdown.

En route to the police station, my phone rang. Luther glanced over at me.

"It's Honey," I said. I took a deep breath and pushed "Accept."

"Hello, Aunt Honey. How are you doing this morning, sweetheart?"

For a long moment, she said nothing. Then she sighed.

"I don't know how I'm doing. Fine, I guess. It's like I'm watching my life as a play right now, from the back row of a big, dark theater. I'm here but gone. I don't know quite how to describe it."

I wished I could think of something to say that could be comforting. She seemed a million miles away. "I love you, Aunt Honey."

"Love you, too, Beatrice. I'm so glad you're home."

I was glad too. Had I not already been on my way to Savannah to see Momma, I knew I would not have chosen to come back to share in this tragedy. I would have found a reason to stay in Los Angeles. The universe was now calling me in. I had to listen no matter how hard the message.

"How are plans for the funeral coming? Is there anything I can do?" I asked.

"We're scheduled to have it this weekend, just got confirmation." A heavy sigh filled a silence. "My choir will be performing Jayden's favorites. We want to make sure your momma will be able to come. She said she hoped to be home by then."

"Yes, she's looking good."

"The medical examiner still hasn't released my baby's body to the funeral home. Maybe Luther could check and see what the holdup is. That would be great."

I'll make sure he does that." Luther could hear the conversation and nodded his head. "We're on our way to the police station right now."

"Okay, I won't keep you. I think I'm going to lie down. I'll probably see you at your momma's later today."

"Okay, Honey. See you soon. Love you."

"Bye, Auntie," Luther said, raising his voice to be heard.

"Bye and thank you both. Don't give up, please, don't give up. I have to know what happened to my son."

"We all do, Auntie. And we will never give up," I promised and glanced over at Luther as the call disconnected.

Talking to Aunt Honey was like talking to an empty husk, her soul being held together by an unraveling thread. First, her husband is killed in Afghanistan, then her only child is murdered in Savannah. We had to find out who did this to Jayden, to her, to us. The maiming shrapnel of his murder and the collateral loss was a bleeding emotional wound.

Luther pulled his Crown Vic into the lot next to the main police building. I opened my door and stepped into the humid morning. Big cumulus clouds lumbered overhead like creamy blimps. Already, my clothes threatened to drip right off my body.

"Now, be good," he said. "I still don't know what O'Hanlon's going to do about you, Bea. Whatever happens, you'll have to roll with it. Hear me?"

"I do, I hear you." I bit my lip, trying to keep my mouth shut. I just had to get the detective to believe that I was the perfect helper—calm and unobtrusive, smart and resourceful. How would I handle it if she cut me out? Probably not well.

I followed Luther into the station. A short, middle-aged white man, high on something, blood from his nose oozing all over the counter, was screaming.

"Chick cops, fuck them all. No fuckin' female should be allowed to touch a gun. They'll get us. In our sleep. Right in the fuckin' balls."

"And you're gonna be the first one I'm goin' after," said a gloved-up female officer about Luther's size. Her name badge flashed *Sergeant Hildy Lopez* before the guy ripped it off her shirt pocket flap with his teeth. She tried to maneuver this misogynist screamer out of our way.

"Keep your goddamned fluids off my paperwork, Dewey," she growled at him.

He spit blood across the counter.

One of Lopez's colleagues jumped in to cuff the guy while she held the perpetrator by his skinny neck.

"Back to the slammer, Dew-boy. And cough up my name tag, asshole," Lopez said.

The guy drooled out the metal badge and shrieked a litany of nastiness until they hauled him off.

The red-haired Detective O'Hanlon appeared in the doorway and rolled her eyes. She motioned for us to follow her down a short hallway and into her office.

A whiteboard with shift schedules and notes hung on the wall across from her old Steelcase desk. There were a few personal items and memorabilia atop a bookshelf filled with criminal justice books. I noted a couple of Flannery O'Connor volumes too.

About 5'8" or so, my height, Mary O'Hanlon was a slim, muscular woman who looked like she could take care of herself on the street. Her movements were economical and spare. Her hair, however, was like a rusty blaze barely under control, despite being slicked back into a bun. Her skin was the color of cream with cinnamon sprinkles and her eyes were green and wary. Not your typical beauty, she was... compelling in an interesting way.

A diploma from UCLA Law School next to a picture of her in military uniform with a big German shepherd was displayed near the whiteboard. She had been K-9 at one time. I liked dog people.

I wanted to like her but I was not at all sure she wanted to like me back.

9

After introductions and inquiries into Momma's recovery, Luther and I sat down on metal chairs at a small round conference table next to O'Hanlon's desk.

She lost no time with small talk. "As you know, Jayden and the GratiFlyers's band manager and agent is a young man who calls himself Evan Doobius." She paged through a file folder while simultaneously glancing at her computer screen. "But his real name actually appears to be Evan Dubinskov. Family from Miami. Looks about seventeen but we found out he's older. Like eight years older. Hasn't been seen since Jayden's murder."

Luther tapped notes onto an iPad. "Has a sheet in South Carolina too," he said. "Drugs, petty theft, aggravated assault. Hangs around that strip club across the river. Small-time coke dealer. Busy man."

"His juvie stuff is sealed," O'Hanlon said, "but I have

a court order in the works to unseal. Should be a matter of hours."

"So, this Doobius guy evidently saw himself as an up-and-coming agent/manager with big plans for Jayden and the band in the music industry," I said, thinking about how vulnerable a fifteen-year-old from Midberry might be in this situation.

"Definitely big plans," O'Hanlon replied. "Saw Jayden as his protégé, his meal ticket. Real bad news."

She pushed a stray tendril of hair behind her ear. It was a losing battle in this sticky weather. It sprung free immediately.

"Bad-news dude but with great taste in music," Luther said, still tapping. His big fingers struggled with the small keys.

O'Hanlon continued, "We also think it's possible that there may be some kind of an Eastern European crime connection with the Dubinskov family. May be part of a cartel based out of South Florida."

Luther stopped typing.

"Like the Russian mob?" I asked. This was getting more complicated by the minute.

"Maybe, but it's all speculation at this point. The Port of Savannah is big, fifth in the nation for traffic, but it's still in some ways far enough off the radar that it could be the perfect place for imports of, let's say a very questionable nature."

"Drugs? Human trafficking? What kind of things?" I asked, waiting for her to shut me down at any moment.

"Today, it's drugs. We're starting to see evidence of a new strain of heroin hitting the area, all outside the purview of our usual suspects in Atlanta and

Jacksonville. It's laced with fentanyl which makes it about eighty times more potent. Evil stuff."

"Fentanyl's used with oncology patients during the last stages of cancer treatment," Luther said. "We seized a ton of that shit from a boat off Melon Bluff last month. Really, really lethal. Just a tiny dose can kill a person."

"Made an arrest, didn't you?" O'Hanlon asked, still paging through the folder. She took out a photo of Doobius and slid it across the table to us.

The guy was skinny as a sprig of swamp grass, had darkish skin, curly black hair, and a wispy, wannabe mustache. He had the feel of emaciation about him— high cheekbones and sunken eyes. Looked vaguely bisexual.

"We did make an arrest," Luther said as he examined the image of Doobius. "The guy was Afghani, not Russian. Managed to kill himself his first night in federal lockup. *Allegedly* killed himself, anyway. The investigation is still ongoing."

"Murdered?" O'Hanlon asked.

"Likely," Luther said.

The detective put her folder down and slumped back in her chair. She looked hard at my brother.

For an instant, I had the distinct feeling that there might be some sort of history between them. But it was probably this awful case.

O'Hanlon's green eyes were translucent marbles. They shifted toward me, assessing.

"We're scheduled to start talking to the kids in Jayden's band in a half hour. We took initial statements from them right after the murder but we have some follow-up to do. I understand you'd like to ride along," she said.

"I would." Was she letting me in? My heart pounded and I tried to stay cool.

O'Hanlon didn't respond. She glanced at Luther. It felt like she was on the verge of rescinding her offer.

"I've got to get back to Shellman County," Luther said. He gathered his iPad, notebook, and car keys. "Beatrice does interviewing every day as part of her job, so she'll be helpful."

"You're welcome to come," O'Hanlon said, looking back at me, "but I'm the one doing the interviewing. Understood?"

"Understood."

"Bye, Sis." Luther gave me a raise of his eyebrows, a peck on the cheek, and abandoned me to the whims of Detective Mary O'Hanlon.

※

I waited patiently while O'Hanlon excused herself, promising to be right back. Officer Hildy Lopez entered the office, hair awry. Probably a result of tussling with Dewey the spitting screamer at the front desk. She placed a list of names, addresses and a folder of notes on O'Hanlon's desk.

"Jayden Middleton, Junior file," she announced, looking askance at me.

Lopez left the office and partially closed the door behind her. It took all of my willpower to keep my eyes to myself. I'm glad I behaved because O'Hanlon was back in no time. Maybe it was a test to see how nosy I'd be.

"Thank you, Hildy," O'Hanlon called over her shoulder as she stepped into the office. She glanced at me then shifted her focus to studying the materials.

I had to step back and trust the detective to do her job. I was grateful that she was willing to take me with her on the interviews. Luther had finagled an entrée for me that I didn't want to blow. She could be looking for any opportunity to send me packing.

"Sure, you want to come with me?" She stood, tucking the file under her arm and heading for the exit.

"Absolutely." I jumped up and followed her down the hall and out the back door of the building.

We exited onto the parking lot next to the Barracks. O'Hanlon wore a conservative gray pants suit, white shell top, and black running shoes meant for business. No high heeled pumps or spiky boots here. This was no TV drama.

We headed toward a silver Ford Taurus waiting at the gas pump on the far edge of the lot. Several squad cars were lined up behind it yet to be fueled. The man with the Bluetooth who was hosing off the vintage cruisers in front of the station a half hour ago placed the pump handle back in its cradle and then screwed on the gas cap as we walked up.

"Morning, Detective O'Hanlon," he said. "Ready to roll."

"Thank you, Mr. Cecil."

He handed her the key fob. We climbed into the newly washed and vacuumed car. A pine tree fragrance hanger dangled from the rearview mirror. A computer and multiple electronic systems were affixed to the dashboard and between the front seats.

We pulled from the lot onto Habersham Street—part of a lovely residential area lined with live oak, crepe myrtle, and magnolia trees. The sidewalks were made of a mixture of crushed seashells in mortar called tabby, rather than the standard concrete, adding to the charm.

In this pricey part of town, residents are required by strict regulations to keep the historic nature of the neighborhood intact. Local college students vied for the carriage houses and small cottages on the sandy back lanes of the district.

Tucked away in a garage nearby on one of those lanes was my favorite little restaurant, Hall's Barbecue. I could barely wait for an opportunity to stop by. The co-proprietor, Miss Vanessa Hall, had also been my math teacher at St. Catherine's. Outside the southern states, lanes are called alleys—same thoroughfare, but a much less appealing image.

Savannah is one of the few cities that was not burned to the ground when Sherman made his bloody march across Georgia. Some say it survived because it was so pretty. One story has it that Sherman gave it to Lincoln as a Christmas gift. Others say the city avoided the torch because Daisy Lowe, founder of the Girl Scouts and Sherman's childhood sweetheart, had a very fine home located right in the middle of downtown.

Lore abounds on this subject. I prefer to think that love saved the day, but the truth is probably something much more cold-blooded.

10

"We're heading over to Gordonston," O'Hanlon said. I snapped back into the moment. "Two of the five kids in the band live there. We'll try to talk to all of them this morning."

Not far from Grayson Stadium where the Sand Gnats, now the Bananas play, is Gordonston, a modest neighborhood of small bungalows and pocket parks, located several miles beyond the Historic District.

"What did the first round of interviews give you?" I asked. She had mentioned previously that these talks were follow-ups from the day of the murder.

"Not much. The kids were all in shock. Their parents were freaking out. It was, as you can imagine, a horror show. They've had a day or two to settle down so, hopefully, we'll be able to have better conversations. And remember, you are an observer, here by my consent, provisionally."

"Of course." I nodded my head.

"I'll introduce you as a consultant. Beyond that, we'll keep it vague."

"Okay, sounds good."

I didn't need to be a mind reader to know that O'Hanlon was very unsure about me. Probably for good reason. I tended to color outside the lines now and then. Maybe she sensed that. I wasn't sure about her, either. Was she really going to include me in the investigation, or go through the motions to placate my brother? I guess we'd find out.

The first two student interviews offered little that could press the investigation forward. Both kids seemed down-to-earth and forthcoming, but without a clue as to why the murder had happened, or who might have pulled the trigger. Both speculated that it was a terrible case of mistaken identity. Someone bad thought Jayden was someone else. Neither boy could believe he had a thousand dollars in his pocket. The band members had gone for Slurpee's earlier and had barely cobbled enough money together to buy the drinks. How Jayden landed the cash remained a complete mystery. As did everything else.

Our third stop was in more affluent Ardsley Park, Savannah's first suburb now ensconced in the larger city, with Rory Ratcliffe. Just graduated from the Arts Academy High School, he was soon to be a first-year student at Armstrong Atlantic University here in Savannah. Annie Allman's Guitar Center on Broughton Street downtown was where he worked part-time. The most sophisticated of the group so far, Rory had frizzy blond hair, wore jeans and flip-flops, and looked like your stereotypical Southern California surfer dude.

His dad, a lawyer, and his mother, a stay-at-home mom, and artist, never left his side. They invited us to join them on an L-shaped slate gray couch. Dad, originally from London, and mom from Hamburg, Germany, had been in the US for ten years. With his good looks and British accent, Rory was clearly the heartthrob of the crew. Every band had one.

"What can you tell us about Evan Doobius?" O'Hanlon asked. "The other band members didn't seem to have had much interaction with him."

"I met him, maybe three times, at gigs," Rory said. "Seemed like a decent guy, low key. Talked mostly with Jayden and myself, not the younger guys. Wanted to have his own label someday. Liked our music, wanted to be our agent, which was fine with us. Thought Jayden was rock star talented, which he was."

A ginger-colored cat jumped onto his lap and he stroked her, scratched her ears. She purred like a hairdryer turned on high. "Doobie, we called him that, was definitely not from the southern US or Europe. I have an ear for accents," Rory said.

"Our son speaks five languages fluently," his proud father told us. "We traveled around Europe and the Middle East quite a bit during his formative years so he picked up a lot. He's also learning Mandarin." A thin man with graying hair and wire-rimmed glasses, he was at least a decade, or maybe two, older than his pretty wife.

"Doobie told us he was originally from Atlanta," Rory continued. "That could be, but still, I didn't buy it. He had this way of speaking—specially narrowing his O's—that was unique."

"What's your guess?" O'Hanlon asked. "Russia? Eastern Europe?"

"Farsi," Rory said. "Definitely, Farsi."

I glanced at O'Hanlon. She gave no readable response. The buzzing in my own brain was enough reaction for both of us.

We didn't speak until we returned to the car.

"If Rory is right and Evan Doobius has a Middle Eastern connection, that's a game-changer." O'Hanlon turned on the ignition.

"What the hell are we into here?" I asked.

"I don't know. But I don't like what I'm thinking."

Neither O'Hanlon or I offered further speculation.

Next stop, Hitch Village and the public housing apartment of Antwone Thomas. His was the last unit still standing as the neighborhood was in the process of being rebuilt onto something tonier. In the class ahead of Jayden at the Arts Academy High School, he was an actor, singer, and keyboardist. A tall, boney kid in a sharkskin suit and red bowtie met us at the door and invited us in.

"Great look," I said. The kid was a fashion plate.

"Thank you so much," he said, beaming.

He offered us soft drinks. We were about floating from the sweet tea we'd had at every house, so we declined.

Throughout the conversation, younger siblings ran in and out demanding various forms of attention from Antwone. He was patient and kind to them despite their whining, crying, and the usual kid-style conflicts. A parent was not to be seen.

Antwone had little to add so we didn't keep him long. He seemed like a good kid, living in impoverished circumstances, trying to keep out of trouble and make something of himself.

I would keep my eye on him, help if I could. I didn't share that with O'Hanlon.

It was almost noon. One more interview to go. I had the distinct feeling that we had learned all we could from these young people.

Last was Trace Jones, a senior at Savannah Christian High School who'd met Jayden through a church group. The drummer in the band, medium height and a bit overweight with stringy red hair, he wore black jeans and an Atlanta Falcons T-shirt. He was shoeless. His parents were divorced—dad military and mom a tax preparer. Trace had two younger brothers away at a YMCA soccer camp for the week. The mother sat quietly while we interviewed her eldest.

The questions and answers droned into a boring litany. O'Hanlon turned another page in her notebook. She doodled sketches of bullets between jotted notes. My mind wandered. The living room of the 1980s split-level was neat and bright. Family photos hung in black frames near a door that opened into the kitchen. Among the images was a man who looked a lot like Trace. About forty years old, he held an imposing, dull gray rifle. There were lots of military folks in the area, but still, hackles rose on the back of my neck.

"That's a nice collection of pictures," I said, interrupting O'Hanlon. "Is that your former husband?" I stood and pointed at the man with the gun.

O'Hanlon was clearly pissed at my interruption. I could see her jaw clench. I ignored her.

"Yep, he's still in the boys' lives," Mrs. Jones said. Her fingers tore at a knitting project she was working on. "He tries to be a good father. Has some issues, though. His fourth tour in Afghanistan put us over the top. Was just too much to recover from."

I could only imagine. Four tours? Crazy. "Which base is he at? Hunter Army Airbase in Hinesville?" I asked.

"Fort Stewart," she said, sighed.

"What does he do there?"

"Special Ops. He's a sniper instructor."

My mouth fell open but I shut it fast. I glanced over at the detective. Her face remained immobile but she chewed on her thumbnail for a second. Maybe she'd forgive me for the interference. This could be a critical lead.

A few minutes and several innocuous questions later, O'Hanlon wrapped up the conversation with the Jones family. She obtained the dad's contact information and promised to keep them updated on the investigation.

We headed for the car. It was spitting rain again. O'Hanlon walked fast toward the curb, then stopped short. I almost fell over her. "What did you think you were doing in there?" she demanded, glowering.

"The photo, you mean? I know it was kind of a Hail Mary, but it looked like a sniper rifle to me."

"It's an M24, used by the Army. I saw it. I didn't need you to draw her attention to that fact."

"I didn't realize that you could see it from where you were sitting. My apologies."

"Let me do my job, Ms. Middleton."

I gritted my teeth and tried not to snap back at her. Clearly, I had been presumptuous to hope for any slack. The car lock chirped and we slid into our opposite sides of the front seat.

"Just trying to help," I said, keeping my voice neutral.

"I'd rather you observe, as we had discussed yesterday. We're not good cop, bad cop. You're not a cop. Period. Do you understand?"

I started to really not like her. "You're right, I'm not a cop. I'm a journalist—and a trained investigator, like you. What is it? Why is it such a burden to have someone along who could actually help you?"

"I brought you on because I owed your brother a favor. What I don't need is for you to come in here and, and screw this up for me. This is not Fox News."

My blood pressure skyrocketed.

"I never worked for Fox News. I worked for an NBC network affiliate, and I won an Emmy for my work on the Los Angeles School Board scandal last year. I got an email last night that I'm under consideration for a job at CNN. I'm not a hack. I have a picture of Walter freakin' Cronkite on my desk."

O'Hanlon cracked a flicker of a smile. She sighed as the rain hit the windshield, harder now. "I'm under a lot of pressure here with this case. I don't want to blow it."

"I understand pressure. And this is my nephew, I don't want to have it blown either."

11

O'Hanlon's anger seemed to cool. She turned on the computer and shifted her attitude into professional mode. "I'm checking the database for priors on the kid's dad, Kiefer Jones, the sniper. And with the possible Farsi connection Rory gave us, I might actually have something to work with."

I didn't know if O'Hanlon's sudden refocus on the work at hand meant that this crisis was over or not. I crossed my arms over my chest and looked at her.

"We'll move forward, all right?" she said, not raising her eyes from the screen.

"Am I still onboard?"

She nodded.

"Okay," I said, skeptical. "We'll move forward."

While O'Hanlon was entering Jones's information, my phone beeped. It was Dexter.

"Mind if I take this? It's my son."

"No problem," she said, intent on her typing.

I clicked on my cell phone. "Hi, honey."

"Hey, mom. How's the investigation going?"

"Going okay. Slow."

"I spoke with Aunt Honey."

"She called you?"

"No, I called her. She's at Gram's."

"Yeah, I know." I was surprised he'd reached out, they barely knew each other. "That was sweet of you, babe."

"She's a nice lady."

"She is. Glad you're in Los Angeles though. Tough times down here."

"Well, speaking of Los Angeles, we have a situation." Dexter's voice cracked. That didn't happen much anymore unless he was anxious.

"A situation?" I could feel my own stress responses niggling. "What kind of a situation?"

"Daddy's going to Iceland."

"Ireland?"

"No, Ice-land."

"Iceland? When?"

"Tomorrow."

"What?" My ex was wildly impulsive in every area of his life. It had charmed me at first. "Iceland, uh, what a surprise, huh? Sounds like it will be quite an adventure for you, sweetheart."

"It'll be an adventure for Dad, but not for me. Her name is Brigitta and she lives on an alpaca farm outside of Reykjavik. Dad wants me to go along and help shear alpacas. I don't want to go. He'll be with the lady and I'll be mucking alpaca stalls. That's always the way it goes with him."

I knew he was right. "You're supposed to be together all month." Only my first ex-husband would find a nubile, alpaca-shearing, Nordic goddess to pursue in lieu of caring for his son.

"They're supposed to have very soft fur and they're cute. It sounds kinda cool and all but when there's a girl involved, Dad usually shoves cash into my hand and dumps me onto some random person, then and he and the girlfriend disappear."

I could not believe that my ex had only lasted a week and a half with Dexter before creating an excuse to bail. Actually, I could.

"But anyhow, Mom, I was going to do the UCLA high school film summer workshop next week and now I can't. I can't find anybody I can crash with and I don't want to stay alone at Dad's place. But guess what," Dexter continued, finding his voice again. "I was researching on the Web and came across the same kind of program at Savannah College of Art and Design. It starts this week. We live in the dorms for two weeks and I get to make a documentary. Sounds good, right?"

Wrong. This would be a terrible time for Dexter to come to Savannah. With Momma sick, Aunt Honey barely functioning, and Luther and I working with O'Hanlon, I couldn't handle someone else to worry about.

"Dexter, go get your father."

"He's over at the driving range shooting golf balls. He'll be back in about an hour, I think."

"Have him call me the minute he gets in. We'll

talk about this later today, okay? Gotta run now. The detective and I are heading back to the station."

I was seething.

"'K, mom. Love you. Be careful out there."

"Always. Love you, too, baby boy. Miss you, tons." The kid had a way of always melting my heart.

I clicked off and tried not to grit my teeth. Scanned my texts, checking for something from Dexter's father, Kevin Jackson, about his plans for Iceland and the *Sigridsdottir* chick. Nothing. I dropped the iPhone back into my purse.

O'Hanlon looked over at me. "How old?"

"Fifteen," I said. "Both of them."

She actually chuckled.

You got kids?" I asked.

"Nineteen-year-old daughter at UCLA, doing study abroad in London."

I looked over at her, she was biting her lip.

"My ex-husband, you may know him," she said, turning down the radio. "He was the prosecuting attorney on that school board case. I didn't realize you'd covered that."

I knew that O'Hanlon and I shared a history of being long-time Angelinos, but this news was stunning. "Whoa, you mean Brandon Doyle?"

"That's him. I'd heard at one point that you had been, uh, involved with him."

My mouth opened in shock.

"What? You can't be serious. No way in hell was I involved with him or 99 percent of the men the local gossip rags had me paired with. No way. I probably shouldn't say this, I know things are, well, uncomfortable enough between us, but Doyle, man, he's a very, very, nasty son of a bitch."

"You're being too kind," she said.

"I could tell you how I *really* feel about the slimeball."

"I think I might be getting to like you," O'Hanlon said. I sensed relief in her response. Then the computer beeped. She immediately shifted focus to the screen—scrolled and read. "Oh, jeez. Interesting."

"What is it?"

"Kiefer Jones. Priors. Mostly domestics, charges dropped every time. Aggravated assault at a bar in Statesville. Settled out of court. Suspected PTSD."

"All that, and he still has total access to firearms," I commented. "Gun laws in this country, and definitely in this state, never fail to amaze me."

O'Hanlon nodded her head, her red hair curled like loopy copper wire as the humidity rose. Mine was even worse.

"I'll set up a meeting with him as soon as possible," she said, firing up the ignition. "I'll go through the databases and see what else I can find. Got your cell number—I'll text you if there's anything. Can I drop you off at your house?" She pulled out onto the street.

It was starting to rain in earnest. I had forgotten how much it could rain here. Decades of Los Angeles drought had become my normal. Thunder rumbled in the distance. The wipers started their thump-thump cadence. The radio crackled.

"That would be great. My mother's place is over in midtown near the corner of Henry and Vine."

"I know," she said.

Why was I surprised that she knew exactly where we

lived? Anyway, I was still in the investigation. Despite my gaffe at the sniper's home, she was keeping me with her. It was enough for now, but I knew I would be fast getting sick of walking on eggshells around this woman.

12

Blasts of wind beat the foliage as we drove in silence to Henry Street. A row of crepe myrtle trees along the way resembled dancing old ladies on spindly legs. Their long gray hair of Spanish moss, laced with fading pink blossoms, shimmied and whipped like dervishes.

Detective O'Hanlon pulled up to the curb. Water ran down the sidewalk, roiling like an open artery. I took off my suede shoes and stuffed them in my purse. I thanked O'Hanlon for the ride and then slamming the car door behind me, made a dash to the porch in my bare feet. It was only a twenty-yard dash, but I got soaked. I remembered doing this very same thing as a youngster, so many times before.

As I opened the unlocked front door, I ran a hand through my hair so I wouldn't drip on the wood floors like a sheepdog. A wet and muddy pair of men's athletic shoes rested askew next to the doormat, black and silver Nikes, size twelvish. I wondered who was visiting.

I fished the iPhone out of my bag on my way into the vestibule. I still hadn't heard a thing from Dexter or his delinquent father and I was starting to really boil. Then I heard a familiar voice.

"S'up, Mom."

Dexter waved from the couch, holding Aunt Honey's hand like they had known each other forever.

I blinked my eyes, sure I was hallucinating. "Dex? What the—"

I sighed. He was a handsome boy, several years from growing into a man's full body but his feet predicted he could reach his father's height. He wore baggy Los Angeles Clippers T-shirt and sweatpants.

"You have such a fine son, Bea. He has been so kind and comforting. My Lord, it's been ten years since he was here, at least." Honey's eyes held a faint glimmer of light. I dropped my bag onto a chair, dashed to the couch, and hugged them both with all my might.

"Yes, it's been way, way too long," I said, pushing back the guilt that always lurked right around the corner. "It's so great to see your face, baby," I said, pinching my boy's sweet cheeks then feigning an attempt to strangle him. "But I'm also angry. I want to know exactly how the heck you managed to get here. Hear me?"

"Yes, ma'am." He gulped hard. I could see his Adam's apple bounce.

Two minutes in Georgia and Dexter was already saying, "yes, ma'am." I liked it. The kids all still do exactly what you tell them not to do, but it feels more civilized somehow when they're so polite about it.

I wanted to immediately press Dexter for the details of his arrival, but I contained myself and poured us all sweet tea and made some sandwiches first. My stomach growled from the fragrance of fresh sourdough. I piled on sliced barbequed turkey, Swiss cheese, lettuce, tomato, and mustard. Oh, yeah. I've never been one of those people who pick at their food when stressed. I tore into a bag of sour cream and chive potato chips, only remembering to pass them around after I had done some serious damage to the contents.

"Will y'all excuse me?" Honey suddenly looked exhausted. "I'm going to lay down for a bit." She squeezed Dexter's hand, rose from the couch, and headed for the stairway. She had been staying with Momma much of the time so she could be near her son. She had a little house in Shellman Corners that she'd put on the market but no offers were coming in.

"Of course, sweetheart," I said. "Can I help you with anything?"

"No, dear. Talk with your son. I love you both. So happy you're here."

"So are we, Aunt Honey, so are we." My heart broke for all of us.

I sat on the couch and embraced my son, who, over the last week, had grown taller than I was. He patiently allowed me my motherly moment, then I let him go and went for more ice cubes, dabbing my eyes. He knew that in the next breath I would demand a very persuasive explanation as to his unexpected arrival.

"Okay, Dexter, spill it," I said. "When I talked to you about forty-five minutes ago, I thought you were in Los Angeles. Unless you beamed yourself across the country, you were already here."

His typical guilty face emerged. It involved lip chewing and nose scratching. "Well, Dad's friend, Tyrell Barnes, had to go to Jacksonville, Florida this morning. He plays for the Jaguars."

"I know Tyrell." Another man-child.

"He has a private plane. We left Santa Monica really early. Played video games and had tons of great snacks. It was way cool. His daughter came with us. She's nineteen, really nice."

Older women. Look out little man, I thought to myself. "Well I'm glad you had a good flight, but I wish you would have told me what was going on. I don't want you to get in the habit of not being forthright."

"Yes, ma'am. I was afraid you'd say no, and I'd have to go to Iceland. I couldn't do it."

"Okay, I understand. I'll take this up with your father later. He never should have put you in this position, but I still expect you to be honest with me. Always."

"Yes, ma'am, I'm sorry."

I sighed, he sighed, we hugged, and it was over.

"So," I said, "tell me about this program at SCAD."

The next morning, after a quick trip to Target for missing essentials, I checked Dexter into a mid-century modern residence hall at Savannah College of Art and Design about three miles from Henry Street. A pulsing neon-light sculpture of faces merging and re-emerging in multiple hues moved across the lobby walls. Made my stomach a little queasy, but the kids loved it.

Dexter's roommate, Jonathan Cohen, was a fellow film student from Atlanta. A perky, pony-tailed resident assistant named Tess Ramirez made the introductions and helped Dexter set up his computer, activate his cafeteria card, and review his class schedule.

With a peck on the cheek and a "Don't worry, Mom," Dexter and Jonathan hustled off to a floor meeting.

A sharp, unexpected stab of loss sent my heart aching. This moment opened a quick view into the near future when Dexter would be heading to college for real. I was not ready for this. Where had the time gone? Life was moving way, way too fast. I'd make Dexter live at home and go to UCLA. Alyssa, too. Sadly, Aunt Honey would never have the opportunity to see Jayden make this transition. He would be forever fifteen.

As I walked slowly down the steps toward Momma's silver Camry, my phone sounded. It was Detective O'Hanlon. "We're leaving for Fort Stewart in thirty minutes to talk with Kiefer Jones."

"On my way," I said. I wondered what Jones, the Special Ops sniper instructor, would have to say. I also wondered what favor O'Hanlon had done for my brother that got her to agree to put up with me.

13

Resembling a corpse ready for embalming, Emad Al Alequi, also known as Evan Doobius, lay naked amid a tangle of shiny black sheets, moldering food containers, and empty bottles of Jack Daniels. The bluish light of a laptop illuminated the dark room. The screensaver image featured skeletons dancing to the tune of the old spiritual, "Dem Bones."

A yellow-eyed tabby cat used the reeking litter box, as hard as a slab of concrete from overuse.

There was a knock at Emad's door. He twitched, coming up from the depths of a drunken sleep. Scratching his genitals, he opened a gritty eye and glanced at the clock. It was 5:07 a.m. and still dark as pitch outside.

The knocking became pounding.

"Emad, open this door."

The voice was deep, male, and angry.

Father had arrived.

Emad's eyes opened wide. Nausea rose into his throat. He knew this confrontation was going to happen, but he was never really ready for a discussion with Daddy. "Go away, leave me alone."

The door to his little house shuddered. The pounding became increasingly insistent. Evan tried not to panic.

No neighbor would be calling the police to investigate the commotion. He lived too far out on an isolated, woodsy edge of Wilmington Island, about five miles from Savannah proper.

"Emad, open up or I'll rip this door off the hinges," his father roared.

Emad knew he would do it.

He threw off his covers.

The cat yowled and ran into the closet.

Grabbing a pair of running shorts that were wadded up on a chair, he hoisted them over his bony hips then pulled a beer-sodden Atlanta Falcons T-shirt over his head. A couple of condoms lay on the floor from a visit by a big-assed wannabe rock starlet earlier in the evening. The bitch was relentless.

Emad picked up the shriveled rubbers and stuffed them into the trash beneath a pizza box. Not the behavior of a good Islamic-fundamentalist boy, but she had helped alleviate the grief, if only for a moment, over his friend and protégée, Jayden Middleton. They would have conquered the world together.

He rubbed grit from his eyes and took a deep breath. Father would not be leaving until he could humiliate his son, again.

"Emad. Open up." His father's English turned to

Farsi. "Now! I'm asking you for the last time."

"Shit," the son muttered. He knew the old man would be coming for him when he didn't show up for work. His father was always breathing down his neck. He didn't give a flying fuck though, not anymore. The man had gone too far this time, way too far.

Emad opened the door.

Farouk stepped toward his son. Looming overhead, he was all fury, vibrating at a dangerous pitch. Two of his men remained on the porch, pretending to mind their own business. Evan knew them both from other nasty times. He hated them.

Farouk glanced around the trashed living room where Evan had been sleeping on a pull-out couch. He saw the bottles of booze spilling from the trash. His fingers jerked toward the holster beneath his jacket. Jaw clenched, he appeared as if he was almost ready to do the unspeakable.

"Go ahead. You know you want to," Emad taunted.

Backhanding his son across the face, Farouk sent him stumbling, twisting, and falling face-first onto the coffee table. Emad's flattened nose began to gush, splattering blood onto the floor. A coppery taste filled his mouth. Struggling to stand back up, the son refused to prostrate himself in front of his father.

"Wipe your face," Farouk snarled. "Enough of your fairy boy self-pity."

Emad's father was a big man, twice the size of his son. Emad had his mother's bird-like features, her artistic nature, and passive brown eyes. Unlike his older brother, Shimon, who had almost been his father's clone, and thus, the golden child.

But Shimon was dead. Killed in a drone attack along with his wife and young kids. The Americans were responsible. Why Shimon? Why not Emad? Why the strong and not the weak? It made no sense to his father. As if sense could be made of random death.

Emad wiped his face with his shirt.

His father stepped outside onto the sagging porch and lifted his chin toward his son. "Take him."

The two guards grabbed Evan by the arms. They dragged him down the steps and across the driveway of crushed shells as the sky lightened toward dawn.

Emad's dark eyes smoldered with contained rage. "You didn't know that Jayden Middleton's uncle was a sheriff, did you? And his aunt's a news reporter. They'll find you, old man, all of you. You'll pay."

Farouk hesitated for a split second. His son smiled. Like the vampire Lestat, Emad's teeth were red, fresh blood dribbling from the corners of his mouth. The two bodyguards hurled him into the backseat of a black Lincoln Town Car. His head cracked hard against the door jamb.

"You thought killing Jayden would stop me? There's only one thing that can stop me." Emad's words spit out in a bloody foam as he struggled to sit up.

His father looked over his shoulder, recognizing the challenge. "You think I wouldn't do it? Think again."

The air inside the car was freezing. As the locks shut with a bank-vault *clunk,* Evan Doobius, aka Emad Al Alequi, began to shiver uncontrollably.

14

I finished looking at the photos Alyssa had texted from Hawaii. Seeing my almost thirteen-year-old wearing a way too teeny bikini, with her new little infant sister and the picture-perfect version of the Strauss clan, was kind of depressing.

Unlike Dexter, Alyssa had always had a precarious self-image. I knew she wanted a "real family," the traditional kind from the storybooks, in a deep way that I never quite understood. I could provide a lot of what she needed, but not that.

Eli Strauss, my second ex-husband and Alyssa's father, had been my news director at a TV station in Los Angeles. With Eli, a devout Jew, I found solace in the liturgy and fundamentals of that faith after my painful and contentious split from Kevin. But it had all happened too fast. The infamous rebound effect had been in play.

We divorced shortly after Alyssa was born and had shared custody, very effectively for the most part.

Eli remarried two years ago to a rather abrasive Israeli woman, a psychiatrist at Cedars-Sinai Medical Center. I think she's cold and all in her head, but Eli seems happy. I'm not sure what her effect on my daughter has been.

Alyssa is also a frighteningly beautiful girl. Cocoa skin, much lighter than mine, her father's piercing blue eyes and her Grandmother Strauss's loose, dark curls, she's stunningly beautiful. I was afraid that as she grew, somehow Los Angeles would eat her up. She could easily spin off somewhere bad, seeking images of perfection that didn't exist, and blame herself for never being able to measure up.

As I pondered my family situation, what the future held and how Savannah figured in, my cell phone rang. I checked the ID and accepted the call.

"Hi, Aunt Honey. Sorry I slipped out so early this morning. I left you a cinnamon roll from Clausen's."

"Thanks, dear. Just wanted to let you know," she cleared her throat, "that the coroner released Jayden's body. He's been delivered to the funeral home. The service is set for Friday afternoon at our church, 2:00 p.m."

I wanted to share something wise and comforting but again I could think of absolutely nothing. For some agonies, there simply are no words.

"Thank you, Aunt Honey," I finally said. "I'll let Detective O'Hanlon know about the funeral so she can pass it on to her people. We're about ready to leave for Fort Stewart to talk with someone who might have a lead."

"You and Luther, and this Detective O'Hanlon, you'll bring the murderer to justice real soon. I know you will."

I could hear tears forming in her words.

"Yes, real soon, Auntie, real soon." If only that could be true. I felt the dry mouth and hammering heart of desperation—a frame of mind that had never served me well.

Dexter and his roomie and new BFF, Jonathan, wandered into Biggie's Bean Project, a hip-looking, distressed-wood, and corrugated-metal coffee house two blocks from their residence hall. It looked like they were feeling a bit sophisticated, out on their own around town. They gave the photography-filled space an appreciative look. Complicated coffee orders rolled off their tongues with practiced ease. Both tall and lanky, they were high school basketball players as well as budding artists. Savannah was a place where it was fine to be both.

After receiving their drinks and hefty slices of fresh key lime pie with extra whip, they planted themselves at a wobbly wooden table in front a large window where they could watch the girls coming and going from the health club across the street. Jonathan insisted on stabilizing the table with a couple of sugar packets.

The boys discussed hot women, hometowns, and high schools. Eventually, talk turned to sports and basketball—Lakers versus Clippers, and the Atlanta Hawks.

"My dad played for the Lakers for six years until he totally blew out his knee," Dexter said between mouthfuls.

"So your Dad is Kevin Jackson?"

"Uh-huh."

"He was really good."

"Yup," Dexter said, "but you never know in pro sports. It can all end in an instant. I'd never go in that direction."

"But all the money and the action. Whoa." Jonathan's eyes were glassy, far off into imagining how good all that cash and fame might be.

"I'd rather be poor and happy," Dexter said. Then he smiled. "Well, not too poor, though. You want to split another piece? We don't have food like this in Los Angeles. This stuff is seriously sick."

"I'm in for more."

"I'll get it." Dexter rose and took off toward the counter.

He lined up behind an attractive Asian girl about his age. His raised eyebrows indicated profound admiration for her very short skirt and great legs in fishnet tights and black ankle boots.

She turned toward him and smiled.

For a moment, Dexter was tongue-tied. His cool evaporated. "Are you a, uh, a SCAD student?" he asked her.

"I'd like to be, someday," she said, tossing her long, shiny hair. "Are you?"

"What?" It hadn't even registered what she had asked him. She was definitely hot.

"Are you a student there?" the girl asked again.

She smelled slightly of something flowery. "Oh, uh, yes, in the high school summer program," Dexter said.

"Nice."

"Yeah, so far so good. It's only been a day. I'm going to do a documentary." *Was he as big a dork as he sounded? Probably.*

She stared at Dexter, eyes intense. Her head cocked to the side, taking him in. She had dimples. Oh, God.

"Can I buy you a coffee or a piece of pie? The key lime is awesome. Would you like to join me and my friend?"

He glanced back at Jonathan, who flashed him a not-so-subtle thumbs-up. Dexter flushed and turned back to the girl.

"You're actually the one I want to talk to," she said, reaching into her purse, rooting around for a few dollar bills.

Dexter's eyes widened. "Really? You wanted to talk to me?" He could feel sweat gathering on the back of his neck.

"Are you doing a documentary on Jayden Middleton?" she asked. "You're his cousin, aren't you?"

Shocked at the question, Dexter swallowed.

"How did you know that?"

"I live in your grandma's neighborhood. Word gets around. I was—er—a very good friend of his and a real fan."

"I'm Dexter Jackson. It's nice to meet a friend of Jayden's. I haven't seen him since we were both little, so I never really knew him. I wish I had."

"Cornelia Chan. Nice to meet you too. Your cousin was amazing."

She smiled, perfect white teeth gleamed. They shook hands.

"Doing a documentary on him is a really interesting thought," Dexter said, suddenly captivated by the idea as well as the girl.

He ordered two more pie slices. Cornelia got her own coffee, and they joined Jonathan for introductions. Jon agreed that the documentary idea was a good one. "I'm in," he said. They clinked their coffee cups together. "To the Three Musketeers."

"More like Mousekateers," Dexter said. "I'm always the realist."

Cornelia giggled. Her dimples were amazing.

15

Big, gray turboprops, military jets, and a Coast Guard helicopter came and went as we approached the entrance to Fort Stewart.

"Stewart's about three hundred thousand acres," O'Hanlon said. "Biggest base east of the Mississippi. Add on Hunter Army Airfield and it's massive."

"Passed by it plenty of times but I've never been inside." I craned my neck to watch a big chopper overhead. "This will be interesting. I remember from back in grade school that the main runway was an alternative spot for landing the space shuttle."

"Yeah, I think it's around three miles long," O'Hanlon said. We drove up to the guard house.

The gatekeepers were heavily armed, their movements vigilant. Our IDs were carefully inspected, phone calls made, and directions given to the sniper range.

The detective drove about a mile before turning a hard right off from the main road that took visitors into the heart of the base. We were immediately enveloped by a thick slash of pine forest. The sunlight shone dim through the canopy. A coyote paused by the roadside as we drew near, then disappeared back into the underbrush.

About five more miles, on progressively less-maintained roads, a broad grassy field opened before us. O'Hanlon pulled into a crushed-shell parking lot and joined less than a dozen other vehicles. The smell of pine mingled with brackish gunpowder.

Behind a shallow berm, maybe fifteen camouflage-clad men lay prone on the ground with rifles balanced on tripods, spotters with scopes at their sides.

No one turned to acknowledge us, but they knew we'd arrived. Somehow you could feel their intense awareness. Slow and methodical, the teams studied their targets. Then the snipers took shots at distant human-shaped forms that moved back and forth like tiny puppets near a rocky outcrop more than a quarter mile down the field.

Except for the explosive *pfft* when a trigger was squeezed and a bullet discharged, the place was eerily quiet. The vibe was strange and tense; warriors were practicing to kill. Even the birds and crickets seemed to have abandoned this meadow. The men and they were all men, were lean, stone-faced, and all business.

Nervous and antsy after a half hour of watching, I wanted to find Kiefer Jones and get the interview over with. The shooting was getting to me, bringing up feelings I'd rather keep filed away. I watched the soldiers study their targets, strategizing, and setting up for a successful hit. I probably had a lot to learn from the sniper's stoic patience. The best shot was likely the one worth waiting for. I breathed out, trying to imagine being in this profession. I'm not sure that I could.

Finally, the training practice was over. The men packed up and put their gear away. Some sat on a bench under a canvas awning and began disassembling their firearms. From deathly stillness to picnic chatter in a matter of moments. Still no birds.

Kiefer Jones removed a sweat-stained, khaki fishing hat and ran a hand through his reddish blond hair. I recognized him from his photograph. His skin was sun-beaten and leathery. Although he seemed to be only in his early forties, he was probably a candidate for melanoma. We walked out to meet him as he headed our way.

"You must be Detective O'Hanlon." He offered his hand to her. "And..." he looked at me with intelligent blue eyes.

"This is my colleague, Beatrice Middleton. She's here as an observer," O'Hanlon said.

"Yes, ma'am, pleasure to meet you both. Would you care to join me in the office? It's much cooler and I can get us some sodas."

We agreed and followed Jones to a small, cement brick office building. It was painted a drab gray except for a black, red, and white sniper logo, involving crosshairs and a skull, over the door. Inside, all was the same bloodless color, except for Jones's shrine to his children.

Crayon drawings, plaster molds of small hands painted in electric hues, photos of the boys in team uniforms and school pics from every grade adorned the walls. He was definitely not feeling like a guy who could kill a kid.

We thanked him for the cold drinks and sat down on wooden chairs across from his desk. Bare bones, but not uncomfortable.

"So, what brings y'all out to Fort Stewart this morning?" Kiefer Jones asked. "My wife, ex-wife, says it has something to do with the death of my son's friend, Jayden Middleton."

Did you know the boy?" O'Hanlon asked.

"I did. About couple months ago I took the whole band fishing out here on the Canoochee River. Caught bluegills and sunfish. We fried 'em up, ate 'em all. Jayden was a good kid, very talented. I loved seeing all those boys from such different backgrounds playing music together and loving it. We could learn a lot from this next generation. They care about the music, not the color of the keys, know what I mean?"

O'Hanlon nodded her head. "That's really good to hear, sir, but somebody didn't feel quite that optimistic. We have reason to believe that the boy was killed, by a sniper."

I heard a quick intake of air. "What?" he asked, eyes wide, appearing truly shocked.

"Can you give us any insight, Lieutenant Jones?"

"Like what?" He leaned forward, hands gripped the desktop. "You can't think that I was involved."

"We're checking every possibility, sir," O'Hanlon said, unmoved. "Are there any among your group who would ever, even as a remote possibility, take on, shall we say, freelance work?"

Jones's face turned red. He sat quietly for a moment, shaking his head, collecting himself. "There is no one, absolutely no one I know, who would ever accept the kind of offer you are talking about. We're soldiers, Detective, sworn to protect this country. We're not murderers, although some might call us that. Ultimately, we save American lives. Every shot taken is about saving Americans."

"Okay, okay, sir. I had to ask. We have to pose the tough questions even if they seem offensive."

Jones relaxed a bit. He studied an invisible spot on the wall. "Tell me about the shot."

"The shot?" His request seemed to take the detective by surprise. She stopped scribbling in her notebook.

My eyes narrowed, not sure what he was asking. Then, I understood.

"The shot, tell me about it. Where did it hit him? What was the round?"

"It's an ongoing investigation," O'Hanlon said. "We can't discuss those details with you, sir. I'm sorry."

"Detective, excuse me," I said, done walking on eggshells. "If Lieutenant Jones is told exactly what happened to Jayden, then maybe he can offer his expert opinion on whom, or what type of person, might have murdered my nephew."

"Jayden was your nephew?" Jones asked.

I nodded.

All at once he seemed to soften. His eyes shifted to the photos of his children. "I am so sorry, Ms. Middleton."

Detective O'Hanlon was quiet, weighing the decision. She glanced at me, sighed, and then filled him in.

"The shooter is definitely not US military," Jones

said, after hearing the story. He sounded sure.

"Why do you say that?" I asked.

"We would never have made the second shot, the one to the violin case. 'One shot, one kill.' That's what we say, and that's how we do it."

"Then who—" O'Hanlon began.

"Drug cartels are known to be active in this area, both Russian and Afghan, maybe others."

O'Hanlon nodded in agreement. "We know. It's easy for them to hide in all these swamps and creeks."

"Any of them could have a sniper-trained operative on their team. I'd look there if I were you. And if any news comes my way, you'll be the first to know."

We thanked Jones for his help, then headed for the car. As O'Hanlon and I drove away, something came clear to me. "It's about the violin case, something about the case or the music," I said. "That's where we need to look. The music. Who hated the music?"

16

My cell phone rang. It was Momma, she'd been discharged and was on her way home. *Hallelujah.* Luther had picked her up at the hospital and they were arriving at Henry Street. I assured her that I'd be there momentarily.

Aunt Freddie May's pale blue Ford Fairlane, Luther's cop car, and Honey's Prius all filled the driveway. I parked the Camry in front of the residence across the street. A high-school-aged girl with long, black hair scuttled from the porch and disappeared into the backyard. *Sneaking an illegal toke? Kids.*

I rushed up the steps into the house and into the arms of my small, frail mother. She seemed almost skeletal. Her skin was sallow and translucent. But her eyes sparkled once again in that old familiar way that told you that you were special and loved, and she was so glad to see you. How did Luther and I get so lucky?

After Momma was ensconced in her rocking chair, feet up, with a glass of sweet tea in her hand and Fig Newtons on a plate at her side, talk turned to the investigation.

I was not sure of what and how much to share. The grim reality was that we had little to go on. I didn't want to depress everyone with our slow progress or raise false hopes through speculation. Fortunately, Luther took the lead. Evidently, O'Hanlon had been keeping him updated by the hour.

A short while later, Aunt Hattie arrived with Dexter, toting a pan of lasagna, garlic bread, more garlic bread, and a bowl of salad. Dexter seemed to be enthusiastically reaching out to his relatives without my help or prompting. I was proud of him.

Luther grabbed the boy and gave him a noogie and a big hug.

"Too long, youngster. Gotta put a brick on your head to make sure you don't get taller than me."

The sweet gesture was heartbreaking because Jayden should be here for his brick as well.

Aunt Freddie May hustled into the kitchen. She braced herself against the fridge for a moment, seeming to collect herself, then pulled out a sweet potato pie that a well-wisher had dropped off earlier in the week. We filled our plates and followed Honey's lead. She wanted to discuss the upcoming funeral.

"Actually, Dexter has been helping me brainstorm something interesting," Aunt Honey said like she was sharing a secret with him. He beamed. "And I'm turning the musical program over to Harris Tyde. He'll be working with the musicians and the choir. He's wonderful."

"Is Tyde your assistant director?" I asked.

Aunt Honey nodded, pulled a crumpled tissue from her sleeve and wiped her eyes. "Such a kind man. He's gay but God made him that way and who are we not to celebrate all of His children?" she said with great conviction. We all nodded our heads in agreement.

"It's going to be a wonderful funeral. No eulogies, just his music, that's what my boy would have wanted." She took Dexter's hand and kissed his fingers. "I am so remarkably blessed to have such a loving family, friends at the church, the choir, the whole community." She stopped for a moment in silent prayer. My eyes dampened with tears.

The lasagna was delicious but I couldn't eat much of it. My stomach felt queasy. Aunt Hattie noticed my half-filled plate, but she didn't go after me about not eating enough like she had back at the hospital. All you had to do was look at me and know that food consumption had never been a problem.

It was almost 10:00 p.m. before the family meeting broke up. We ended in a long giant hug, holding each other up amid the tears. Aunts Freddie May and Hattie volunteered to drop Dexter at the residence hall. He'd been raised in a world of skinny women, kale smoothies, Beemers, and Audis, yet I could see that he loved riding in the old Fairlane with his two great-aunties and a container of leftover bread and lasagna on his lap.

As Aunt Honey took Momma up to bed, I followed Luther outside and cornered him before he could crawl back into his squad car. The night was soft and moist with the earthy scent of decomposing leaves and the first hint of a change of season. The quick *snick* of bicycle tires on wet pavement came and went down the empty street.

"O'Hanlon likes you, thinks you're good," Luther said, leaning back against the vehicle.

"Well, of course, I'm good. I came so close to walking away and telling her what she could do with her stupid attitude yesterday." I crossed my arms over my chest and planted my feet. "Forgive me, but she can be such a bitch."

Luther smiled, playing some private scenario in his head. "Well bless your sassy little heart, Beatrice Middleton. I'm glad you didn't walk away. I vouched for you big time, but you're still a complete wild card to her. She knows she's walking the line by bringing a civvie into a murder investigation, especially a civvie directly related to the victim."

I shrugged, knowing he was right. "What I don't understand, is why she's doing it? What kind of favor are you calling in, big brother?"

"Why do you think it's a favor?"

"Because I know you, Luther, that's why. And she told me it was a favor."

He outright laughed at that one. "Whatever *favor* that may or may not exist, is between me and Mary."

"*Mary?* So, you call her Mary? Do you two have a 'thing' going on? I should have known—I felt some kind of one-off vibe from the very beginning."

"No way." Luther shook his head, vehemently denying it.

I knew I'd hit pay dirt here. He was the worst liar.

"You two *do* have a thing, don't you? Oh, my God. You and Detective O'Hanlon. Pepper and spice, what a vision."

"Uh-uh, little snoop, it's not like that. Not like that at all."

"Then what?"

"Why do I always end up telling you everything?"

"Because I tell you everything. Now, what is it with this woman? What's going on, Luther?"

He moved from the car door and we went to sit on the porch step together, like old times. The house was dark now except for the kitchen light. Momma and Aunt Honey were probably already fast asleep. It had been an exhausting day.

"Okay," he began, "if you must know, here's the deal. I met O'Hanlon at a national police convention in Phoenix, maybe three or four years ago."

"You've known her for that long?" I was quite surprised.

Luther nodded. "We were registered for the same workshop on workforce diversity. The group got into a great discussion about the different values around law enforcement in various parts of the country. When she found out I was from Georgia, we got to talking and I invited her to join me for lunch. Turns out her dad was a cop in Macon when she was a kid before they moved to southern California. He ended up as an assistant chief in Santa Monica."

"Oh, my God, Walter O'Hanlon?" I said, finally recognizing the name. "I know who he is, even interviewed him a few times for various stories. And I knew her sleazebag former husband too. She and I talked about him."

"Yeah, well, that sleazebag former husband was stalking her at the time. Her father had died of testicular cancer and then Doyle was terrorizing her. Her mom had passed away early on. Mary was trying to leave Los Angeles with her daughter, Holly, a junior in high school then, but things were going to hell all around. I guess he's a lawyer with heavy connections."

"He's powerful and ruthless. A complete control-freak. She's lucky she got out alive."

"That bad?" His jaw clenched.

"Very possibly. He was finally put on probation last year for taking sexual favors from under-age clients. He's up for disbarment but he'll weasel out of it somehow and turn up as head of a major movie studio or something. He's one of those shape-shifters who'll reinvent himself whenever he needs to. Those types do well in Los Angeles."

"I wonder how she married such a snake." Luther sighed and rubbed his head, seeming to search for an answer that wouldn't come.

"He's a total Prince Charming, Luther. Great looking, funny, hobnobs with all the *glitterati*. Takes a while before you realize he's also a total sociopath."

I was truly pained for what O'Hanlon must have endured. I knew about wrong choices.

Luther took a swig from a water bottle he had stuffed in his pocket. Offered it to me but I passed. We suspended conversation as a gaggle of students walked, skipped, and staggered by, singing the Tina Turner classic, "What's Love Got to Do with It." *Eau de* sour beer with the barest hint of marijuana wafted along with them.

"When Mary started the job here in Savannah, about a year ago," Luther continued after the singing kids had moved along down the block, "she brought her daughter with her. The girl was in terrible shape emotionally. A week after they arrived in Savannah she totaled her car on Veteran's Parkway, blood alcohol level off the goddamn charts. That alone should've killed her, but the accident was nasty. Broke her up real bad. The only bright spots are that no one was in the vehicle with her, and she didn't hurt anyone else."

"Small mercies."

"Yep and her car landed in a ditch about twenty yards or so into Chatham County, practically on the Shellman-Chatham county line. I was driving home from Momma's and heard the call on my radio. The EMTs arrived first but I was the only law enforcement on the scene for about ten minutes. I insisted that her vehicle was over the county line into Shellman County, my county. I made sure the EMTs took her to Regional Medical Center in Midberry rather than to Savannah. Midberry's technically closer to the crash site and has a top trauma unit, but it wasn't where she was officially supposed to be transported."

"Why did you insist on the change of venue?" I asked, not quite sure what he was telling me. "Why keep her in Shellman county, why not let her go to Savannah?"

"Her ex-husband was fighting for full custody, simply for spite. I was trying to protect O'Hanlon's privacy. If her daughter would have been taken to Savannah Memorial where Momma was, it would have been all over the news, maybe even hit the national media.

Her husband would have used it as evidence of Mary's incompetence as a parent and hauled the kid back to Los Angeles. Midberry, on the other hand, is pretty much off the radar. "

"Sounds just like Brandon Doyle," I said, wondering if he had abused his daughter as he had many of his young clients.

"Mary's grateful for my help."

"She said her daughter is studying abroad in London now. She must be doing all right," I said.

"No, Molly's not in London. She's actually at the spinal rehab center at Emory in Atlanta, trying to learn to walk again."

I leaned my head against his shoulder, too stunned to respond. He pulled me in tight.

"And Beazy?"

"Yeah?"

"You're right. We have a thing."

17

The day of the funeral arrived. A limousine picked us up at the house. Momma and Aunt Honey's friend, Mr. Winn Crawford, the kind taxi driver who I met at the airport, chauffeured. The car was impeccably kept, smelled of leather polish and peach blossom air freshener. We said little as he drove us to the All Glory and Mercy Baptist Church in Midberry, the church my father had pastored for ten years before being called to Savannah.

The building was a traditional, white-washed clapboard edifice with window panes of blue and yellow glass. My father had said that our congregation couldn't afford to install full-out stained glass. And even if we could've afforded it, it was better to give the money to those in real need anyway.

I used to stand beside him, the Reverend Dr. Luther

Middleton III, and hold the edge of his silky black liturgical robe as he greeted Sunday worshipers. I'd bask in their approval. There was a piece of me that still wanted to hang on to the silky robe of a glorious man everyone adored. With two divorces from men who gleamed like comets in their fields, this behavior obviously hadn't served me well.

Built during the Civil War, the Old Church, as everyone now called it, later spawned a conglomeration of boxy additions, highlighted by the latest—a large brick auditorium which served as the main place of worship. The Old Church also had one heck of a history—it was a stop on the Underground Railroad during slavery. I know the family was proud of the big brick addition, but the soul of that church to me would always where my daddy came to the pulpit and preached every Sunday. If God had a physical voice, it would be my daddy's—deep, sure, and true. The actor James Earl Jones, with his sonorous velvety words, could only hope to run a close second place.

"The congregation has really grown in the last decade," Momma said to me. "Gotta give Honey and Pastor Raymond lots of credit for that. They know how to light up a meeting, bring in the Holy Spirit. Yes, they do."

I squeezed her hand, proud of the lives of service my mother and father had led. I needed to be more like them.

The crowd parted as we disembarked from the limo. We made our way past a memory garden of tea roses and into the church building. Several of Luther's uniformed officers patrolled the periphery of the parking lot.

My brother had Momma on one arm and Aunt Honey on the other. He looked distinguished in his dark navy, chalk-striped civilian suit. Dexter and I entered the sanctuary together. Black dresses and big hats, men in dark suits, youngsters in everything from khakis and sport coats to prom gowns, and blue jeans. All of Arts Academy High School seemed to be in attendance.

We accepted memorial programs with a picture of Jayden, intense and dreamy, playing the violin, from the ushers. Then we proceeded down the long middle aisle to the front rows. The church held about 400 visitors. People stood in every available space, packed the balcony, and still more filed in behind us. I saw Rory, the surfer-boy member of Jayden's band, the language expert. I gave him a little wave. He smiled back at me.

Aunt Honey settled into the front row flanked by my momma and Edna, Honey's white-haired grandmother who pushed a walker with yellow tennis balls on the skids. Aunt Freddie May joined them with her second husband, Skinny Rufus. Aunt Hattie sat at the end of the row crowned with a black silk hat the size of a hovercraft. I admired her style and *chutzpah,* as my second husband would have said.

Luther, Dexter, and I sat at the end of the second row, which was filled by a passel of other relations I hadn't seen in ages. Members of the funeral congregation chatted quietly as they proceeded into the church. Bouquets of sunflowers and greenery graced the altar. The faint scent of magnolia hung in the air.

Students walked somberly to the closed casket, leaving little mementos—stuffed animals, pictures, flowers, notes, and other trinkets. The pipe organ played a familiar sacred tune, Beethoven's Ode to Joy from his Symphony No. 9. The piece was both haunting and hopeful, interpreted by a genius who'd known that joy was made of not just happiness, but the whole cloth of human experience.

I brushed back tears and focused on the memorial program, which highlighted wonderful pictures of Jayden, our family and friends, and references to various social media outlets for more information and links to his music.

I glanced over my shoulder at the congregation again and spotted Detective O'Hanlon in plain clothes with a half-dozen uniformed officers crammed into a back pew.

The lights dimmed. The audience quieted.

From the balcony, a young voice, as clear and flawless as a cut diamond, began to sing *a capella*. It was a dear, simple song, one we had all grown up with and learned as children. *You are m sunshine, my only sunshine,* he sang. A collective gasp rippled through the congregation at the first sound of his beautiful rendition. People cried out in anguish.

I looked over my shoulder again to see the singer—it was Antwone Thomas, the tall, skinny kid from Jayden's band that O'Hanlon and I had interviewed in Hitch Village. In his charcoal suit and striped bow tie, he channeled the angels. The song touched a chord we all shared—innocence, so beautiful and fragile. Lost.

Rio Deakins slipped into the far end of our pew. He wiped his moist eyes. I wanted him nearer; I wanted to hold his solid, masculine hand. I wanted to get to know who he was now, beyond the brother figure I had grown up with. Would I ever have the opportunity? Did I really want it? Doubt crept in.

Antwone's voice pulled me back to the moment. I turned again and glanced up at him—so young and vulnerable, so much stacked against him. An eerily familiar face partially obscured at the edge of the spotlight, caught my eye. Where had I seen it before? Who the hell—

A chill shook my body. Pieces of recognition started to fall into place. A mugshot in O'Hanlon's office. A skeletal visage with prominent cheekbones and deep-set sad eyes. Evan Doobius. Emad. He stood at the rear of the balcony wearing a black hoodie.

How would I get to him? I wasn't going to disrupt the sacred space of the funeral by screaming down the aisle. Luther, deep in meditation, soundlessly moved his lips in prayer. I pulled out my cell phone and texted O'Hanlon, hoping she had her phone on.

Dexter glimpsed at my texting and gave me a disapproving look. That was usually my role.

As I waited for a response, a young Asian teenaged girl in a black mini-dress walked quickly down the center aisle and slid in next to Dexter. We all packed in tighter to give her space. Mascara streamed down her grief-filled face. Dexter put his arm around her and pulled her near.

Who was this little damsel in distress? He'd only been in town a few days, yet they seemed to know each other well.

I took a quick look over my shoulder to see if O'Hanlon had received my message. She and the uniforms were disappearing out a side door. She'd got it.

I drew closer to my brother and whispered, "Doobius

was in the balcony. O'Hanlon's after him. I texted her."

Luther froze, then excused himself and made his way across our row of mourners. He struggled to avoid stepping on toes, banging knees, or knocking Bibles onto the floor. As he squeezed past Rio, they exchanged a nod. My brother exited our row and headed calmly down the side aisle toward the church foyer. Rio followed in his wake. That was the way it had always been with them.

Aunt Honey turned at the commotion.

I reached forward and squeezed her shoulder. "It's okay," I whispered. It wasn't okay at all. I tried to concentrate on the funeral service and let O'Hanlon and Luther do their jobs.

As the lights came back up, the choir began a soulful and passionate version of "Comforter," a gospel song I had first heard CeCe Winans sing years ago. The choir was amazing. God bless our Baptist church. We knew how to make a joyful noise even in pain, maybe especially in pain.

I peeked at my iPhone, hoping for a text. The pastor, a prematurely white-haired man in his mid-fifties, had an air of calm and kindness about him. He read the 23rd Psalm. I loved those verses but I could barely concentrate.

"What's up, Mom?" Dexter asked, quiet as a mouse but definitely irritated.

I whispered, "Evan Doobius was in the balcony. He's the guy who—"

"I know who he is."

The girl shot Dexter a questioning look.

"Doobius," he mouthed to her.

"I came in late and saw him in the parking lot," she

whispered.

I was shocked that she knew who he was and had seen him. "Do you have any idea what he was wearing or was driving?"

"A black Nissan SUV. Had on a long black trench coat over a dark hoodie."

I texted this information to O'Hanlon and Luther.

"License plate?" Dexter asked.

The girl shook her head, pulled a tissue out of her leopardskin purse and blew her nose.

This time, Momma turned around, lips pursed. We stopped talking.

The next section of the service was entitled "Eulogy for Jayden Middleton." Production credits listed included Jayden, Aunt Honey, Cornelia Chan, and my son.

I glanced at him. A proud smile flickered on his lips. The girl slipped her hand into his. Very likely this was the Cornelia listed in the eulogy.

An orchestra of violins, bass, keyboard, drummers, and percussion began the opening strains of "Hallelujah" written by Leonard Cohen many years ago. Aunt Honey rose to direct the choir for this selection. Her assistant choir director helped her up into the chancel. She raised her arms. Voices rose on the air, pitch-perfect, filling the church with a visceral power that only music can convey.

As the lights went down, a large screen lowered, filled by a YouTube video. A teenage boy, thin like Momma and Honey, big black-rimmed glasses, baggy pants, and a Ziggy Marley *Love Tour* T-shirt, began to sing. The choir, the orchestra, and Jayden Middleton on video performed the soul-rending hymn of self-discovery, struggle, and redemption. The lyrics had been rewritten by the kids and touched on a common theme of both tragedy and hope. Jayden was indeed everything they said he was. His talent had been otherworldly.

Soon, the entire gathering sang along, crying out and moving to the sound. His classmates waved cell phones in the air, shining like candles with pictures of Jayden playing his violin.

When the performance concluded, the crowd demanded to experience it all again. Spontaneously, the singing recommenced, *a capella*. The orchestra joined in. Jayden's classmates danced in the pews and down the aisles. A young life was celebrated and released into a higher sphere.

Too soon, the service was over. Congregants filed out crying, laughing, and of course, singing. There would be a burial at Laurel Grove North Cemetery in the family plot, then a reception and lots of food, food, food, back at the church's fellowship hall.

My cell phone vibrated. It brought up a message from Luther. *We lost him.*

18

"You have *got* to tell my mom and Uncle Luther," Dexter said. "You can't withhold this information, Cornelia. It's too important." He dropped his pie-filled fork to his plate with a clatter. "I mean, you actually *saw* the shooting?"

Keep your voice down." Cornelia's almond eyes narrowed to angry slits.

Dexter looked around the café, they were alone in a far corner. At the register, a couple of postal workers were ordering sweet tea. The place was otherwise vacant.

She continued. "If I tell anyone I'll be dead. My whole family too." She peeled blue-sparkled polish from her bitten nails leaving a detritus of shiny specks on the table.

"The police can protect you."

She shook her head, dismayed. "For someone from

Los Angeles, you are way naïve. Come on, Dexter, gimme a break. You've seen enough episodes of *CSI* to know that if I testify, I'm toast. The police can never really protect crime witnesses. Or they send them off to WITSEC somewhere totally grim. My grandparents came here after being in an internment camp in California after World War II. My family has been running a Chinese restaurant on Tybee Island since 1953. We're doing well. We won't move. No way."

"But you saw a *murder*." Dexter scrubbed his hands through his short hair in frustration. "My *cousin's* murder. Jesus, Cornelia."

"Yeah, but we're not going to be shipped off to North Dakota to freeze our butts off and start a Mexican restaurant as the Gonzalez family. You promised that you wouldn't tell. No one else can know."

"My roommate knows," Dexter said.

Cornelia sighed. All the blue on her nails was gone. "Okay, Adam. He did a great job with the sound recording at the funeral, didn't he?"

"Yeah, awesome." Dexter shook his head, picked up the fork and stuffed the last piece of peach pie in his mouth. "So, what are we gonna do? They think Doobius did it."

"Doobie's a stoner who loves music. Thought he had a winner with the GratiFlyers. He's too mellow to start anything bad with anybody."

"Could you see who was in the car?"

Cornelia scanned the café again. "They were two men I'd never seen before. Looked like Doobie's ethnic group to me. Dark."

He frowned. "I'm dark."

"Duh. Not your kind of dark. Maybe from India or the Middle East or something. Hard to really tell. But I'd recognize the shooter. Definitely."

"Oh man, this is bad." Dexter pushed his plate away.

"Another piece?" Cornelia asked. "You love the pie."

"Huh-uh. I don't feel too good."

"Listen, Dexter. Your mom, your uncle, and that O'Hanlon detective, they're smart enough to put it all together. We need to figure out a way to help shift their focus in the right direction. They don't need to hear it from me."

"Are you kidding? They don't need to hear from an *eyewitness?* Your story could be the difference between nailing these assholes or letting them off."

It was Cornelia's turn to be quiet. She opened her purse and took out a pack of Winston Lights. "I have an idea."

"Yeah, what?"

"Come on. I need a cigarette."

"Shit'll kill you."

"Better than a bullet to the head at fifteen." She took his hand and yanked him out of his seat, then let go and headed for the door. Dexter grabbed his backpack, and with a skeptical raise of his eyebrows, followed.

The two teenagers wandered down Liberty Street past gracious Colonial-era homes; some still residential, others now restaurants, boutiques, spas, and offices.

"I'm still in total culture shock," Dexter said. He gazed up at an elegant brick edifice and tripped on the cobblestone sidewalk in the process. "You can't believe how different this is from Los Angeles. It's crazy. Out there we're pretty removed from local history, except for our California Mission projects we have to do when we're in middle school. History—here it's everywhere."

"I've never been out of Georgia. I like Savannah. But I'd like to visit Los Angeles sometime. I'd like to see the Hollywood Walk of Fame and all."

"You can stay with us in Santa Monica. It's cool," Dexter said with a shy smile on his face. "Just a quick walk to the beach."

They made their way to the Colonial Park Cemetery in the heart of the Historic District. Dexter paused to skim the information at the kiosk. Established in 1750, many of Savannah's earliest citizens buried beneath that lawn included victims of a terrible yellow fever epidemic. Bordering the old Savannah jail, which was presently part of a school, the cemetery also bumped up against a dueling range, where for over a century, many sought justice for crimes and breaches of honor, imagined or real. The convenience of a burial ground right next to the jail and the dueling field was ironic.

An advertisement for an evening ghost tour hung on the wrought-iron gate. Dog walkers played ball with their pets and tourists took pictures amid the gravestones. A mob of middle-school-aged girls in neon-pink *Ohio Girl Scouting* T-shirts ambled among the gravestones sucking on runny ice cream cones.

Dexter and Cornelia sat together atop a brick crypt, a few feet from a No Smoking sign.

"So, what's your bright idea, Miss Cornelia?"

"You're starting to sound like a Southern boy, sir."

Dexter smiled for a moment until an unexpected Frisbee hit him in the shin. He picked it up and sent it flying back toward a bouncing Jack Russell terrier.

"Sorry!" the dog owner called.

"No problem." Dexter gave him a wave.

Cornelia finally lit up, took a dramatic draw on her cigarette. "Okay, when Doobie lived on Tybee, and he still may live there—I don't know—but he'd order out from our restaurant. At least weekly."

"What's that got to do with the hit?" Dexter asked. Frustration with her slow speech and the glacial unraveling of her idea was apparent as he chewed at a hangnail.

"I can get his address from credit card receipts. We can drive by his place. See if Doobie's around. Check things out. What do you think?"

"That's it, that's your idea?"

"Yeah," she said. "You know, do a little investigating on our own."

He pulled a Red Bull out of his backpack, popped the tab and took a long swallow. "Sounds dangerous. And how are we gonna get out there? Do you drive?" Dexter asked.

"No, but I have my permit. Do you drive?"

"No, but I have my permit too. I took driver's ed but I'm not sixteen yet."

"Do two permits make a whole license?"

Dexter laughed. "I'm sure the cops will go for that idea. But hey, guess what? My mom is going to be in Atlanta tomorrow. A friend called and there might be a job with CNN. She's gonna fly up and stay overnight, fly back in the morning."

"Perfect."

"She won't be taking Gran's Camry, and Grans can't drive it right now cause of her heart attack. It'll be sitting there in that *dark* driveway. Can't even see it from their bedrooms."

"We shouldn't," Cornelia said, eyes bright. She took a final puff and blew smoke toward the No Smoking sign.

"You're right, we shouldn't," Dexter agreed. "But actually, this is part of my class assignment, the tribute to my cousin."

"I like that thought. And Dexter, let's hope it's not a stick shift." She gave him a little peck on the cheek and ground her cigarette into the base of the grave marker.

19

"I'm pretty sure that girl knows a whole lot more than she's letting on," I said over my iPhone to Detective O'Hanlon. I sat in the rear of a taxi on my way to Hilton Head Airport and then to Atlanta. "I'll be anxious to know what you find out. Be back tomorrow around noon. Call or text me if anything comes up."

I didn't trust that young Miss Cordelia, or Camellia, or was it Cornelia? I'm not sure what it was about her, but I was alarmed at how in a few short days, she had wormed her way into my son's life. I strongly suspected she knew something about Jayden that she wasn't coming forward with. I would not have my son become an accessory to withholding evidence. All I could picture was the two of them being carted off to the slammer together in orange jumpsuits.

Or was I being a crazy mom who didn't want her son to

grow up and leave her? Dexter had never had a girlfriend before, and was there anything more susceptible to the wiles of a lovely shape and a sweet feminine mouth than a fifteen-year-old boy? Maybe guys were all fifteen-year-old boys at heart, but they weren't mine. A new world was opening up for both of us. I didn't like it.

I hadn't expected to be on my way to Atlanta today. Things in Savannah were far too volatile. Momma had settled into the house again. Aunt Honey was with her and trying to be a rock but Honey's inner strength was already almost stretched to the breaking point. The shooter was still on the loose and Dexter had taken up with a beautiful mystery woman-child who was likely hiding something.

But in five months my money would run out, bills would pile up, the house would be foreclosed on. I needed to find a job. I should have taken my exes for all they were worth. California law would have given me 50 percent of everything, but that's not who I am. I settled for a modest amount of child support and a trust fund to guarantee the kids could go to whatever college they could get into. I would not be financially beholden to anyone if I didn't have to be. I started to feel my chest squeeze tight, like a pair of pliers going to work on a stubborn splinter. *Calm down, pull it together, Bea. Focus on this job possibility. It's all going to be okay.*

Now descending fast from 30,000 feet, the constantly developing skyline of Atlanta appeared beneath dull, low-hanging clouds. Giant construction cranes were as numerous as high-rises.

I would be meeting Lindsay Vargas at baggage claim. We had worked together five years previously at KLAK-TV in Los Angeles when she was a summer intern and I was her supervisor. After the internship, she landed her first real job in Sacramento. Now she's at CNN in Atlanta. TV newsies tend to move around a lot, particularly early in their careers.

Her brother, my dear friend, and colleague, Ernie Vargas, was still a senior field producer at KLAK. He chose to stay in Los Angeles after the buyout and accepted a major pay cut for the sake of family stability. Maybe I should have done that. Too late.

Now I was looking to my former intern for a break.

Lindsay had arranged for me to meet with the national CNN News Director, Grant Levine. Although it was still technically off the record, a new West Coast correspondent position was rumored to be available soon. Lindsay's insider connection gave me the advantageous entrée that I needed.

As our plane lowered its landing gear on final approach, I kept thinking about Rio. I'd barely had a chance to talk with him at the funeral. For some reason, I couldn't get him off my mind. It would be fun to see his school and the kids he taught. Maybe I could let go of the shining-robe-of-the-adored-man syndrome and be happy with a school teacher. Probably not. What was wrong with me?

Lindsay met me as scheduled. She looked fantastic. Always a fashionista, she had neatly coiffed curly brown hair and perfect skin. And a perfect smile. And she was smart as hell. Between beautiful Miss Cornelia stealing my son and glamorous, employed Lindsay, I was feeling uncomfortably off-kilter and unsure of myself.

She treated me to dinner at Rosa's Mexican Restaurant, which included pomegranate margaritas, a variety of appetizers, and blue-crab enchiladas with guacamole made fresh at the table. How in the world did she stay so slim? I'd gained pounds in the few days I'd been in Georgia and hadn't worked out once.

Lindsay loaded a taco chip with salsa. "It's so great to see you, Bea. I heard all about what happened at the station from my brother. I thought maybe you could give this CNN gig a look-see. Word through my inside sources is that the job opening is imminent. Might as well throw your hat in the ring as early as possible, right?"

"Absolutely. I so appreciate your connecting me with the news director. At this point, I'm wide open to any possibility."

"I went to Berkeley with Grant Levine's son, so we have that Cal connection along with working together at CNN," she said. "I gave you high praise so he's looking forward to meeting you tomorrow."

I could tell she enjoyed cluing me in on her fast-developing professional network. Lindsay had always had a bit of a superior attitude, but right now I was in no place to be anything but grateful.

We talked further about the job, which was making me increasingly nervous. What if CNN didn't like me? What if I couldn't even get a job in a small market? What if? What if?

I had to stop my panicked brain from flying into the Nethersphere. I changed the subject as fast as possible.

"So, Lindsay, how's the love life? I hear they don't

call it 'Hotlanta' for nothing."

Belatedly, I noticed her large diamond ring. I'm not sure why I directed the conversation from jobs, which I don't have, to relationships, which I also don't have. Where was a therapist when I needed one?

Lindsay laughed. "Well, actually I was going to ask you if you'd like to go over to Emory University with me after dinner. My fiancé is giving a lecture on veterans and the latest in PTSD treatment. I remember you did a story on that when I interned with you in Los Angeles." She pulled a mirror out of her Gucci handbag and applied a generous swipe of mocha-colored lipstick. Picked at something invisible on her teeth.

"Sounds great. I'd love to go. And congratulations on your engagement. How wonderful." I was truly very happy for her.

"I'd like you to meet him. I live right near Emory in Druid Hills so it'll only be a ten-minute drive to my place afterward." With a subtle wave of the hand, her sparkly ring caught the attention of our waiter and she motioned for the bill. "But I'm sure you're tired because you've been through so much in the last few days. Please, don't feel obligated."

"No, truly, I'd love to go, it'll get my mind off family things. And I'd be honored to meet your fiancé. Your brother will expect a report back, of course." I gulped down the last remnants of the big margarita, enjoying the mellowing effect. I wasn't much of a drinker and it didn't take much to make my bones begin to melt.

"You'll like him. So will Ernie. Can't wait for the two of them to meet. Ernie and the family will be out here next month. Time goes by so quickly. We don't see each other enough. And suddenly, years have slipped by."

I knew exactly what she meant, and more.

20

The drive to the garden-like Emory campus in the suburban Druid Hills section of Atlanta took less than half an hour. As we trolled for a parking space near the entrance to the Rollins School of Public Health, Lindsay and I continued to chat about her brother, Ernie, in Los Angeles, about the corporate culture at CNN, and about living in Atlanta with its rich African-American roots. I also got the low-down on wedding venues.

After ten long minutes of weaving up and down narrow parking lanes, we nailed a spot. When we finally arrived at the lecture hall, the only seats left were in the second row, practically on top of the dais and podium. Two video cameras were set up for recording. We squeezed in up front, excusing ourselves as we went.

As we settled, I checked my phone—a message from Alyssa. Pictures of my youngest with her pretty baby sister and the Strauss family tugged at my heartstrings. I loved my daughter in a way that was baked into my DNA, as fundamental as the shape of my nose and the color of my hair. I missed her desperately. How would she do if I had to take a job outside of Los Angeles and we had to move?

The lecture hall hushed. I put my fears for my daughter and my complicated protectiveness of her away as the speaker, Lindsay's fiancé, was introduced by the executive director of the Veterans Health Research Institute. As I looked up to see Lindsay's man, I almost fell off my chair.

Dr. Rio Deakins, Public Health Fellow, and Chair of the American Studies Department, walked up to the lectern. Black leather biker garb had been replaced by gray trousers, a navy blazer, light blue shirt, and striped bow tie. My brother, my protector, my family, the school teacher I couldn't fall for, was an Emory professor and engaged to Miss Perfect.

He saw me and startled, then smiled broadly. Rio excused himself from the podium to step down and give both Lindsay and I a hug. I suddenly felt quite light-headed.

"Two of my favorite women in the world. What the hay? We'll talk after the lecture."

"Okay baby." Lindsay said to Rio. He gave her a peck on the cheek then made his way back up to the dais. She turned to me, eyes wide and a little wary. "How do you know him?"

"You didn't say your fiancé was from Savannah. Oh, my God. You never mentioned his name. We grew up together. He's my brother's best friend. He's family."

"Luther Middleton is your brother?"

"Yep, my big brother."

"Your last name's Jackson, or was when we worked together, not Middleton—I never made the connection. You still use Jackson on TV. Unreal. Bea, you and I'll be relatives soon."

I nodded and squeezed her hand, not quite sure I wanted to welcome her to the family tree. At that moment I decided to take Middleton back, permanently. I had been Strauss and Jackson, but Middleton—that was blood, now and forever.

Rio's research was probably fascinating but I couldn't concentrate. I could see that he captivated the audience with his warmth and enthusiasm. Afterward we grabbed drinks at a local sports bar and talked about Jayden's murder and our frustrating lack of progress.

Lindsay and I chatted back and forth but Rio, usually the extrovert, became uncharacteristically quiet. Trauma and pain was the impetus for his work, but it brought an airless darkness to him as well. I never knew the extent of the abuse he'd suffered as a child before he came to live with us, but I knew it was bad.

X

The glimmer of raindrops sparkled on Dexter's cottony dark hair. Big, water-balloonish splats hit the sidewalk, spitting like distant gunshots. Reflections from red and white lights painted impressionistic patterns across Henry Street as cars rolled through a drive-in liquor store on the corner.

Cornelia, almost invisible in a black nylon parka and black leggings, approached the parked Camry from the rear. Dexter had managed to sneak the extra set of keys from the key hook at the back door. Cornelia toted a well-used supermarket eco-bag with a peace sign on the front. Bottles clinked.

Dexter gave her the eye.

"For the stakeout. Chinese food, Diet Cokes, and two beers," she said.

"Oh great, we can get busted for under-age booze as well as driving without licenses."

Cornelia shrugged, pulled out two Kirin beers and tucked them behind a bush bordering the driveway. "Killjoy."

Dexter pointed the key fob toward the car.

"No. No beeper," Cornelia reminded him. "No noise and flashing lights popping on."

"Oh, yeah. Sorry." Dexter carefully inserted the key in the driver's door lock and braced for a brash horn or a nasty mechanical voice shouting, *stand back from the car*.

Nothing alarming happened. The lock opened. They paused and let the wet, quiet night settle around them like a gauzy cloak.

"Gotta start thinking like professionals," Cornelia whispered. She banged the shopping bag noisily into the side of the car.

"Like you?" he said, grinning.

"Uh-huh," she said. "Watch and learn."

They slid into the front seats. Winced as the car doors closed with a decisive clunk. Dexter doused the cabin light. He turned toward Cornelia; both were clearly stressed out, and they hadn't even left the driveway. Reaching over, he gave her hand a pat, turned on the ignition and backed out of the driveway—in front of a pickup truck that had turned the corner. The driver leaned on the horn and swerved around the Camry, barely missing them.

"Holy shit. Dexter," Cornelia hissed.

"Girl, this was your lame idea. Do you wanna drive this stupid car?" Dexter was shaking, more completely unnerved than angry.

"No, no, you'll do fine. Let's go. Take it slow. Left on Habersham. Don't forget to use your blinker when we turn."

"What?"

"Blinker. Now."

"Okay, okay. You're more annoying than my driver's ed teacher." Dexter drove slowly down the wet street and managed to turn in the right direction.

It was a few miles before they spoke again.

The city receded. The darkness of the two-lane road through the marshlands out to Tybee Island finally engulfed them.

Cornelia opened a take-out carton of egg rolls. She offered them over to Dexter.

"Been gripping the damn steering wheel so hard my fingers are paralyzed." He wiggled them back to life enough to grab an egg roll and dip it in mustard sauce.

"We bad," Cornelia said, with a tentative smile.

"We idiots," Dexter returned and shook his head.

Finally, on their way to scope out a suspect—they looked at each other and laughed.

21

The fifth prayer cycle of the day. Almost done.

In the middle of his living room floor, beneath the big flat screen TV, Emad knelt one final time. His forehead dipped to the blood-colored paisley border of the Persian prayer rug. Sighing deeply, he prayed for deliverance from evil.

You are my sunshine, my only sunshine...

He couldn't shake the refrain. Ever since the funeral, the song had worm-holed into his brain. It was starting to really drive him crazy.

As Emad raised his head from the final prayer, a lug-soled boot crushed down on his neck and smashed his face deep into the rug's pile where coarse hand-tied knots upbraided his face.

"Grow the beard and I'll stop stomping those creamy, bitch-cheeks," Muhammed said, as he pressed down harder.

Emad gritted his teeth and refused to succumb to the humiliation and anger roiling in his gut. There was now not one, but two handlers living with him. Sick assholes his father proclaimed as "real men" who would show him what it meant to be a proper Muslim son.

He was harassed every waking minute, even throughout the eight-hour graveyard shift he worked at the Georgia Ports Authority in north Savannah. He was the accountant on his father's crew—cooking the books, manipulating the recordkeeping. He'd hated every minute of getting his Bachelor of Science in Accounting, *summa cum laude,* from the University of Miami. At least the degree was one thing the old man gave him a little credit for. It was not enough. Had he pulled the trigger that had put Jayden Middleton in the ground, he might have earned an approving nod.

"More prayer," Muhammed demanded. His boot ground Emad's head with vengeance—his ear felt like it was ripping off. "Louder."

"Leave me the fuck alone." Emad crawled off the prayer rug amid kicks and laughter. One blow caught him hard in the side. The sharp pain made him gasp. The cracked ribs from last week's beatdown when his attendance at the funeral had been found out, were far from healed. He wasn't sure he could survive this shit much longer.

Sama and Muhammed were both highly entertained by inflicting misery. Sama, in pressed jeans and a white shirt, with manicured fingernails and a fancy Swiss watch he loved to flash, seldom sullied himself with inflicting physical abuse. His expertise was psychological warfare.

Muhammed was a different story. A local Savannah boy, with a decade in Special Ops and then time with the mercenary contractor, Blackshear, he had a sadistic streak a mile wide. He targeted Emad with stinging slaps as Emad made a break for it, out the door into the cold, rainy night. Barefoot from prayer observance, Emad couldn't go far, but neither could he stay inside for another second.

"We're leaving for the port in fifteen, asshole," Sama growled, gazing at the solid gold timepiece sparking on his wrist. Muhammed, African American, the smaller, more muscular and quieter of the two, barely spoke. There was nothing behind his deep-set eyes but emptiness.

Misty spirits whispered through the woods surrounding Emad's isolated duplex. Spanish moss drifted and undulated in unseen drafts. It was as if hell was breathing.

Emad stumbled to the crushed-shell driveway, coughing. His feet bloodied on the shards of tabby, his ribs twinging in pain. He glanced back at his home. The next-door neighbors had suddenly moved out two weeks ago.

A quarter mile along the road to the east, an old couple and their fortyish Down syndrome daughter lived in a white-frame bungalow. In the other direction was a fishing shack adjoining a broken-down boat ramp. Snapping turtles liked to sleep there on warm days.

Cars rarely stopped on the road, so the light-colored Camry down near that old dock with its parking lights on, drew his attention. Then the lights extinguished. Were they small-time dealers shooting up or counting their pills? Or kids doin' the dirty?

"Asswipe," Sama called. "Unless you want me ripping off your fucking toes, you better get your shoes on. Now. We're leaving." He stepped out onto the stoop and lit up a cigarette. Specks of tobacco ember vanished into his formidable beard. Car keys jingled in Sama's hand. His eyes narrowed as Emad approached. "You're going back home next week, after the big drop."

"No fucking way. This is my home." Emad returned from the driveway and trudged back up his front steps, footfalls tenuous, anxiety building. He would not go back to Afghanistan, ever. He loved his little duplex in the woods. He loved America. Despite its flaws, he goddamn loved it.

Muhammed backhanded him across the face. Emad bounced off the porch wall. Fighting back was useless. The dizzy spells were the result of his last attempt to confront these assholes.

"You're going to marry your cousin, Fatima, immediately—as soon as you get back to the village. Her HIV is in remission."

"Fatima?" Emad laughed out loud. He was living in an insane sitcom. She was twice his age and sick, with four kids and two dead husbands, one his own father had probably murdered. Emad would rather die than hook up with Fatima. Would it come to that?

He skulked back into his room, now devoid of any décor—no posters with Falcons logos, no Beyoncé, no books other than an edited Koran. All traces of the life he loved were gone. He was disappearing as well. He had to make a break for it soon. Real soon, or there would be nothing left.

Emad pushed his feet into his black trainers and shuffled toward the front door. He had to full-out run after Muhammed as the dull gray panel van pulled away without him. They slowed down enough so he could jump in. He gashed his shin on the edge of the door.

As they passed the Camry in the gloom, Emad caught the eye of someone familiar. The Asian chick who hung around Jayden Middleton. Was it really her? Yeah, had to be. What the hell was she doing out here? Emad wanted to scream a warning to the kids but nothing, no sound would emerge. Overcome with despair, it was probably too late for them anyway.

$$\text{\Y}$$

"Oh, my God, I think he saw me," Cornelia cried, dismay edging her voice.

"When the person you're spying on drives by, two feet from your face, you duck. Surveillance 101. Shit, girl."

"I was so shocked. I'm new at this."

"That, I doubt," Dexter said. "I think you have plenty of experience putting your cute little nose where it doesn't belong." He reached for a cold egg roll.

"What are you doing?" Cornelia slammed the lid of the cooler dangerously close to his outreached fingers. "Don't you do anything but eat? Let's go. Come on, follow them."

"Oh yeah, like I really want to get my ass kicked by some homicidal jihadists. Those guys were beyond nasty-looking."

"Man-up, Dexter, go. Step on it. We're gonna lose them."

With a shrug, Dexter turned the keys in the ignition and the car sputtered to life. He pulled a decent U-turn and followed the red pinpricks receding in the distance.

Cornelia and Dexter followed the van across the dark salt marshes. The road off the island etched a black rip through the rising tidal waters that were the color of old pewter in the pale ambient light. They drove with the windows down. The brackish smell of saltwater and pluff mud was almost sweet, not a bit like Santa Monica, Dexter mused. Rain spit in their faces but it was warm and soothing.

Soon back into the city, they followed Doobius and his posse in the van onto Bay Street which took them along the Savannah River bluff. It was a main thoroughfare traversing the downtown Historic District and part of the route to both the port and the bridge across the river into South Carolina. Where were they headed with Doobie?

"There's the Moon River Brewery, and City Hall," Cornelia narrated like a tour guide. "The dome's covered in twenty-three-karat gold. Mega bling. Always wanted to climb up there and scrape some off."

"Real interesting, Cor, but there's about ten cop cars up ahead. We're gonna get stopped." The noodles and egg rolls suddenly felt like rocks in Dexter's stomach. "My mother's gonna kill me. My iPad'll be gone forever."

Cornelia looked over at him, touched his knee.

Dexter let out a little breath.

"It's a traffic accident," she said. "You're gonna drive right by all those flashing lights, right on by. Dexter, you truly look like you've been driving forever, baby. You feel me? You can do this."

He nodded and took her hand. The downpour intensified so they rolled the windows up. The sound was cut in half and the sirens ahead quieted. The two teens followed the van through the district to the edge of downtown where Bay Street turned into a much less-traveled two-lane highway. All was now quiet except for the slap, slap of windshield wipers that needed replacing.

"Looks like we're going toward Garden City," Cornelia said. "Tiny place but the Port of Savannah is there. Fourth largest seaport in the country, or maybe the fifth."

"Wow, a lot bigger than I thought. Like Long Beach in Los Angeles," Dexter said. The scale of everything seemed to be expanding. Sneaking off in Gran's car with a hot chick and Chinese food was feeling much more serious with every minute that passed.

For about six miles they kept their distance from Doobie's panel van. Finally, it turned into the highly secured main gates of the Georgia Ports Authority, Garden City Terminal. A guard waved the van through.

"There they go. They must work here," Dexter said, eyes wide, impressed by the huge ships from distant countries across the world that lined the docks. Mountains of apartment-sized steel containers rose up alongside giant loading cranes, all under acres of sulfurous lights.

He pulled over into the dingy shadows beside the Lucky Clover gas station across from the entrance. "If Doobius and friends work at the Port of Savannah, it seems awfully convenient for trafficking shit."

Cornelia nodded. Dexter noticed her picking at her nails again even though all the polish was gone. Seemed to be what she did when she was stressed. Little slivery flecks had accumulated on her back leggings.

Cars and trucks came and went in droves through the big gates. "Looks like maybe a shift change," Dexter said. He turned the windshield wipers to an intermittent swipe.

"You think they figured us out?" she asked, now chewing at her cuticles.

"I think Doobius made you when he jumped into the van. He didn't seem too solid with the other guys, though. They practically ran him over when he was trying to get in. Didn't seem like they were joking around either."

"I'm scared. Should we be scared?" Her lower lip quivered in the greenish illumination from the dashboard.

"They killed my cousin. That pretty much says it all. I'm calling my uncle Luther." Dexter pulled out his cell phone. "Even if I'm grounded forever. I gotta do this. We're in over our heads."

They didn't take notice of the truck pulling in behind them at the rear of the gas station. Three men got out and disappeared into the rainy gloom. As Dexter dialed Luther, the Camry door was ripped open. The phone flew from his hand and bounced under the seat. Cornelia was pulled from the passenger side and thrown to the ground.

A cloth was pressed over Dexter's face. A foul smell of something nauseating and medicinal filled his nostrils. Cornelia cried out. He reached toward the sound. Then there was blackness.

22

Coppery curls washed across Luther's broad chest like bright waves on a shore of dark stone. Black and white, yin and yang, wrapped together in a complement of energies.

"I can never quite get used to seeing us naked together," Mary O'Hanlon said. She laughed and curled her fingers in his. "Couldn't be more of a contrast."

"I live for contrast." Luther lightly kissed her love-bruised lips. "Chocolate and cinnamon forever."

"The Mayans invented chocolate and always mixed in cinnamon to make it the most divine sweet in the world." She kissed his wrist where the pulse thumped a soft steady rhythm.

Luther chucked. "You know such random stuff, baby."

"I watch the History channel." O'Hanlon raised

herself up on one elbow and covered her pink breasts with the sheet. She looked intently at her lover. "Where the hell are we going with this, Luther?"

"Mexico, I guess. Gotta try their recipe."

"No, I'm serious."

"Wherever it takes us, sweet mama, I'm there." His smile was happy but his eyes were sad. "I asked you to marry me, and you disappeared for two weeks. My balls are in your court, Detective. Literally."

"*Luther,* you're making fun."

He hoisted himself up to lean back against the headboard and drew her into his arms. "I totally am *not* making fun."

From a side table, Luther's cell phone sounded a blaring siren.

"I don't know how you can stand to hear that *every* time you get a call," O'Hanlon said. She pulled back from Luther and reached for the phone.

"Just my bizarre sense of humor. Maybe someday you'll get used to it."

She held the phone up for him to view. He squinted and honed in on the screen. "It's my nephew. Kinda strange. It's late."

"Kids don't know late."

"True dat, Miss Mary O. It's early. I'm getting old." Luther took the cell and punched the callback access code. The number picked up.

"Dexter?" he asked. "S'up, young'un?" In the background he heard loud voices, scraping, then the phone knocked hard against something. Silence.

"Dexter?"

Disconnected.

He pressed *Callback*. No pickup. Call again. *Nada.* "Probably butt-dialed me by mistake."

"Happens all the time." O'Hanlon kissed his neck.

Luther squeezed her fingers then moved to the edge of the bed and stared out the window. Rain dripped down the panes.

"What is it, Luther?" she asked.

"It's nothing, but my sister's in Atlanta, and I feel kinda responsible. Just being paranoid."

Just then, another call came in. Momma was on the caller ID.

"Oh, Jesus," Luther gasped.

"Momma? You okay?"

"I'm fine, Luther."

"You scare me when you call so late."

"Sorry to frighten you, honey," she said, "but my car's gone from the driveway, and I have a suspicion Dexter's the culprit. That little Asian girl might be with him."

"Okay, don't worry now, Momma. I'll take care of it. Probably a little teenage joyriding. I'll swing by his dorm. G'night now. Call you later."

"Goodnight, son. Love to Mary."

Luther looked over at Mary as he hung up. "How does that woman manage to know *everything?*" he grumbled.

χ

"Let's take my unmarked." O'Hanlon tied her hair up into a high ponytail. She wore khakis and a white SCPD polo shirt. Luther nodded, strapped on his shoulder holster, his hair damp from a quick shower. O'Hanlon's bungalow was in Ardsley Park, ten or fifteen minutes from where many of the Art College residence halls were clustered.

"You want to check out his res hall first?" she asked.

"Yeah. I think he's in, uh... where did he tell me? Boundary Village." Luther scrolled through the contact list on his iPhone. "He's in the Hive. Over by the bridge."

The rain had stopped and thin clouds hung before a waning moon. They drove into the Historic District. At almost midnight on a warm, humid evening, people still strolled the streets, gathered outside of clubs, and dined *al fresco*.

The Hive was a former Holiday Inn updated and renovated to look like a hip, new, W Hotel but with honey-yellow doors. They pulled into a No Parking zone.

The lobby of the residence hall resembled a mini-museum of neon art. A giant metal bee had been mounted on the wall behind the front desk. A tired-looking work-study student tapped on her laptop. She had short, spiky black hair and a rose tattoo that started at her neck and vined across her clavicle toward her shoulder then disappeared beneath her shirt.

"May I help you?" she asked, politely. "We close to visitors in about five minutes."

O'Hanlon displayed her credentials. "We're here to talk with Dexter Jackson," she said.

The student's eyes widened and she sat up straighter.

"Dexter? He's not in trouble, is he?" she asked, biting her pierced lip.

"No, he's not in trouble, we're doing a safety check. Is he here?"

"Uh, no. I think he left around eight o'clock." She glanced up at the clock on the wall across from her desk. Took a quick glimpse at a sign-in sheet.

"By himself?" O'Hanlon asked.

"I think so, but I was pretty busy then. I'm his RA so I know him, but I wasn't, like, paying close attention. Kids come and go as they like."

"He say where he was going?" Luther leaned onto the desk. The student leaned away.

"Nuh-uh, not to me. Maybe his roommate knows something. Want me to, uh, call him?"

"That would be great," Luther moved closer to the RA. His sheer size could be persuasive.

She picked up the house phone and punched in a number and pulled at the silver skull-shaped stud in her earlobe. Finally, she connected. "Jon? It's Britt. The, uh, police are here looking for Dexter. Can you come down? Okay." She hung up the phone.

"He'll be here in a sec. Name's Jonathan Cohen, from Atlanta."

Luther nodded. "Thank you."

The young woman powered down her computer and loaded odds and ends into her backpack. Her eyes cut again to the wall clock.

"Sorry, but it's past time for me to close up—gotta go study," she said. "I have a project due at 8:00 a.m. and I haven't started it yet."

"Can you leave us your contact information, please?" Mary asked.

Britt hesitated, then wrote her phone number and email on the back of a flyer for free pizza. She then punched in a code to lock the dorm's front entrance and slipped quickly down the hallway.

"Assignment due at 8:00 a.m. and not started yet— some things never change," O'Hanlon whispered to

Luther.

"I never put assignments off 'til the night before," he said.

O'Hanlon snickered.

"I'm serious. Try having a high school principal for a mother."

O'Hanlon and Luther moved from the front desk to a lounge area that overlooked residence hall parking. The two-mile long Tallmadge Memorial Bridge to South Carolina glittered several blocks away. The massive high-rise bulk of a container ship floated beneath it, effortlessly.

A group of students, toting a full-sized mannequin dressed in what looked like an evening gown made of rhinestone-adorned candy bar wrappers, made their way across the parking lot. They swiped IDs at the door, then spilled into the lobby, laughing and animated.

At the same time, a tall, skinny young man wearing baggy basketball shorts, flip-flops, and a faded Pearl Jam T-shirt emerged from the elevator. "Hey, guys," he greeted the boisterous crew.

"Hi Jonathan," called out a girl who wore a gold mini-dress and teal pumps. "Hunter was rejected from Project Runway. They said this was the nastiest design they'd ever seen." The group cheered and pounded a purple-haired student, evidently the designer, on the back. "We're celebrating. Come on up and join us."

"Maybe later." He caught the eye of O'Hanlon and Luther and seemed to shrink with the sighting. The other students disappeared into the elevator Jon had come down in.

"Jonathan Cohen?" O'Hanlon asked.

"That's me," he said and offered his hand. Introductions were made.

"So, Jonathan, we're trying to find your roommate, Dexter," O'Hanlon said, good-cop style. "His grandmother called us, afraid that he's out joyriding in her car. He doesn't have a license, let alone permission. You know anything about that?"

"Ah, man, well, I'm not really sure..." His face paled. Wrapping his arms across his chest, he tucked his hands beneath his armpits and shuffled his long, narrow feet.

"Jonathan," she continued, "if anything happens to him, or if there's a car accident where others are hurt, or God forbid, killed, he'll do time in juvie, or worse."

Luther's fingers skimmed across the shiny badge clipped to his belt. "Georgia is pretty loose when it comes to charging teenagers as adults. This isn't California."

Jonathan's twitchy body language screamed anxiety. He sucked in a deep breath. "Okay, he did borrow his grandma's car. He and Cornelia needed to go somewhere."

"Cornelia Chan?" O'Hanlon jotted notes in an old-school notebook.

He nodded.

"Where'd they plan on going?"

"Well, this is bad." Jonathan closed his eyes for an instant. He tugged at his messy hair, then tucked his hands back beneath his armpits again.

"Go on," Luther said. "Let's hear it."

Jonathan glanced around as if seeking somewhere to run. "You're Dexter's uncle, right?"

Luther barely nodded. He became quiet and ominously still.

"Let's sit over there and talk," O'Hanlon said. She pointed to a scruffy, overstuffed collection of easy chairs and couches near an abandoned pool table. They followed her over. Jonathan perched on the arm of a chair and looked increasingly miserable.

"Okay, here's the thing," he said. "Dex and Cornelia were headed out to Tybee Island."

"To the beach?" O'Hanlon asked.

"If only." He pulled at his hair again. "They were, uh, planning to do surveillance on a guy."

"They were WHAT?" Luther jumped up. He towered over everyone.

Jonathan's eyes popped. "Yeah, uh, surveillance, sir. You know, sitting in the car and—"

"I know what the hell surveillance is, young man." Luther's fists clenched and unclenched.

"What *guy* are we talking about?" O'Hanlon asked. She flashed Luther a warning glance.

"His name is, uh, Doobius, or something like that. They thought he might know something about Dexter's cousin's murder."

"And you didn't alert anyone when Dexter said he was going after a criminal?" Luther grabbed Jonathan by the shirt, pushed him against the wall.

"Luther," O'Hanlon clenched his arm.

He released his grip on Jonathan. The boy's face was drained of color.

"How did they know where this guy lived?" O'Hanlon asked. "We've been trying to find him for questioning. Murder one."

Jonathan edged closer to O'Hanlon and wrapped his arms around himself again. "Well, uh, Cornelia found his address through old receipts at her parent's restaurant out on the island. Szechuan Paradise, I think it's called. This Doobius dude used to have food delivered from there."

"And they're *following* this asshole?" Luther shook his head.

"We know you, uh, think he killed Jayden," Jonathan said, "but he didn't do it."

"And you know this, *how?*" O'Hanlon asked.

"Cornelia saw who did it. She was there."

"Fuck." Luther jumped up and started punching numbers into his phone. In seconds he had a response. "I want a BOLO on a silver 2011 Camry, license plate number Alpha-Bravo-Foxtrot-555, Georgia, Chatham County. Registered to Florence Rose Middleton of Savannah. He finished the description and closed out the call. "Anything else you want to tell us? These kids are in serious shit. I can't believe you didn't share this with us. It's called criminal obstruction of justice."

Moisture began to pool in Jonathan's eyes. "Dexter and I wanted to tell the cops but Cornelia is scared shitless that she'll have to testify. Then she'll get murdered too." His voice raised an octave. "And she thinks the witness protection program will destroy everything her family has built here over generations. Her grandparents were in concentration camps back in California during World War II, I mean I can relate to that. My family... we're Jewish. It's complicated. We didn't really know what to do."

"Okay, okay," Luther said. He took a deep breath and attempted to calm down. "Don't talk to anyone about this. You hear me? No one."

"Yes, sir. I mean, no sir, I won't talk to anybody. But would you let me know when you find them?"

Luther's phone buzzed. "Sheriff Middleton," he said. As he listened, he pressed his fingers hard against the bridge of his nose, then shut off the phone. He turned to O'Hanlon. "Garden City PD found the car about five minutes ago. Abandoned near the terminal. Signs of a struggle."

Luther and O'Hanlon sprinted for the door. Jonathan slumped against the dark, empty front desk and broke down in tears.

23

At 7:00 a.m., Lindsay Vargas and I headed off to CNN Center from her magazine-worthy, Frank Lloyd Wright-inspired home in Druid Hills. The woman was definitely living way above my pay-grade—even when I had one. Miraculously, we made it through the city to her office with time to spare. She maneuvered the side streets as if she were a city native. As many times as I'd visited Atlanta, all the Peachtree-named roads, avenues, courts, and circles still confused me. I'd read somewhere that there were over seventy variants of the name for roadways in this city.

CNN headquarters was an ultra-modern, hotel-type structure with a gigantic red CNN logo out front. A big open atrium, composed of a lot of steel and glass, was adorned with an eye-numbing array of TV screens presenting live feeds from around the world, dazzling visitors. The last time I'd been here, a tornado had passed through and ripped the front off of the place. That quasi-war-zone look felt more appropriate for a news organization than the wannabe Disneyland incarnation front of me. Pure entertainment, however, was more the state of the news industry today than I wanted to acknowledge.

As we headed for an escalator, a group of sleepy-looking grade-schoolers on a field trip marched by. The beleaguered teacher, a curly-haired Hispanic woman in her twenties, and perky parent volunteers tried to keep them in line. They checked us out, probably wondering if we were somebody they could recognize from the tube. Sorry kids.

I was dressed for success in my one and only Armani pants suit—a slate gray classic. I felt sophisticated and professional, something I hadn't felt twenty-four hours ago. Lindsay wore a deep red jewel-tone wrap dress. It swirled nicely around her hips as she walked down the hall in front of me. Of course, it did. Rio had found himself a gorgeous woman.

When we arrived at Lindsay's office, I turned down a third cup of coffee. My head was already buzzing like a hot wire. Sitting on a caramel-colored leather couch across from her blond-oak and stainless-steel desk, she filled me in on how best to make news director, Grant Levine, want to offer me a job at a fat salary.

My phone chimed. It was Luther. I'd have to call back after the interview. Even if it was news on Jayden's case, it would have to wait an hour. I turned off the ringer.

If I couldn't land this position, I didn't have anything else up my sleeve. Adjunct teaching in journalism at USC was always an option, but it would be only part-time, offering barely enough income to cover the mortgage and it didn't include any health benefits. The kids were on their father's plans, but I had nothing. God knows how life could change in a blink.

I had to stop working myself into a frenzy. I took a breath and mentally snapped myself back into focus. I am who I am. My experience is what it is. I let go of the worry as much as I could and did what I'm best at—just being myself. It is either good enough, or it isn't. Lindsay was reassuring and upbeat as she led me up to the top floor to meet my fate.

Grant Levine hadn't arrived by the time we got to his office. Introducing himself as Orson, Grant's administrative assistant, a young man in a slim suit and an apricot-colored tie, apologized profusely on behalf of his boss.

Before he could take our refreshment orders, Grant zoomed through the door, overcoat flying.

"Good morning, sir," Orson said. "Ms. Vargas and Ms. Jackson are here to see you."

I would legally change my name back to Middleton this week.

"Thank you, Orson. So sorry to keep you waiting, ladies. I'll be right with you," Grant said.

Distinguished-looking but not handsome, Grant was in his mid-fifties with prematurely gray hair and a goatee. He tossed his coat to Orson who quickly hung it up, pressed the start button on the office microwave and had a breakfast sandwich and a latte in front of the news director before we could stand up and follow him into his inner office. Felt like a scene from *The Devil Wears*

Prada.

I politely refused Orson's offering from a pink bakery box that he pulled magically from somewhere behind his desk. Lindsay and Grant spoke briefly about a story they were working on, and then she patted my arm and scooted out the door.

Grant motioned me to a worn leather armchair. The administrative assistant exited the office, quietly shutting the door. Behind me, a wall display of TV monitors streamed live but silent, with subtitles scrolling. He could interview me while not missing a beat at the news desk. I would have to compete for his attention with an array of lovely anchor people hawking bombings, political hi-jinks, and weather disasters. Damn.

He took a bite of his breakfast sandwich, grabbed his coffee and sat in the matching chair opposite mine.

"So, Beatrice... may I call you that?"

"Of course. Bea is fine, too."

His smile was feline. The hairs on my neck rose. I could envision the caterpillar in *Alice in Wonderland* saying *"Whoooo... are... you?"* while puffing God-knows-what-kind of smoke from his hookah.

I hated being critical of someone I'd met, someone who could actually give me the opportunity to support my family again.

"I'm glad we could chat today," he said. I'm very interested in your approach to your nephew's story. It's garnered national attention."

My stomach knotted. How dare the bastard ask me about Jayden.

I tried to stay calm. "You know I can't share details, Mr. Levine. It's an investigation in progress."

"Call me Grant, please."

"Grant, I'm actually rather shocked that you'd ask me about this, given our family is still in a state of grief and disbelief. I'm not covering the murder as a reporter here. I'm his aunt."

"Yes, his aunt, who is also a highly-regarded journalist, unemployed or not. And whose brother is a county sheriff."

A piece of me wanted to walk out, but I couldn't afford to squander this opportunity.

Grant took a deep draught of coffee and looked me over as if he were deciding which tomato to pluck from a bin. "Well, Beatrice, we have to ask the hard questions, don't we? Everything pertaining to a current story is fair game. Doesn't mean anything you share with me will go beyond these walls."

I shook my head in dismay. Condescending asshole. "You're right, Grant—I am a reporter, and I know how this works. Don't bullshit me. Information is a commodity up for grabs."

My hand flew to my mouth—I couldn't believe I'd said *bullshit* in a job interview.

He set his cup down with a clunk.

"Wait a minute now," he said, "I expect Lindsay has vouched for my integrity." The arrogant smirk that had been frozen on his lips softened. "I do, truly, want to understand your thinking. How you're approaching this challenge. How the stress affects you. The job for which you're being considered will be very tough. There are times when it may become personally uncomfortable."

I rolled my eyes. I was now full-on pissed. He was talking to me like I was a goddamned intern.

"Anyone can give me a cherry-picked news piece, Bea. Lots of journalists can put together a great-looking story. Doesn't mean it's accurate or worth a shit. I want to know what kind of a person collected the material, how they determined what was important, and why. I want to understand how you see the world. It may fit our work culture. It may not."

I nodded but didn't rush to respond. Not the kind of interview I'd expected. I tried to quell the steam that was probably coming out of my ears.

Grant finished his coffee and removed his horn-rimmed glasses for quick cleaning with a tissue. I resented this guy. My personal life was none of his business. But dammit, I needed the job.

I took a deep breath and tried to step back from the precipice of completely blowing this opportunity. Likely I was overreacting, given how vulnerable I was feeling in all parts of my life right now. I couldn't let my professionalism slip away.

My phone vibrated. I thought I had turned it off.

"Okay," I finally said, "let me tell you what we have."

Our discussion turned toward what I did well—report the facts, identify the players, and brainstorm the possibilities. In the next hour, I must say that I hadn't felt so energized in months, maybe more. Grant completely engaged with me—asked pertinent questions, offered feedback, suggestions, and helped me frame the next steps.

Someone knocked on the office door. *Ugh.*

I glanced at my wristwatch. The time had flown by.

Orson stuck his head in. "So sorry to bother you ma'am, but your brother called. Seems quite important."

"He called me here?" I asked, startled.

"He's been trying to reach you and says to call him, stat. He insisted that I interrupt you."

Orson shut the door.

"Please feel free to take the call," Grant said. He rose and moved to his desk.

"Thank you." I looked at my phone. Multiple missed calls from Luther came up on the screen.

I keyed in his number and he picked right up.

I struggled to follow his rushed words. I could feel beads of perspiration begin to rise on my skin. They'd found Momma's car open and abandoned near the Garden City Terminal early this morning. Momma thought Dexter was driving it. His friend Cornelia had likely been with him.

Understanding began to take hold. I broke into a full-on cold sweat, my chest constricting. The kids were gone. Signs of a struggle. An APB had been issued.

"No. No, no, no, no." Sparks pocked my vision as if I had been hit in the head. "I'm on my way." I disconnected. My hands shook.

"Are you all right?" Grant asked, a concerned frown on his face.

"No. God, no. My son, my baby boy. He's gone."

24

I roared up to the crime scene in my rental car. Momma's silver Camry was on a flatbed truck pulling out of the weed-choked Lucky Clover gas station parking lot. It looked to me like one of the unluckiest places on earth. Yellow crime scene tape snapped like gunshots in the wind gusting off the Savannah River.

Luther, O'Hanlon, a gaggle of officers in uniform, and various media types lingered and talked near a rusted-out car wash. It surely hadn't seen any kind of vehicle in decades.

An Asian couple, accompanied by an elderly white-haired woman, walked across the lot toward me. Their faces were pinched with anxiety. Cornelia Chan's relatives.

I had to remind myself that there were at least two insanely terrified families involved here. I started toward Luther, eager for news that our children had been found, but took a quick U-turn and rushed to the Chan's. I needed to connect.

"I'm Dexter's mother," I said as I jogged up to them.

Wordlessly, we all embraced. It was that simple.

Luther and O'Hanlon quickly caught up with us. My brother made official introductions. "Bea, this is Cornelia's mother and father, Elliott and Nancy Chan, and Nancy's mother, Esther Nakai."

We murmured acknowledgments.

"Mr. and Mrs. Chan gave us the food delivery records their daughter had discovered," Luther explained, all business. "Now we know where Evan Doobius lives. Detective O'Hanlon has confirmed that his legal name is Emad Al Alequi. The search warrant arrived so we should be able to get into his place within the hour. We're heading out to Tybee right now."

Elliott Chan clung to his wife. "As you get more information, please, *please* let us know what is happening," he said.

"We'll be in touch as soon as we know anything," Luther assured them. "We will find these kids. I promise you that."

O'Hanlon rushed to her unmarked car on the edge of the field and jumped in. Luther followed. They pulled up to me. I stood dazed, in the middle of the crumbling parking lot.

"Hop in, Bea," Luther said.

"I'm good. I want my car." I needed to get far, far away from the Lucky Clover but felt too disconnected from reality to do anything about it.

Luther got out and hugged me tight then guided me

over to O'Hanlon's car. "One of the uniforms will drop your rental off at Momma's," he said. "I don't think you should drive right now."

"No, no, I'm fine," I said. I took off for my car, but Luther managed to corral me and take the key fob. In a few seconds, I found myself in the back seat of O'Hanlon's vehicle, on the way to Evan Doobius's place on north Tybee Island. Two squad cars followed.

"We'll meet Crime Scene there," Luther said.

O'Hanlon was on the radio, dispatching a critical incident team for backup. She turned on her siren and picked up the speed. I moved forward in my seat behind Luther and threw my arms around his shoulders, pressed my face into the side of his prickly neck. He squeezed my hands in his.

A great deep sob rose up from my core. I could easily disintegrate here and now.

"We're gonna find them," he said. "This address is a helluva lead. We're way ahead of where we were a half hour ago."

I nodded, sat back and buckled my seatbelt. We navigated through the Historic District, regularly getting cut off by random clueless drivers, lookey-loo tourists, and oblivious bicyclists. O'Hanlon was scary-good behind the wheel. Probably all those years of driving in Los Angeles traffic.

As I watched the city fly by, I reeled myself back in. Flailing around, way the hell out there on an emotional tether, was no way to be effective. I moved from pure agony to anger. We were gonna get our children back and nail these assholes for Jayden's murder. Or die trying.

Finally, the city fell away. O'Hanlon accelerated as we approached the straightaway through the saltwater marshes. Past Fort Pulaski and the north Tybee marina, we flew toward our first real lead.

"How was the interview?" Luther asked, no doubt hoping to distract me for a moment.

I sighed and struggled to remember *anything* about *anything* beyond my lost child. "I think we kinda liked each other by the end, but I said 'bullshit' in the first five minutes, so I think that job's history. I highly doubt that he's looking for somebody quite like me."

"You mean, smart, tenacious, and great at their job," Luther said.

I wiped tears from my eyes. "I can't handle anyone saying anything nice to me right now. My son has disappeared. He stole Momma's car and drove it without a license to spy on a killer. I thought I'd raised a pretty level-headed young man. Evidently, not. Maybe if I had been at home more, hadn't got divorced, had been a better person like my mother."

"Beatrice, he's fifteen," Luther said. "We were all idiots at that age. There's nothing you could have done. At some point, they fly on their own, at least the ones that were raised right."

I managed a sad smile.

We turned onto Sandy Point. Bouncing along the rutted gravel and tabby road, we passed small, isolated frame houses, and weathered fish shacks with salt-stained docks. Some reached almost a quarter mile out across the seagrass and pluff mud into the shallow tidal creeks. The air held the earthy scent of decomposition.

Doobius's duplex was constructed of greenish pine

clapboards blackened from mold and lichen. We pulled into the driveway. The single unit to the right of his appeared abandoned. The black-and-whites came in around us. O'Hanlon and Luther exited our car. I tried to follow.

"Stay right there until we secure the place," my brother ordered. "Hear me?"

I undid my seatbelt then tried to roll down the window so I could hear and see everything, but they were locked. My entire being felt like a rocket honing in on some yet-to-be-defined target, ready to explode. Calming myself was critical. *Namaste.*

A Savannah-Chatham County Metro Police Department van swerved in tight next to our vehicle. Four SWAT team members with POLICE stenciled on their black bulletproof vests jumped out and conferred with Luther and O'Hanlon. The uniforms surrounded the duplex and peeked in windows, guns drawn, trying to get a sense if anyone was in the area, more specifically, inside either of the residential units.

Luther backed up by his team, pounded on the front door and loudly announced, "Savannah-Chatham County Metro Police—open up."

No response. The places felt empty. All was silent; even the birds failed to sing. A buzzing insect was the only sound I could hear.

Then, BANG.

Wood splintered. Hinges groaned and gave way. A battering ram ripped open the door.

The SWAT team swarmed into Doobius's condo, Luther and O'Hanlon right behind them. I waited, praying. Finally, after about ten long minutes, O'Hanlon returned to the front porch.

"We're clear," she called out.

I blew out the air I'd been holding in my lungs. Light-headed, I sucked in oxygen. As I jumped out of the car, a battered navy-blue panel van with an SCMPD logo on the side pulled in behind us.

A young man in jeans and a worn gray SCMPD Softball Champions T-shirt climbed out of the truck, a video camera tucked under his arm. He hung back, appearing to take in the whole scene, like my photojournalist friend, Lucy, always did in Los Angeles.

The driver of the van was introduced to me as Annabelle Borchard, county crime scene investigator. A spare, skittish woman of color with a mass of curly gray hair, she was in her early 60s. She projected a no-nonsense intensity. Her eyes darted around like hummingbirds looking for a feeder.

Her assistant, Horvath, the man with the video camera, soon joined us. Next to his tightly-wound boss, he seemed to move in slow motion.

The SWAT team and local cops vacated the duplex but continued to monitor the perimeter of the property. O'Hanlon instructed the local uniforms to go house-to-house along the road and interview residents for pertinent information. Luther got on the radio again, talking to someone about another warrant.

I followed the crime scene folks up onto the porch. Annabelle handed me booties to put over my shoes and warned me to stay out of the way. I'd heard that before.

The house was stripped of decoration. It smelled of beer, mold, and unwashed body. Bare bones and stark, the walls were riddled with nail holes and dried masking tape where posters and pictures must have once been attached. An empty pizza box lay open on the coffee table. A rolled-up rug was tucked next to the couch. Other than the remnants of fast food and a collection of worn furniture, the place had been cleaned out.

Annabelle and her assistant snapped photos, vacuumed, collected kitchen and bathroom detritus into baggies, and scavenged surfaces and handles for fingerprints. An hour and a half into the search, everything was covered with black fingerprint powder.

Annabelle processed the prints onto strips of clear tape and affixed them to cards where she noted date, time, and location. Horvath photographed the prints and then digitally sent them directly to the AFIS database for possible ID.

"Any idea how many people lived here?" I asked.

"Well, at first glance, there seems to be one suspect's fingerprints all over the place," Annabelle said. "I picked up a good print from what might be a second subject on the toilet seat. Got a couple more partials—it's hard to tell much. We sent the images priority, so we could hear something soon, or it could be hours."

"Or never," Horvath said, eyes droopy. He reminded me of a big sloth. A sloth who maybe smoked a bit of dope.

I left the booties in one of Annabelle's HAZMAT bags, worried that Horvath could be right. What if all the prints came to nothing? I couldn't go there.

As I walked down the road to where O'Hanlon was talking with two extremely fit-looking SWAT guys, Luther came up unexpectedly behind me and threw his arm around my shoulders.

"How ya doin', baby girl?"

Hadn't been "baby girl" in decades, but it was kind of nice knowing there was somebody who still thought about me that way.

"Hangin' in," I said and took his hand. Grimy black dust from my once lovely job interview suit streaked my fingers. "What do you think happened in there?"

"I'd say they moved Doobie out real fast, late last night or early this morning. Maybe happened when they realized the kids were following them. We're gonna leave a couple guys here to keep an eye on the place for the next few days."

I nodded, glad to hear that they would continue surveillance. "Annabelle packed up a prayer rug that was left behind. A nice one. She said it looked like silk fibers, natural dyes. Strange that it got left behind."

"Yeah, there may well be a religious component mixed in here," Luther said. "Rugs are often passed down through the family, have a lot of meaning. Who knows, maybe they'll try to come back for it."

"We can only hope," I said as we approached the car.

"Let's get you back to the station. You can pick up your rental and head back to Momma's." Luther opened O'Hanlon's rear door for me and I crawled in. He slid into the front.

My cell phone chirped with a newsy little text from Alyssa with attached photos of her baby sister. Sweet innocence. I'd call my daughter later with the bad news about her brother.

The front doors clunked shut. O'Hanlon pulled out around the crime scene van and headed back along the road toward the highway. Beneath our tires, gravel and crushed seashells crunched and crackled like corn in a popper.

"Have you called Kevin yet?" Luther asked.

"Oh, jeez." My heart sank. I'd been so obsessed with the abduction I hadn't even tried to reach Dexter's father. Then anger kicked in. "If he had been a responsible parent and hadn't abandoned his son to run off to Iceland with some hot Nordic sheepherder—"

"Bea," Luther said as if he were commanding his officers to attention. "The blame game is worthless. People are who they are. You two have to be on the same page here, not at each other's throats."

I knew he was right, but I wasn't ready to actually say it. I punched in Kevin's number. I'd had international calling since Dexter was born. It went to voicemail.

"Kevin, call me as soon as you can. This is an emergency concerning our son." I hit the disconnect button hard.

"Kevin Jackson, the NBA player? He's Dexter's dad?" O'Hanlon asked.

"Yeah." My voice came out as a whisper.

"Shit." O'Hanlon jumped on the phone. Drummed her fingers on the steering wheel as we pulled onto the highway. She connected with someone at the police station named Sergeant Afton and gave him succinct orders.

"Listen to me carefully—no media. Hear me? Absolutely no media around these kids' situation. Understand? Heads will roll if I hear an ID. Okay, we'll be back at the station at about 1500."

Luther glanced back at me, then over at O'Hanlon. "You thinking that this could turn into a hostage situation if the perp knows Dexter has a rich papa?"

"Who the fuck knows," she said, agitated, "but we can't take any chances. There may come a point where we can use it to our advantage, but we have to be strategic, not throw it out there."

Luther nodded. His radio squawked. It was Annabelle. He put the call on speaker.

"Sheriff Middleton, we got a hit on one of the prints already."

We all quieted, intent on the report.

"Print found on the toilet seat belongs to a Marcus Trotter, aka Marcus Hunter, aka Muhammed Al-Sadr, and Muhammed Hussein. Seems to have spent at least a decade as a Marine in Special Ops then went with Blackshear as an independent contractor. Technically, a mercenary. Hardcore sniper trained. You won't believe this, but he's a Savannah man."

My brain seemed to leave my body as Annabelle continued to speak. Her words became garbled white noise.

Marcus Trotter. I was fifteen when he raped and tried to murder me. And now, he had my son.

25

"Cornelia, wake up," Dexter pleaded, his voice was raspy and hoarse. "Cor, please."

His friend's clammy coldness was chilly against his hot skin. He elbowed her as hard as he could within the confines of their cramped, claustrophobic cage. Zip ties cut into his wrists and ankles. He couldn't feel his feet. Maybe they would turn green and fall off. A tear slid down his cheek as he contemplated being footless and never being able to play basketball again.

Cornelia moaned.

Dexter sighed with relief. She wasn't dead.

In the pitch blackness, the air was cloying—it stunk of urine, sweat, and something coppery.

"Mom?" she whispered.

"No, Cornelia, it's Dexter. You're not at home. Don't know where the hell we are, or if anybody even knows we're gone."

"Dexter?"

"I'm right here, next to you." He nudged her, more gently this time.

"Dex? I'm going to throw up."

"Ah, shit, really? Okay, try to puke through the wire, outside the cage, okay?"

"Cage?"

"Feel the wire next to you? Aim out that way. Come on, that way, please."

She started to gag.

"Oh, God," he choked. "I'm gonna hurl, too."

As they both vomited, Dexter heard the scraping of a latch lifting, then the high-pitched groan of metal doors opening. Then blinding brilliance sliced through the darkness and pierced his retinas like a luminous scalpel.

The person loomed at the end of the large shipping container. "Stinks like hell in there. Ketamine always makes people puke their guts out," he said to someone nearby.

A few moments later, Dexter, hands bound in front of him, wiped his mouth on his sleeve. The light blindness began to fade. The speaker took form. He recognized the guy who had been with Doobius—the driver of the car they'd followed to the port.

"Ketamine is what they use to put animals to sleep," Cornelia whispered to Dexter. "Our dog had an operation last term and I did a report on it for school. I got an A. Do you think they are going to kill us?"

"Shut up, bitch," the big man said, "or I'll cut your goddamned tongue out."

Dexter felt Cornelia squeeze closer to him. The rusted

wire of the kennel bit into his flesh. He noticed the dead body of a brindle-colored pit bull pup decomposing a few feet away. The sad sight was incredibly disturbing. Who were these hideous men?

The door to the shipping container slammed shut with a hollow clang. Dexter and Cornelia were again plunged into the foul darkness.

)(

"So, what the hell are we going to do with those kids?" Farouk addressed an elderly man who sat next to him in their wood-paneled construction trailer. Whiteboards with schedules, a large calendar, and worn religious posters filled the walls. *Garden City Imports* was stenciled on the partially opened front window. The office overlooked stacks of Maersk shipping containers. The rumbling of huge cranes created vibrations in their cups of thick, black coffee. Dirty mini blinds tapped against the glass.

"You never should have killed that boy. How many times have I told you this kind of action would only bring trouble?" Grandfather Parsa stroked his gray beard. His eyes were cloudy—blue-yolked boiled eggs behind thick glasses. Despite his aged appearance, the man had the sharp, intimidating demeanor of a patriarch. His fifty-year-old son, Farouk, was balding and stocky, his fingers nervous and nicotine-stained.

"Father, it was the only way to stop Emad. He had to be taught a lesson. He is not an American playboy, with the stupid name of Doobius, here to be a rock and roll star. Emad has a job to do for the family. He is Afghan, a Muslim—my son."

"And my grandson."

"Yes, of course, Father." Farouk looked away and unhappily sipped from his Styrofoam cup.

"You failed to consider the fact that the dead boy's family is prominent in the area. Sloppy, Farouk, very sloppy. You should have sent Emad home to the village like I told you."

"I'm sorry, Father—"

"Stop this whining." Grandfather Parsa, held up his arthritic hand, shook his head at his errant son and sighed. "It is what it is now, Farouk. Things have been done that need to be fixed. You need to fix them."

"I will fix them, Father." Farouk's face was ashen.

Emad stepped through the doorway into the office with a Subway sandwich bag and a soda in his hand. He barely acknowledged his father and grandfather as he plunked down at a computer on the far end of the trailer. Sliding an expensive set of headphones over his ears, he appeared to enter his own world. The phones were, however, enough ajar so he could hear everything the men discussed.

Farouk shook his head and didn't bother to conceal disgust for his disrespectful son. A knock sounded at the office door. "Yes, come in."

Muhammed, or Marcus Trotter, entered the trailer and closed the door behind him.

The air in the room changed, it hummed with his intensity. "*Assalam Alaikum.*" Muhammed offered the traditional greeting.

"*Wa Alaikum Assalam,*" Farouk replied. "So, how are they? He popped the top on a plastic container and dug into a salad of couscous, hummus, and cucumbers with yogurt.

"Awake. Heaving, big time."

Farouk took a generous forkful of salad. Cucumbers crunched. He wiped his mouth with a paper napkin.

"Do we know any more about who they are and their connections in the community?" Grandfather Parsa asked.

Muhammed's eyes darkened. "We do."

"And?"

Muhammed hesitated an instant too long. The force of the men's sudden attention hit him like a slap to the head. "The girl's name is Cornelia Chan."

Emad ripped off his earphones. "What? You fucking kidnapped the Chinese girl?"

Muhammed ignored him. "Her parents own a restaurant on Tybee. The other kid is Dexter Jackson, SCAD summer school student. And, uh, Jayden Middleton's cousin from California."

"Whose uncle is a Shellman County sheriff, and whose mother is a reporter. Correct?" Grandfather Parsa's voice was deadly calm.

"This is true, but no worries. I'll take care of it." Muhammed's eyes narrowed. "I've dealt with much worse."

"And you call me the idiot?" Emad exclaimed. He rose from his desk, pushed Muhammed aside, and stormed from the trailer. The door slammed behind him with a sharp crack.

The old man's eyes became angry pink slits. "We need to move them immediately, Muhammed. Out to the fishing camp, away from the city. Tonight."

"Of course, Grandfather Parsa, sir."

Muhammed escaped the trailer as quickly as he could while still observing expected courtesies. The trace of a sneer flickered on his lips then spread into a full-on grin. "Her son. The boy is for sure her fucking son."

26

Completely overwhelmed after the mad dash from Atlanta and the unfolding horror of my child's abduction, I greeted Momma and Aunt Honey back at home, then immediately tromped upstairs to seek oblivion, if only for an hour. Did I really think I could sleep? I would never sleep again.

I left my clothes on the floor and crawled in between fresh sheets. I'd probably streak them with lingering fingerprint dust but I was too tired to care. I was not one of these people who could be up for days straight and still function.

As I lay down, a long-repressed episode in my life ripped wide open. I was fifteen when I met him.

Marcus Trotter was nineteen and the most gorgeous, worldly man I'd ever met. I'd only known boys from "good families" up to that point, selected for me from our church rosters. I hadn't dated much and my knowledge of men, was, to say the very least, limited. Trotter was a high school dropout who had never darkened the doorway of a church. My mother was beyond dismayed by my interest in him. My overly-protective brother, assisted by equally over-protective Rio Deakins, refused to let me near him.

A beautiful bad boy. Family disapproval. That's all my newly-erupting teenage hormones needed to propel me into wild, soul-mate, French-kissing, third-base love.

It didn't matter that his father was in jail, wrongly convicted for the third time of armed robbery. His mother was a drug addict because she couldn't deal with her beloved husband being in prison for life, and his older brother hadn't really killed a man. He'd been framed by dirty cops. His sixteen-year-old sister already had two kids. I'd heard he had several of his own but he denied it. Actually, cried about wanting to be a good father someday—with the right woman. This right woman was, of course, *moi*.

Poor, abused Marcus. My heart reached out to him. Helping others, saving others—it was the Christian thing to do, I remember telling my mother. I still can see her face after hearing that one.

We'd been secretly going out for about three weeks when, on a warm summer evening after work at his uncle's auto-part reclamation business, aka chop shop, he decided to drive me to his special place, out near Tybee. It was a place so special he'd never taken any girl there before.

I was a little surprised by the twelve-pack of Budweiser in the back seat and the flask of hard cider he offered me. I hesitated, but it was really quite delicious, and I felt more grown-up and delicious myself with every sip.

We turned onto a vegetation-clogged dirt road that narrowed after about a half mile into a rutted track. I remember palmettos scraping against the car as we plunged deeper into the undergrowth until his aging Camaro disappeared within the mosquito, sand gnat, and no-see-ums-infested forest.

We got out of the car and walked another half mile up what was now a sandy path. We sprayed each other with Deep Woods Off! and laughed at our cute antics. I, who had only sipped beer once and hated it, polished off half the contents of the flask of cider. Marcus had beers in every pocket but didn't seem to be drinking them.

My speech became thick and I started to stumble. If this was what being drunk was, I was not going to be a drinker.

I had never heard of Rohypnol.

Something was going so wrong.

A clearing that overlooked the Wilmington River spun in front of me. I remember a picnic blanket, the growing darkness, fighting for my clothes. I was seized by panic, I was losing control of my body. Then things got worse.

I tried to scream, but his hands around my neck strangled any attempt. Biting hard on my shoulder, then again harder on my breast, he tore down my new white shorts and rammed himself into me. I gagged in pain. I raked his jaw with my fingernails. He winced.

I am strong and I tried to fight, but whatever was in that flask practically paralyzed me. He was stronger and monstrous. I was nothing to him. Not the special girl at all, just a virginal victim to break and snuff out.

All light was leaking away. I couldn't breathe, blackness was closing in. I was going to die.

Then, somehow, Marcus Trotter rose into the air like a bloody-beaked vulture being ripped from its roadkill. Air returned to my lungs with a blast of hope.

Rio's face appeared. An avenging angel. Fury. Blood. Bones smashing against hard surfaces. Not mine, someone else's. Again, and again.

When it was over he picked up Marcus's limp body, spun it around like a hammer thrower, then launched it into the river. It skipped like a stone.

Rio had killed him.

The next thing I remember was slumping in the front seat of Rio's old Chevy truck, holding my bloody white shorts and pulling on an old UGA T-shirt that came down to my knees.

Rio fired up the ignition and maneuvered the stick shift for traction. He pushed Trotter's Camaro over rocks and bushes until it balanced on a boulder, then tipped slowly toward the river. I held my breath as it slid down the bank and disappeared into the channel.

Rio and I never discussed that night of horror. I began to pull away from him, from my family, from this town, burying the incident, like the car, like Trotter, in the deep watery back creeks of my brain.

How many crimes had this river claimed? How many secrets had been drowned here for good? I'm sure many, but evidently not this one.

27

I crawled out of bed and glanced at the clock on the nightstand. I'd been asleep, if you could call it that, for several hours. My skin was clammy and the sheets were damp with sweat and streaked with fingerprint dust.

I couldn't deal with what had happened between Trotter, Rio, and me all those years ago. Another time, another place, and the events of that day would have to be addressed. The box had been opened but I slammed it shut for now. It was necessary to focus on the present.

Saving Dexter and Cornelia and finding Jayden's murderer was all that mattered right now. Time was ticking away and I was feeling unsettled about the security tapes O'Hanlon's people had reviewed from the port. Maybe they had missed something.

Grabbing a pair of gray yoga leggings and an orange T-shirt, I headed to the bathroom. After the fantastic hot shower, I turned the water knob to cold to wake myself up. It was crucial to get back to the station as soon as possible. Another day couldn't fade into evening with nothing to show for it.

Quickly, I toweled my hair and glanced at the array of skin lotions, hair products, and makeup that were a routine part of my life in Los Angeles. Masks, meaningless masks. When the knife wound of a dead or lost child cuts you down to brutal, visceral reality, you're simply flesh, bone, and raw emotion, humbled and on your knees.

I threw on my clothes and headed for the stairs. As I approached the landing, I was stunned to see the family looking up at me from around the table. Honey, Aunts Freddie May and Hattie, Skinny Rufus, Luther, and Momma.

"It's Sunday night, child," Momma said.

Sunday night. Oh no. I wouldn't be speeding down to police HQ yet. Our tradition of Sunday night supper had been going on for generations. No crisis, however catastrophic, was reason enough not to come together as a family and support one another.

"Just grilled some chicken and some of Rufus's homemade sausages. Come on now and sit down. We all need sustenance to keep us strong." She pointed to plates of food that would feed an army for a week.

"Uh-huh, yes, indeed," the aunts said, almost in chorus.

"We were about to say grace. Luther's going to lead us." Momma indicated a chair for me. I was beyond frustrated but there was no escape from Sunday supper.

Luther sat at the head of the table, Momma was at

the other end across from him. We joined hands and bowed our heads. I slipped into a chair between Momma and Honey and laced my fingers into their strength and warmth, the fabric of my family. In my panic to follow every lead to save my son and find Jayden's murderer, I had forgotten about the power of prayer.

In the circle of my family, Luther's deeply familiar heartfelt words soothed my jagged nerves, mania began to fade. We prayed not just for our own, but for all those in need of strength and comfort. Although I am no longer a particularly religious person, in the doctrinal sense at least, I felt many spiritual hands holding me up at that moment.

The food definitely added renewed energy—I had been pretty much running on empty since early in the morning. I've never been one to function well on sleep deprivation and starvation. I tried to stay away from the carbs. Fat chance. Pass the cornbread. I'd hit the caffeine later to compensate.

"Luther, we need to go back down to the station tonight and look at the tapes from the Ports Authority," I said as dinner concluded.

"I already made arrangements for that." He took one more sausage.

I was relieved that we both appeared to be in sync with what had to be done next.

"I think I should come along," Aunt Hattie stated, her forkful of red velvet cake hanging in midair.

I looked over at her. Tried to hide my skepticism but failed.

"Don't give me that look, young lady," she said. The cake disappeared into her generous, ruby-lipped mouth.

How did her lipstick manage to remain in place after all that eating? Her eyes narrowed. I suddenly felt queasy.

"You're not the only one who knows how to investigate crime," Hattie said. "I'm head of our neighborhood watch in Shellman Corners. I saw Joe Pickett's watermelon truck get hijacked. Must have been fifty melons in there. He depends on that money. I followed the perpetrator in my car and called the police on my cell phone. Received a Citizen of the Month award."

The meal I'd eaten turned to lead in my stomach. I knew better than to cross either of the aunties—ever. It always turned out badly for me. Hattie was the scariest. "Aunt Hattie, that's amazing. Congratulations, but this is a murder investigation."

"Well if you're trying to find somebody who looks like that awful picture I've seen on TV of the Doobius kid, y'all will never find him. He ain't looked like that in a couple months."

Luther stopped chewing. "You've seen him?"

She sat up straighter so it felt like she was looking down on the rest of us. "I first met the young man when Jayden played in Forsyth Park. Honey was out of town so I insisted that Jayden introduce me to all of his musician friends. Basic courtesy. Then, a couple weeks ago, I ran into Mr. Doobius at Hall's Barbeque. Could see he'd got himself a haircut. Lightning bolt on the side. Was very polite. Went on about Jayden and the band. I told him to come over to Shellman Corners for his next haircut for free."

"How come you never mentioned this, Aunt Hattie?" Luther pushed away his plate.

"Well, y'all seemed to have everything so well in

hand," she said, patting her blond-highlighted wig, a hint of sheepishness in her voice. Only Luther could elicit that.

He glanced over at me and I knew we'd have to take her with us, for the sake of family relations. "Okay, Auntie," he said, "you're coming with me and Bea. We're heading down to the station right now. Is there anything else you haven't told us? Anything else that seems, *so well in hand?*"

She pursed her full lips and sat up even straighter. Didn't even finish her dessert. "No, nothing. That's it, dear."

We all thanked Momma for hosting the great meal. Rufus helped her to the recliner as Aunts Honey and Freddie May began hauling the plates and dishes into the kitchen. We all kissed, hugged, and then Luther and I hit the road in his cruiser. Aunt Hattie refused to ride in a police car. She followed in her Fairlane. Got to give her credit for being independent.

Felt like we waited for hours in the lot adjacent to the station as Aunt Hattie redid her makeup, organized her handbag, and then shifted her heft from behind the wheel to join us. She also took her time walking down the sidewalk to the main entrance. The irritating glare of blue-green fluorescent lights just inside the door spilled onto the sidewalk. Azalea bushes appeared crushed and spiritless, like ex-cons heading for their next incarceration.

The night clerk buzzed us in. A harried-looking woman in her forties with prematurely graying hair, her nameplate said Officer Grace Pinckney. She handed Luther a thumb drive.

"Down the hall. Use the small conference room," she said without a greeting. "It's all on there, the computer's set up with the projection screen like Detective O'Hanlon asked."

She returned to the pile of paperwork on the desk.

"Thank you very much, Officer," Luther said. I knew he was making sure he communicated gratitude for her effort. We were guests of the SCMPD and worked here at their pleasure.

Aunt Hattie looked Grace up and down, and sniffed, eyebrows raised, about to say something. Turning Hattie loose to share comments with Officer Pinckney wasn't going to lead anywhere good but she refused to be moved. She fished a business card from her salon from her purse and handed it to Grace.

"Call me," she said. "I can do wonders for that mousy hair of yours and any police officer gets a 20 percent discount."

Grace looked at Aunt Hattie like she was talking in Swahili but accepted the card.

"Let's go," I said, pushing Luther and Hattie ahead. Aunt Hattie didn't need to alienate the desk clerk. You never know whose help you might need in the future.

The conference room was old, dark, and windowless, but the technology looked pretty good. The computer was already on and the projector was easy to fire up with a remote which had been left on the shiny oak table. We each ensconced ourselves in a rolling armchair. There were eight of them, unmatched and stuck permanently at odd heights. Better to use limited funds for the stuff that counted.

The first tape, grainy with faded color, was stamped

at 10:30 p.m. The notes left for us by the previous viewers indicated the time range when the suspected vehicles entered the field of vision. That would be helpful, but we wanted to see it all from start to finish.

"Where is the restroom, and is there someplace I can get a cup of coffee?" Aunt Hattie asked.

"Bathroom's down the hall to the right and ask kind Officer Pinckney at the desk where the coffee might be," Luther said, pressing pause on the console. "But we don't have time to wait on you, with all due respect, Auntie; we have to work fast. Every moment is precious. You sure you wanna do this with us?"

"Of course, of course, dear, let's go ahead," she said, appearing momentarily chastened. She pulled a bottle of water out of her bottomless purse and took a long swig, then tossed a bag of M&Ms on the table. "Chocolate is always good to keep you bright."

The long night began.

28

The door groaned. Dexter and Cornelia, stupefied and soaked in sweat, hardly reacted to the grating of lock and hasp. The influx of cooler air, and of red tail lights shining as a van backed up to the just-opened cargo container, was disorienting.

"What's going on?" Dexter asked, voice frayed, throat aching. He struggled to focus on the dark shape of their handler.

"We're taking a little trip. You get to eat something so you don't croak on us, at least not yet," the man said.

Dexter heard someone call the guy Sama. He was handsome and dark-haired with cologne-advertisement-type beard stubble.

As bad as this guy was, he wasn't the one who oozed pure evil, the one who had checked them out earlier in the day. He was called Muhammed.

Sama dialed in a combination for the kennel, and its lock released. Dexter and Cornelia crawled awkwardly out of the cage and through the shipping container toward the glow of the tail lights, like baby sea turtles hatching on a Tybee Island beach, making their way toward the light of the moon which guided them toward the ocean. Sometimes, however, the light was not the moon, just a streetlight or a tail light on a dark road, with a vehicle ready to squash the misguided little ones in the darkness.

Sama pulled Dexter and Cornelia to their feet, zip ties still binding them. Roughly, he herded them into the back of the same gray panel van they'd followed to the port. When? A day ago? Two days ago?

The smell of pizza wafted their way. It almost made Dexter weep.

His legs nearly paralyzed due to lack of circulation, Dexter moved awkwardly and fell hard on his face. The taste of copper pennies filled his mouth, blood bubbled on his lips. Their captor cut the bindings off their wrists with a box cutter and replaced them with handcuffs attached to the side wall.

Dexter pleaded. "Please, cut the zip ties. I can't feel my feet. I won't run, I swear. I can hardly walk."

No response.

A box of cold cheese pizza and a liter bottle of water was tossed in between them. The door slammed shut. They attacked the food as if their lives depended on it.

※

Coffee cups lay abandoned and the bag of M&Ms was almost empty on the tabletop in the detective's conference room. I dumped the last remnants of the chocolate into my hand. Two reds and a blue—vaguely patriotic.

The lack of air in the small room and the distressing fact that recordings from the Ports Authority security cameras yielded no face matching that of Emad Al Alequi, left us all stymied with frustration. Scenes from the exit gate, a quarter mile farther down the road from where the kids disappeared, were useless. The camera, mounted off-kilter, was pointed toward the heavens rather than the road. Lots of footage of seagull bottoms gliding overhead.

"At least we can see an occasional top of a truck moving by. We can figure out the number of vehicles and the time they exited from the soundtrack." I attempted a tone of hopefulness. "At least the security cams have sound. A lot of them don't."

"And it's worth shit," Luther said, tapping angrily on his iPhone.

"Luther," Aunt Hattie admonished, "your language."

"Sorry, Auntie."

He slipped the phone into his breast pocket and patted her hand. We respected our elders even if they drove us crazy. Payback for all the years we drove them crazy.

"If that Doobius boy was to be seen," Hattie continued, "I definitely would've spotted him. Maybe he was down in the back of one of those trucks or vans. Impossible to know."

With that, she began to pack up. A box of tissues, nail polish top coat, a bottle of cholesterol pills, and other miscellaneous detritus disappeared into her eggplant-colored purse. Seemed almost the size of the gym bag my son hauled his basketball gear around in. My son, all the little things that make up that relationship would haunt me for the rest of my life.

I pressed hard on my eyes to stop the tears. We *had* to find him.

"I think I'll be heading home, children. My first client's at 8:00 a.m. Gotta be fresh for old Mrs. Blake. Has barely a handful of hair nowadays but insists I spend at least an hour and a half coloring and styling it."

I couldn't help but smile. Old Mrs. Blake was practically bald when I had last seen her ten years ago. She had always been hostile to the wig idea which my aunt, on the other hand, had completely embraced. Tonight's version was a mahogany bob.

"Give her my best," I said. "And thanks for your help, Auntie." I was truly grateful for her effort.

"Let me walk you to your car," Luther said. He stood up and stretched his back. The digital clock on the wall read 11:15.

"Oh, no need, dear." She hoisted the purse onto her broad shoulder.

"I insist, Auntie," he said in his no-nonsense tone.

She swooned a bit under his protective gaze. My brother was a man who women felt safe with. Then she stopped and turned to me.

"C'mon out to my salon, honey. I'll do you for some hair extensions and a nice manicure." She displayed her colorful talons. "But maybe you're the more conservative French manicure type."

"I can be adventurous with a little persuasion. And thank you, Auntie." I glanced at my ragged nails.

"Just got the whole place wallpapered in gold-foil leopard print." She beamed with pride.

"Sounds amazing," I said and hugged her goodnight. Sometime soon I'd go and see what her little beauty spa looked like. Who knows? Maybe get extensions too.

As Luther and Hattie left the conference room I cued the recording back up. There was nothing else to do, nowhere to go with what little we had. Something, however, was niggling in my brain but wouldn't take shape.

Finally, a couple of dormant synapses fired and illuminated a thought. Maybe Doobius wasn't the bad guy. He wasn't trained as a sniper and had never been in the military. His name indicated he probably smoked too much dope to be moving too fast and furious. He was even kind to Aunt Hattie. According to those who knew him, all he really seemed to care about was music. We were looking for the wrong man.

※

Luther returned ten minutes later with fresh coffee in hand. It was actually very good. In the break room, they had the stuff in the little cups so you could pick your brew and make it fresh. Evidently, O'Hanlon bought it herself for the staff and made sure it was well stocked.

"Lu, what we're hearing about Doobius tells me he's not a killer. He's a quirky young dude in love with music." I was starting to feel some renewed energy flow back into my tired body. "Maybe that didn't sit well with a father who might hold fundamentalist beliefs. Could be that Doobius didn't want anything to do with the family business. And, I dunno, maybe there's someone else taking the lead here. A trained soldier, a marksman, someone like—" I choked and couldn't say the name.

Luther drummed his fingers on the arm of his chair. I almost recognized the beat. "Maybe somebody like Marcus Trotter? Somebody tough and macho, not a stoner, artist-type."

Hearing that name spoken out loud took my breath away for a moment. "Yeah, a charming, cold-blooded psychopath with Special Ops training."

"A man who worked for Blackshear as a mercenary, a professional killer with no political allegiance. The perfect son-figure for a heroin dealer." Luther took a long swig of coffee. He rubbed his eyes and sighed. "I wonder what Trotter would look like today. We couldn't get anything from Blackshear. And the Trotter family, what there was of it, is long gone from Savannah. The man's a spook."

I envisioned Marcus Trotter's smooth, brown face at nineteen. Images from that horrible time, of my fall from innocence, began to leak out of the box. "No." I slapped it shut with a gasp.

"You okay, Beazy?" Luther looked at me, eyes narrow, probably wondering if I was going to stay intact or fall apart and have to be picked up off the floor. My fists tightened to hard knots. No floor for me.

"Trotter always wanted to be cool, that I know for sure," I said. "If he's losing his hair, he probably shaves his skull. If he has his hair, probably wears it in dreads. Despite any Islamic influence, no beard or mustache is my guess. He always thought his bone structure was too pretty to hide."

I pushed back my chair from the table and paced. It

had been years, but I understood this asshole. "I can see him in jeans, a black T-shirt, and a casual-looking but very expensive sport jacket. Or black leather. Something Euro and designer. He loved labels. Probably has diamonds in his ears."

"Quite the profile, sister. Didn't know you knew him so well."

Well enough to want him dead. I was suddenly so angry it felt like my hair was beginning to sizzle. "Let's look at those tapes one more time." I moved to the console and pressed the green GO button.

A half hour in, we had him. Dreadlocks, dark clothing, and diamond earrings.

29

Luther had to return to Shellman County for the morning so I met O'Hanlon as she entered the Barracks, the Historic District police headquarters. I held a freeze-frame photocopy of Marcus Trotter in my hand.

O'Hanlon had been in Atlanta visiting her daughter at the Emory Med Center. Pale, with purplish bags beneath her eyes, she looked like she'd slept in her clothes.

"How is your baby girl?" I asked, knowing that she suffered from her own family nightmare.

"Doing fine," she said and left it at that. "What do you have there?"

I explained what we'd found.

Within the hour she had a state-wide BOLO issued on Marcus Trotter along with all of his aliases. Now we would wait. Again.

Her phone rang as I was about to depart.

"O'Hanlon."

She listened, brows drawing together with concentration. As I turned to leave, she held up her hand and motioned for me to remain. I stopped in my tracks.

"Okay, so you think you've seen Trotter, at the Garden City Terminal?" she asked the caller.

"We got him entering through Gate 1 at 11:23 p.m. last night," I whispered to her, "according to the time stamp on their security footage." I motioned to the image she held in her hand.

O'Hanlon nodded and slid into the chair behind her desk. She tucked the phone's receiver under her chin as she punched up a screen on her laptop and quickly scanned through several documents. She seemed to find what she was looking for.

The detective then continued her phone conversation. "I see here a white or pale gray 2001 Dodge panel van, couldn't get the plate number. We're pretty sure this Trotter guy left again through Gate 5 seven minutes later, in the same vehicle."

She covered the phone's mouthpiece and turned to me. "Head of terminal security thinks Trotter may be part of an on-site business called the Garden City Import Company. He'll meet us at the main gate in a half hour."

My heart rate accelerated. A possible break?

"Okay, Chief," she continued, back on the phone to ports security. "We're on our way."

Savannah is such small city compared to New York, Boston, or Long Beach—it's easy to forget that the

Georgia Ports Authority, Garden City Terminal, is one of the largest single port facilities in the country. Driving through the main gate, I felt as if we were entering another world, one made of giant Lego-like shipping crates in bright colors and skyscraper-tall cranes that lifted the containers as if they were matchboxes. From China to Johannesburg, company names stenciled in bold letters declared exotic foreign locations. The air smelled of oil, exhaust, and the faint, stultifying mustiness of the ocean.

We parked the car outside of the cement-block main office and went to meet Security Chief John Stoddard. A short, stocky man in neatly pressed khakis, he wore a white golf shirt and a navy blazer with the Georgia Ports Authority logo on the breast pocket. Stoddard moved with the tight formality of a four-star general hosting a visiting dignitary. His accent, however, was completely down home.

"Detective, and Miss Middleton, y'all kindly follow me." His drawl was from somewhere other than Georgia, probably Louisiana. "We're gonna hop in that there Kubota and I'll take y'all over to their office. They always paid on time and never gave us any problems, but when the BOLO came through—I'm pretty sure the guy in the picture, Trotter, or Muhammed, worked for them. When I stopped by this morning, the place had been cleared out."

We settled into the vehicle—I'd call it an industrial grade golf cart. Stoddard turned on the ignition and headed out toward the south end of the facility.

"Garden City Imports? What do they import?" O'Hanlon asked before I could.

"Supposedly, textiles, leather shoes, purses, and dried fruit, mostly dates."

"You say supposedly?" I asked.

"We do intermittent inspections but that's all we ever saw. Seemed legit. That's what's in the records, too. Not to say we catch every shipment of black market goods that come through here, but you can be sure as ticks on a Redbone Coonhound we get most of them. Yessiree."

He pulled out a tablet, punched the little buttons with his fat fingers, and scrolled through records. "Semis left early this morning carrying their products. The office has been stripped down. They also have one locked shipping container we couldn't get into."

"I'm calling in our CSI people," O'Hanlon said, not asking permission.

Stoddard didn't respond, pushed harder on the gas pedal. I had no idea about lines of jurisdiction in a seaport.

"Do you have information on the semis?" I asked. "License plates, ownership, destinations?"

"We do," Stoddard said and took a curve at an alarming speed. My knuckles turned white on the hand grip. We whizzed through the terminal grounds with the chief playing *The Dukes of Hazzard* at every corner. We passed longshore workers of many ethnicities and ages. They wore a uniformly tired, no-nonsense look.

It was a ten-minute ride of terror to Garden City Import's headquarters. I jumped out of the vehicle as fast as I could, not wanting to travel another foot in the chief's little *Mad Max* road machine.

The door to Garden City Imports headquarters gaped open, banging on its hinges in the breeze as we approached. The trailer was modest and dated. The exterior featured rusted-out corrugated metal; inside was nicotine-brown paneling of the cheapest variety. Surfaces of the desks and chairs were clean, but the floors were filthy with dust, grime, and blurred shoe prints. It smelled of cigarettes, vinegar, and pungent spices. O'Hanlon took photos with her cell phone.

We finished up in the trailer then went back outside to follow the chief down a nearby aisle to an aging blue shipping container kitty-corner from the office. Two seagulls landed on the top, did their business, and then flew off, squawking.

The container was identified with an electronic tracking device and secured with a seriously intimidating padlock. Stoddard grabbed a heavy-duty bolt cutter but still struggled with it. Finally, the lock snapped.

He wrenched open the door and we were thrown back by the stench alone. Something had died in there and I prayed to God that it wasn't the children.

Terrified at what we might see, I took a deep breath and peered inside. No human bodies, but a maggot-infested dead dog was sprawled out, covered in what looked and smelled like vomit. Flies rose up from the corpse, circled, and landed again, refusing to leave the feast.

In the gloom, cardboard boxes filled half the container. With Cyrillic printing on the sides along with English and French translations, the cargo was said to be cans of olives. In a canyon between the boxes was a wire pet crate. Filthy towels, old and thin, were piled on the floor. Several appeared to be stained with dried blood.

My throat tightened with a noose-like intensity, and all the oxygen sucked out of me in an instant. My heart was about to rip from my chest. I felt panic hit me like a hammer. O'Hanlon took my arm.

"Listen," she said to Chief Stoddard, "let's get Miss Middleton back to the terminal. This is pretty tough for her."

"Tough for everybody when kids're involved," he said without conviction.

"It's my son who was in that fucking cage." I wanted to hit him, hard. O'Hanlon took my arm again, squeezed it purposefully. *Back off,* it said.

"I'll call my people in and we'll see what went on here," O'Hanlon said. I could see her sweating and her curly hair was exploding out of its ponytail.

"This is my jurisdiction, Detective, I have people, too—state and federal people." Chief Stoddard went to the radio that hung from his belt and called for backup to secure the scene.

In seconds, a Ports Authority truck arrived with two uniformed officers—a tall, rangy bald guy with a sun-scorched face in his fifties, and a young black kid who looked like a trainee, eyes scared and excited. O'Hanlon and Chief Stoddard had words with the men, and with each other. The vibes were tense, so I stepped aside, gasping, trying to get myself back under control.

Stoddard motioned us over to the truck the officers had abandoned and opened the door so we could climb in. The wide bench seat felt like Hattie's Fairlane. Lips tight, face an unhealthy shade of pink, he turned on the ignition and we lurched out onto the main interior road and headed back toward his office.

"Okay, we'll work on this together, we'll figure it out," O'Hanlon said, probably knowing she had to sound collaborative and reasonable or we would lose any influence we had with the feds. "In the meantime, let's get those semis tracked down. See if we can figure out where they're going and what they're carrying."

"I wonder if they have tracking systems." I'd drained my bottle of water in a long, messy gulp. Now I felt like I was going to throw up.

"They do, but they can also be deactivated," Stoddard said. "Better give the highway patrol a heads-up immediately." He pulled out his radio and raised the dispatcher.

Another Ports Authority security truck blew past us toward the scene. Finally, the investigation seemed to be taking on a life of its own.

30

Too many hours had passed since the abduction. I hadn't notified Dexter's father or talked with my baby girl, Alyssa. It would be really bad if they learned about this from some random news feed.

I slid into the front seat of O'Hanlon's SCMPD car, pulled out my cell phone and dialed Kevin, hoping I could bring up a connection to Iceland. He was probably soaking in one of those famous hot mineral springs with the beautiful alpaca farmer. Didn't want to stoop to the blame game, but here I was. If Kevin would have been with his son in Los Angeles for the mere two weeks he had promised, this phone call wouldn't have been necessary. Okay, enough.

I left a voicemail. "Sit down, Kevin, I have some bad news. Our son has been kidnapped by a murderer who is likely the hit man for an Afghani heroin cartel."

Just uttering those words was unreal. I didn't add—*who wants the worst kind of retribution against me and mine for a long-ago rape and attempted murder.*

He called back ten minutes later, about to book a flight down to Savannah. I was able to talk him into sitting tight and promised regular updates. I couldn't imagine having Kevin here right now. Despite his attempts at helpfulness, he was always exhaustingly high-maintenance. He'd need a perfect place to stay, something to do, people to entertain him, constant hand-holding. Even with his son in mortal danger, he'd find a way to make it all about Kevin Jackson. I couldn't and wouldn't take care of him.

"Do not, I repeat, do not, speak to the media," I reminded him. He loved talking to reporters—that was why he married me.

Next call was to ex number two, Eli Strauss, in Santa Monica. I wanted to talk with him before I gave the news to Alyssa. He would support her as we went through whatever was going to unfold. I got him on the first try and told him all that was going on.

He was deeply concerned and interested in every detail, hopefully as a parent, and not as a newsman. My trust issues reared their ugly heads.

He handed the phone to Alyssa. I could hear an old Beyoncé tune in the background about "putting a ring on it," and a baby crying.

"Hi Mom. Something happened to Dexter?" Her voice was small and tentative. I knew the gears would be whirring in her mind faster than our satellite uplink.

The baby quieted and a clack, clack, clack of heels followed Alyssa's question. Probably Deborah, her psychiatrist stepmother, coming into the room to listen in.

I explained to my daughter what had happened, left out the Afghan drug connection and the trained mercenary stuff—just called them "really bad guys."

There was a long silence on her end of the phone when I had finished the story.

"Alyssa?"

"I was going to tell you, ask you something," she said, voice tearful and wavering. "But now, I don't think it would be—" The crying escalated. "Poor Dexter. He'll be okay, won't he, Mom?"

"I hope so, baby. Your uncle Luther and detectives, federal investigators—we're all working hard, around the clock. We're going to find him."

"Oh, my God, he could die." She burst into sobs.

I couldn't deny the possibility even though I wanted to promise her that everything would be all right.

"Let me have that phone, Alyssa," Deborah Strauss said from the background.

Next thing I knew she was on the line.

"I am so sorry to hear about your son," she said. Her voice was always brusque and strident. "It's a nightmare. Anything we can do to help, we're there, anything."

I heard Alyssa ask Deb for the phone back.

"Let me handle this, Alyssa, you're too upset, sweetheart," her stepmother said.

"To handle what?" I asked, concern growing about my daughter. "I want to talk to my child." I slumped down in the seat and covered my head as if waiting for a stone to drop.

"Alyssa planned to tell you that she wants to move

in with us this year, and we have to get things arranged right away. Final application deadline for Beth Shalom Country Day School is this weekend. We need to get her in and registered. I can't be commuting to Santa Monica to drop her off every day. It won't work."

"What do you mean she wants to move in with you? She's my daughter. She lives with me." I felt as if I had been run over by a truck.

"I know this is difficult, but she is so attached to her new little sister now. They're so sweet together. She's also become very interested in exploring her Jewish identity. We thought Beth Shalom would be a great place for her to do that. It's an excellent school. I'm on the board you know. All the graduates go to the Ivies."

"She's not going to a religious school—Jewish, Baptist, or, or Islamic, whatever. We've discussed this before, Deborah. Eli agreed. I want her to be in a school with diversity, with all points of view and backgrounds. And I don't give a shit about the Ivies. Maybe she'll go to UCLA, or Savannah State, or, or maybe a community college..."

Was I screaming? I was. I didn't care. I would not lose both of my children.

"Bea, calm down," Deborah said. She forced a false warmth into her voice that didn't exist in her real personality. Her studied attempts at empathy always came across as disgustingly patronizing.

"I know this is hard, especially with what is going on with Dexter," she continued. "It's horrible, but—"

"But, what? I'm not one of your damn patients," I spat. "How dare you even discuss this with me now. My nephew is dead, my son has been kidnapped by murderers, and now you want to take my daughter."

"I know this isn't a good time, Beatrice—"

"How insightful of you to realize that."

I hung up on her.

Stuffing the phone in my pocket, I trudged over to a nearby chain-link fence. I grabbed the crossbar and hung there, hanging on as if I if were clutching a helicopter skid as it lifted off from a war zone. Tears slowly rolled down my cheeks.

"Get off the cross, Beatrice," O'Hanlon called.

I let go of the fence and turned to face her, feeling as if I'd been slapped. She hopped down the steps from the ports security headquarters, radio in hand and hurried toward the car. Instinctively, I followed.

"The feds say we're out of the investigation and they're going to take it from here on out, so we'd better get moving."

"How can they do that?" I wiped my eyes with my sleeve. Pulled a mangled tissue out of my pocket and blew my nose.

"The ports aren't under our jurisdiction, neither is interstate transportation. I called Luther—we'll meet him at his office in a half hour. We're not gonna be pushed out of this." O'Hanlon jumped into her lead-gray Crown Vic and fired up the engine. I barely made it into the front seat before she peeled out of the parking lot, gravel flying.

I looked back over my shoulder. Chief Stoddard stood in front of his headquarters, feet planted, hands on hips; his slash of a mouth was set in angry protest.

"The Garden City Imports semis were headed south toward Shellman County," Hanlon said. "Stoddard lost all GPS transmission from them beyond the Chatham-Shellman County line."

"Can you call for a helicopter?" I asked. "Maybe they can track the trucks from the sky. But if they already passed through Shellman, they could be almost to Florida in no time."

"I don't think they're taking the trucks to Florida—would be too easy to spot. I think this thing may tie into the bust Luther made the week before last. Cigarette boats trolling backwater streams and bayous, loaded with contraband—Afghani heroin laced with fentanyl."

"It's the same people?"

"Could be," she said. "Gotta get Luther's take on it. He guesses that they pull the semis into a warehouse somewhere, off-load the product into smaller, innocuous-looking vehicles, and then stash the stuff out in remote fish camps. Once they're in the swamps, they're just about impossible to track down."

"Then choppers might be better used monitoring the coastline than the freeway," I said.

O'Hanlon nodded then glanced over at me. "Phone calls go badly?"

I sighed, pressed my temples and closed my eyes. "You could say that. No additional family members have gone dead or missing today, though."

"Then count your blessings," O'Hanlon said, ignoring my sarcasm.

Traffic was building on the highway. She turned on lights and sirens. We flew down the shoulder of the road toward Luther, and God willing, my son.

31

Dexter slumped against a corrugated metal wall in the far corner of a vast, crumbling warehouse. The place reeked with a nauseating cocktail of rotting fish, wet paint, and exhaust fumes. Several decrepit wooden crates covered in bird droppings were the only barriers between Dexter, Cornelia, and the larger warehouse floor where empty-faced workers appeared and disappeared like ants carrying heavy bundles scurrying in and out of their holes. A bank of windows, the glass long ago smashed out, let in dusky light above them.

Cornelia dozed uneasily against Dexter's shoulder. Sometime during the wee hours, they had been rousted from the shipping container, thrown into a van, transported for at least an hour, then dragged into this warehouse and dumped on the gritty cement floor. The two had pressed together to keep themselves warm in the dampness of the night. Now the temperature was rising and they began to perspire, sharing each other's sogginess and filth.

Since first light, one semi-trailer after another pulled in, unloaded pallets of what looked like heroin bricks and reloaded them into an assortment of aging pickups and SUVs that exited out the other end. The shipping containers were immediately repainted with new numbers and company logos and were soon on their way as well. The whole enterprise flowed like a flawless dance.

Dexter and Cornelia were now bound with duct tape rather than plastic zip ties, and despite the black hoods over their heads, it was easy to see through the loose weave. *The assholes must know that we can see everything*. Dexter's thoughts were grim.

"When do you think they'll do it?" Cornelia asked, her voice scratchy and hushed.

"Do what?"

"You know."

Of course, he did. Dexter let out a long, shaky sigh. "I guess they can kill us whenever they want to, so we need to be thinking hard, right now, about how to get the hell out of here."

They were silent for a while. Then Cornelia asked. "Are you a virgin?"

Dexter hesitated. "This question has to do with what exit strategy?" He thought about sex pretty much 24/7 but right now, for once, it wasn't at the top of his mind.

"You can tell me. We have nothing left to prove to anybody." She started to sniffle, then cry outright.

He moved closer, wanting only to comfort her and

calm her down. Even though she tried to act older, she was only fourteen. He was more mature, almost sixteen, and had to help her through this, whichever way it went.

"It's okay, Cornelia. We can talk about whatever you want to talk about. And uh-huh, I'm a virgin," he said and sighed again. "You?"

"Yeah. Wish we didn't have to die without knowing what it was like. You ever have anyone you wanted to, you know, do it with?"

More like was there anyone he *didn't* want to do it with. "Well, what I wanted and what I had the opportunity to do, were two different things. Katie Perry and Rhianna have been kinda hard to hook up with."

Cornelia chuckled amid the tears, then started coughing. Finally, she stopped and cleared her throat. "I thought Los Angeles was full of loose women and hos."

"I don't want no loose women or hos—well maybe a little loose. I want somebody I like. Somebody interesting and nice. I've seen what my dad gets up to, and it's not what I want."

"You want true love, Dex?" Her voice was sad.

"I do, I want true love."

"Oh, my God, you are such a ridiculous romantic. You're like that Nicholas Sparks guy my mom adores." Cornelia sighed. "Maybe we would've been each other's first."

Dexter flushed, imagining.

Cornelia started to cry again, he could hear her sniffling.

Then a door slammed open hard behind them. Its metal hinges screamed as it bounced against the cement-block wall which shuddered from the impact.

Dexter and Cornelia both gasped with fear.

"Yo. Daddy's home," Muhammed shouted.

Dexter sat up as straight as he could, his body crackled with tension. Stomping toward them, hips swaying to his own music, was the really evil guy, the one who always smelled of some strange, fruity aftershave that made Dexter want to puke.

A vicious kick from a metal-tipped boot hit Dexter in the side with a crunch. It took his breath away and seared into his diaphragm. Tears welled in his eyes.

"What're you two little fuck-faces talkin' 'bout, huh?" Muhammed demanded. "And you, boy, you Bea Middleton's brat?"

"Not your business, asshole," Dexter said, infuriated and gulping for breath. How did this guy know of his mother?

"I see y'all got a fuckin' smart mouth. Gonna pay for dat, boy. So's yo' fuckin' mamma. She not gon' get away with shit this time, tight little ass or no. Nuh-uh. She. Gonna. Pay."

"What're you talking about?" Dexter panted, every breath now painful.

"Gonna take every single Middleton down until I get her how I want her." He rubbed at faint scars, like claw marks, on his jaw.

Muhammed planted himself next to Cornelia and rammed his hand up her leg. Her black tights were ripped at the thigh, her skin bloody. She'd caught herself on the edge of the van's bumper the previous night. Dexter could sense her body go rigid. How could he save her from this? His brain burned with the need to destroy this man.

"And y'all gonna be my wifey, China girl. Got a buncha other bitches. Ya gon' love it. I got me a goddamned United Nations of love."

"Muhammed," Sama called.

Through the weave of his hood, Dexter watched the one called Sama as he entered the warehouse along with Doobius, Farouk, and an old man. Several dark-clad guards toting AK-47s stood near wide loading-dock doors where another big rig was pulling in.

"Later, bitches," Muhammed said. "Just gettin' started with y'all." He rose up, turned away, and walked quickly across the vast warehouse floor toward the other men.

When he was out of earshot Cornelia whispered, "What does he mean about your mom?"

"No idea but put everything out of your mind except getting the fuck outta here. Everything. Hear me?"

Cornelia was quiet for a moment. "I think I know how to break out of duct tape. I saw it on YouTube."

"Then start workin' it, Cor. Right now. I don't think we have too much more time."

32

The Shellman County Public Services complex is a series of mid-century modern architectural boxes with floor-to-ceiling reflective windows, like rows of mirrored sunglasses, the kind worn by the highway patrol motorcycle cops I used to see on TV. The building is ringed by a parking lot and fronted with a rose garden. Three huge flagpoles displaying the colors of the state, nation, and county sprouted up from the center of the garden. At the rear of the complex was the entrance to the police department.

We found a spot for the car beneath a spindly, newly planted magnolia tree. Its sparse shade was better than nothing. The rain had cleared for a few hours and the sun beat down unmercifully. *People and pets could die in this heat.* Everything was taking me to thoughts of death.

My cell phone buzzed. I glanced at the caller ID—it was the CNN news department. Were they calling to offer me the job? Reject me? Squeeze me for details of the investigation? I ignored it and tossed the phone back into my purse. The call was linked to a future that I could barely think about—one that was meaningless without my children.

I followed O'Hanlon up the steps to the entrance. The lobby was open and spacious. Photos of all the previous sheriffs adorned the wall across from the main desk. Most were older white men with multiple chins. Then there was Luther. Goosebumps actually raised on my arms. I was so, so proud of my brother.

"Please follow me, Detective, Miss Middleton," an all-business young deputy announced. He held the door to the administrative offices open for us. Blue-eyed with a wispy blonde mustache, he looked barely out of high school. When you start looking at people in their twenties like they're pups, you know you're starting to turn the corner into middle age. Or more likely, you're already well into it.

Luther's office was the physical opposite of the Savannah Historic District Barracks. No dark wood and old-fashioned double-sash windows with wavy panes of glass. Everything was yellow brick and shiny chrome with minimalistic, no-frills furnishings. Big windows overlooked a small grassy area sporting signs to the police department garages and evidence center. Photos of our family, and of Luther with local luminaries, sat on a credenza behind his desk. The only cluttered area of the office was around his computer, where stacks of reports, receipts, law enforcement journals, and file folders looked ready to slide to the floor.

Luther, still on the phone, motioned us to his conference table. A large, bronze, Shellman County logo was mounted on the wall above it. Felt like a courtroom except for the bottles of water and granola bars piled on a large platter in the center of the table, ready for the next meeting. Without waiting for permission, I grabbed one of each and started to chow down, not realizing how hungry I'd become. O'Hanlon followed suit.

Luther finally finished his call. "Want me to order sandwiches? There's a decent place right around the corner."

We both thanked him but refused the offer. Helped ourselves to second granola bars.

"Rio will be joining us," Luther said. He looked at me somberly.

"Rio?" A jolt of fear hit me hard. "Why is he here?" Even though I already knew. This was about Marcus "Muhammed" Trotter.

I put down the granola bar, unfinished. Huh-uh, no fucking way. I'd repressed my experience with this man for two decades—I couldn't face laying it all bare, not even among these good people. I couldn't do it.

I stood up to flee. Grabbed my purse and almost made it to the hallway before Rio materialized, right in front of me.

I shook with anger and fear. "You told him. It was mine to tell. When I was ready."

I would never be ready, and Rio knew it.

Rio shut the door to Luther's office to give us some privacy and pulled me into an empty cubicle. I wanted to knock him over and run like hell. He grabbed me by the arm.

"It was mine to tell, too, Beatrice," Rio said, his voice icy. "I thought I'd killed a man in cold blood. I was a nineteen-year-old murderer. If anybody found out, my whole future would be over; my scholarship to UGA would be history. But now, telling what we know could help the case, could save your boy. We have to do it. They have to fully understand who they are up against. We have to trust Luther and Mary with this information."

Suddenly, long, anguished sobs wracked my whole body. He put his arms around me and held me tight, trying to calm me down. After several miserable moments of weeping, I pulled away from him, embarrassed and humiliated. I carried such shame for the stupid child I had been. No matter how young and clueless, I somehow blamed myself. Intellectually, it was clear to me that classic sexual-assault survivor behavior was cropping up. When this was over, I had to get some help. I needed to crawl out of denial and understand how this horrible incident had affected every bad choice I had made in my life. But emotionally, at this instant, I wanted to hit and run.

"Come on, Beazley," Rio said. He mopped my face with a wad of tissues he pulled from a box on the desk. They smelled like eucalyptus.

"You know I hate it when you call me Beazley, and I hate you for doing this."

"Beatrice, we can face what happened, kick its ass once and for all. Together. We have to. It's toxic crap. We can't carry it anymore."

"I don't know..." I took a deep breath and turned to him. "They have enough on Trotter. They don't need this. They really don't."

"They really do, and you know it. Let's go, girl. Let's get this done."

He was right and again, I hated him for it. And I was madly in love with him. I felt sixteen and vulnerable. He saved me back then. I had to try and trust him with this.

"There must be another way," I said, a desperate last appeal.

"There's not, honey, there's not. Let's do it now, like ripping a big mutha Band-Aid off, get it over with."

I was beaten. I would do this. For my son.

I pulled away from him and straightened my hair.

"Alright. Will you hold my hand? Sounds so lame, I know, but it would really help."

He smiled. He was so beautiful.

He intertwined his fingers in mine. "Let's go. You're gonna be okay, Beazley."

"You shit."

He smiled again, and we walked back into Luther's office. Luther and Mary moved to the chairs across from the couch when they realized that Rio and I were going to stay planted next to each other, hand in hand. My brother looked particularly quizzical.

"Okay, before you two fill us in on Muhammed El-Sadr, also known as Marcus Trotter," Luther said, "let's take a quick look at the sequence of events." He went to a whiteboard on the wall at the end of the conference table and began to draw a timeline. "The MO strongly suggests that the person running the Afghan heroin ring's the major player. They first came onto our radar two weeks ago when we picked up a boat stuffed with fentanyl-laced heroin off Watermelon Bluff, headed for Jacksonville. We arrested four men—two Mexican, two Afghanis. They aren't talking. We made one earlier arrest, but he died in custody."

O'Hanlon took a turn. "We know that Evan Doobius, aka Emad Al Alequi, is the son of one of the kingpins, Farouk Al Alequi. Doobius likely did not kill Jayden. He has no military, Special Ops, or sharpshooter training. Trotter does, though. Tons of it.

"Doobius, Emad Al Alequi, may not be in his father's camp. The family sent him to the University of Miami to get his business degree and looks like he accidentally fell in love with the American culture, particularly the music. Thus, his relationship with Jayden. If he is, in fact, a friendly maybe we can get some help. If we can find him.

"The band members, and Jones, the sniper instructor from the base—nothing likely from them," O'Hanlon continued. "All had alibis and no one seemed to have any reason to hurt Jayden. Just the opposite, in fact." She studied the notes on her iPad. Her phone beeped and she checked a text.

"They probably have Doobius on a very tight leash," I said.

Luther nodded and continued. "Dexter and Cornelia are inexperienced, curious, and they stumbled way too close to the action." He tried to draw an image on the whiteboard of two stick people but his marker was seriously dried up. He tossed it into the garbage can halfway across the room and nailed it with a clunk. My brother was always a dead-on shot. He picked up another marker, barely better than the last one, and continued to write.

"I was notified that the Ports Authority guys couldn't get a forensic team until tomorrow," O'Hanlon said. She tucked her phone back into her pocket. "They let us send over Annabelle Borchard to get samples from the dog cage and collect any other evidence she can get her hands on from the Garden City Imports office and the shipping container. She'll give us the results as soon as anything pops."

"I'm so glad that she ended up being the CSI in charge," I said, beginning to brighten a bit.

"Great news," Luther said, "but let's continue. I want you all to know that because interstate transportation's involved, the feds want us to immediately stand down and let them take the lead. This is our case, however, so we're gonna keep on keepin' on till we take out these slime bags and get our young'uns back safe and sound. The feds don't know this place like we do."

We all nodded in agreement.

"So, about Trotter," Luther said. He looked directly at Rio and me, waiting for answers. I felt as if I was going to throw up.

Rio jumped in before I could bolt for the bathroom. He turned to me, then to O'Hanlon.

"Luther and I were on the phone last night talking about the whole situation with the kids being abducted when Lu mentioned Marcus Trotter." Rio closed his eyes like he was trying to picture it all in his mind. "Hadn't heard that name in a long, long time, but Bea and I know this asshole. We go way back—like to high school. There's some stuff y'all need to understand about him. It could impact the investigation."

"Go on." Luther rubbed his chin uneasily.

Rio looked at O'Hanlon, then at Luther and continued. "A long time ago I thought I'd killed him." Rio turned and looked at me again, pressed my hand. "Killed him for raping and trying to murder Bea."

"What?" Luther's eyes popped large and incredulous.

O'Hanlon gasped, almost dropping her iPad to the floor.

"I've repressed it all since I was sixteen." My voice was shaky. "That's when it happened. This week, when fingerprints came back IDing him. Only Rio, Trotter, and I ever knew what happened."

I started to tremble again. My body was experiencing an insane adrenaline rush. Fight or flight, and I could do neither. Rio put his arm around me. Luther handed me another bottle of water then stood, started pacing, eyes hooded.

"Twenty years ago," Rio explained," I'd been driving down the highway from the beach, headed for town when I passed Bea and Marcus in his old jigged-up Charger. I knew Bea was gonna be in deep shit. The guy had a really fucked up reputation and I figured she was pretty much clueless about it. I pulled over, but by the time I got my car turned around, they'd disappeared. I figured that Trotter might have been headed down toward Fugitive Point—it's remote." He turned to O'Hanlon to explain. "Some think it's haunted from slavery times. There's been a few gators seen out there too, so most stay away. I followed that old sandy trail through the palmettos 'til I couldn't drive any further, then I got out and walked—ran actually like I was after a fucking TD pass against Georgia Tech or something. Passed Trotter's car along the way."

Luther finally sat down, barely. He perched on the edge of his desk.

"When I got to the clearing," Rio continued, "at the very end of the peninsula along the river, he was on top of her, pants down to his ankles, strangling her. She was going blue. I pulled him off, bashed his head in with a log, threw him in the river, and sunk his car. I thought he was dead."

"Then I brought Bea home. She'd been drugged and was barely conscious, half-naked, bleeding."

"Was that the night you told me she'd been drinking for the first time, so we snuck her upstairs and put her to bed?" Luther asked. "That explanation felt off but I let it go."

Rio nodded.

"Why didn't you both go to the police?" Luther asked.

"Because I thought I had murdered a man," Rio said after a long pause. "Was a week before I was supposed to start at UGA on my football scholarship. If I'd gone to the cops, my life would have been over. That was a long time ago, things were different, worse than now. I wouldn't have had a chance in hell."

Luther nodded.

"And I told him I'd deny everything if he told. I shut down," I said. "Packed it all the hell away. Until yesterday."

"It's not unusual for victims of something that traumatic to repress the whole experience," Rio said.

I had forgotten that I sat next to an expert on PTSD.

I felt wooden and disconnected from reality but knew in my gut that getting the story out there, to people who cared about me, was a huge step. I sighed deeply and gripped Rio's hand in mine. Then reluctantly, I let him go. We had work to do. "Marcus Trotter is an opportunistic monster," I said, "and I think he knows that Dexter is mine."

"Oh, my God," O'Hanlon whispered.

"And if he figures out that a rich NBA star is Dexter's father," Luther said, "that will create another potentially lethal complication."

Silence filled the room.

33

O'Hanlon glanced at her phone again—it was another text message. "We have something new," she said. "Honey found out from your aunt Hattie, who found out from one of her beauty parlor clients, that Ellery Trotter, Marcus Trotter's grandfather, owned a fish camp in Shellman County."

I gasped—what a network. Maybe this was the break we needed. Aunt Hattie clearly deserved the Shellman Corners Citizen's Watch award that she'd bragged about at the Sunday dinner table.

"Good to know," Luther said, "but a backwater fish camp could be almost impossible to find."

He grabbed his phone and started to dial. "There aren't any records on lots of places, particularly the old ones, but I'll put my staff on it right away. Don't get your hopes up too high," he warned us, "because even if we can find it, and it hasn't crumbled into the swamp, it may have nothing to do with what's going on here."

"It's still a lead," O'Hanlon said. She said, and chuckled, breaking the room's grim spell. "The feds don't have Aunt Hattie on their team."

"Nobody knows a community better than the pastor, the police chief, and the owner of the most popular beauty shop in town," I said. I realized that my small-town aunt Hattie, with her rainbow fingernails and endless array of wigs, was as sharp as her hair scissors. It was a truth that I should have been taking more seriously.

"I'll call Hattie and see if we can brainstorm anybody who might know more about Ellery Trotter and the fish camp," Luther said. "In the meantime, I think y'all should go home and take a break. I'll let you know the minute we have anything from county records. As I said, it could take a while to go back so far."

He gave instructions to someone on the other end of the line, then hung up, turning to us all.

Rio stood up and stretched his back. "I've got a plane to catch, so I'd better head out." He squeezed my shoulder then moved toward the door.

"Savannah Hilton Head?" O'Hanlon asked. "We can give you a lift."

"Thanks, Detective, but I've got a car. I'll drop it off at the airport. Lindsey's supposed to pick me up on the other end. Please, keep me in the loop," he said, looking at Luther.

My mood sunk even lower at the mention of his smart and beautiful fiancée.

"No need to even ask, brother." Luther came around his desk toward us. He looked exhausted. "And Bea,

Rio—I'm blown away, so upset about what you've gone through." He wiped his hand across his eyes and shook his head. "I don't know what to say except, Rio, thank you for saving my sister. I owe you everything. And Bea, I'm so sorry that you, both of you, had to carry this all these years. Incredibly sorry." He gathered us into his big, wide embrace and held us for a moment.

"Let's put it aside for now," I said, compartmentalizing as fast as I could. I knew the blowback from this event would be with us for a while, in ways we might not yet even anticipate. "The only thing that matters is that we have children to save, and pure evil to find and destroy."

Three generations of Al Alequi men—Emad Al Alequi, his father Farouk, and his Grandfather Parsa, along with their colleague Marcus Trotter aka Muhammed Al-Sadr—sat together in a tight, humid office overlooking the floor of the warehouse. The last semi was unloading. As they sipped harsh coffee, Emad noticed his father gaze longingly at a pack of cigarettes. Marlboro Gold was his poison of choice. Grandfather Parsa was getting less and less tolerant of Farouk's small vice. Grandfather didn't know about the gambling and the women.

"So, we move to the fish camps tonight," Farouk said. "We're almost done with our end of things. Went smooth as silk—once we got out of the port." He folded up an Afghani newspaper he had been reading. "We've dealt with a lot worse."

The old man nodded, engrossed in a map of the local low country.

Muhammed drank Diet Coke and checked the charge

on his burner phone. Appeared to be about gone.

Emad, earphones dangling from around his neck, walked over to the window and gazed across the warehouse to where Dexter and Cornelia slumped against the far wall. They looked small and crumpled. They almost looked dead. He couldn't let that happen.

"So, will we leave them here to be found later?" Emad asked, eyes fixed on the two captives.

"Who?" His father Farouk finally reached for a cigarette. Grandfather Parsa shook his head in disapproval.

"You know, the kids—Dexter and Cornelia," Emad said. "If we're really going to be out of here and heading back home after this last deal, then there's nothing they can do to us. We'll be gone."

"They know way too much." Muhammed's pupils were like pinpricks. He tore open a package of two new burner phones and handed one to Farouk.

He must be using, despite his denials. Emad had seen plenty of addicts—Muhammed was one of them. "They know next to nothing. One dead kid is enough." Then he thought about the heroin overdoses that were probably being racked up as a result of his family business. Soon, he would be done with it all.

"Muhammed will handle it," Farouk said, "I'll leave it up to him." He took a long, grateful drag on his cigarette and inspected his new phone.

Emad turned to the other men, then homed in on Muhammed. "Then no doubt we'll have more blood on our hands. With all due disrespect, Muhammed, you're a sociopathic asshole and I can't believe the rest of you—"

Muhammed jumped up, knocked over a metal chair.

"Shut the fuck up, you pussy piece of shit."

"Muhammed, Emad, enough," Grandfather Parsa said, pushing the map away. His dry, quiet voice was like a loaded gun. The room went deathly still.

Grudgingly, Muhammed picked up his chair then sat back down. He glared at Emad with his black, ball-bearing eyes.

Cousin Sadam, all three-hundred-fifty solid pounds of him, entered the office. Unwittingly, he broke the standoff. Sadam was the family muscle. Dumb as cement but lethal as a land mine, he sat at the back of the office and played a game on his cell phone—Angry Birds and Candy Crush were his favorites.

No more was said about the kids, but it was clear to Emad that after indulging in some perverted entertainment, Muhammed would kill Dexter and Cornelia. He wouldn't do it here at the warehouse—too many people around. He'd wait until they were out at the fish camps. They'd all be leaving the warehouse soon, heading into the labyrinthine low country swamps. Emad guessed he had about twelve hours to think of something that could save them, and maybe save himself as well.

With feigned nonchalance, he put his earbuds back in his ears and left the office. Strains of Alicia Key's "You Don't Know My Name," wafted through the grim atmosphere behind him. He needed out, just out. Anywhere but here.

❌

After the door clicked shut, Farouk said to Muhammed, "I don't trust Emad right now. He might try something stupid. Keep your eye on him." Farouk ripped open three packets of Splenda and added them to his half-consumed cup of espresso.

Muhammed nodded. He'd figure out a way to eliminate Emad along with the China girl and Bea Middleton's brat. They were three of a kind. This was the part of the job he lived for. The wet work.

After finishing another can of Diet Coke, he poured himself a cup of strong coffee, and like Farouk, loaded in the sweetener.

Bea Middleton—that was a disaster he could never quite forget, a satisfaction he craved that had nothing to do with sex and everything to do with retribution. He would make sure she knew how her boy had suffered because of her arrogance and the Middleton family's holier-than-thou attitudes. She'd deserved to be raped and snuffed out, and now so did her boy.

There was something else about Bea that he couldn't quite remember. Something important. His mind pulled at the end of a black kite string in a sky devoid of light.

He recalled that Bea'd left Savannah right after high school and he'd gone directly into the military a week after Rio-fucking-Deakins tried to kill him for having a little fun. And the car—he had ruined the Charger. He would never, ever forgive Deakins for that.

"Did you hear me?" Farouk said loudly.

"What?" Muhammed was startled, caught in a murderous daydream, one he wanted to linger on and savor, but now was not the time.

"I said, in ten minutes I want you to load the boy and girl into the van and head out. Too bad we're stuck with this complication. Anyhow, I want to get to the camp before dark. We have much to do in the night."

"Yeah, man, I'll have 'em ready," Muhammed said, his mind still clinging to an incomplete thought. Then it came to him. The kid was the son of Kevin Jackson, an NBA superstar. He was loaded with fucking piles of cash. He was beginning to feel physically aroused— money *and* payback, but mostly payback. He turned to Farouk and Grandfather Parsa.

"The boy has a famous father, a pro basketball player who is very wealthy," Muhammed said, eyes sparkling with more than a little madness. "I think we should take advantage. Could bring us millions if we do it right." This was insanely better shit than he could have imagined. Kill the boy and take Bea's NBA sugar daddy for the ride of his golden life. That'll be the end of the precious brat and precious fat alimony checks for the bitch. She was probably raking in her own millions from the chump. He laughed out loud. "I'll arrange everything."

Grandfather Parsa again drew away from his map. He frowned at Farouk, then at Muhammed. "No, that is out of the question. We will complete our plans. Hand off to the Russians tomorrow as scheduled and be back in Afghanistan by Saturday. We will not waste our time negotiating a kidnapping. That is not our business. We finish here, and that's all we do. Do you agree, Farouk?"

"Of course, father." Farouk averted his eyes for a moment then blew cigarette smoke up toward a useless ceiling vent.

Muhammed's groin ached with the anticipation of taking Kevin Jackson for all he was worth. "But it would be easy."

"It would be stupid, like shooting the Middleton boy.

Think of it no more."

Grandfather Parsa had laid down the law.

Muhammed turned away and looked out at the hostages. Emad was bending down talking to them. The dipshit. If Farouk and Grandfather would not shake down Kevin Jackson for easy millions, he would do it alone and take the whole profit. Muhammed understood that a ransom payoff would be peanuts for the Al Alequis compared to their heroin deal—but they did not have humiliation to avenge. "Yes, Grandfather Parsa," he finally said. "I will think of it no more."

Muhammed excused himself from the office and tromped down a back stairwell. Black mold and rust stained old cement-block walls. A salamander skittered into a corner. The radio switched on up in the office; a Bollywood tune pounded out a tinny rhythm. They ragged on Emad for listening to music, but they loved this shit. Fucking hypocrites.

Pulling out his fresh phone, he punched in a number. Emad answered from across the warehouse on the first ring.

"Asshole," Muhammed growled, "ask the kid for his daddy's personal phone number. If I don't hear back from you in three minutes, tell him I'm gonna fuck up China girl real bad. And if you open your mouth to anybody, it'll be the last thing you do."

34

As I climbed into O'Hanlon's Crown Vic she immediately turned on the ignition and rolled down the windows. The heat was deadening. The air conditioner blasted only hot air, but at least something was circulating. I was physically and emotionally drained from the morning's forced revelations. My head throbbed. I popped a couple Advil, hoping for some relief.

"Anytime you want to talk, or if there is anything I can do..." O'Hanlon said, then dropped the gear shift into drive and pulled out of the lot.

"Thanks, Mary, but let's focus on Dexter and Cornelia for now." The last thing in the world I needed was to sink further into the horror that Trotter had created for me back then. He was probably spinning enough evil at this very moment to put me away forever.

"You got it bad for Rio, don't you." she said. "Gorgeous man, smart, kind. Wants to take care of you."

"No way." I vigorously shook my head in denial. I pulled on my seatbelt knowing she'd hit the nail on the head. I, however, couldn't deal with anymore heavy truths today. "What I have for him is called 'transference.'"

"Transference?" She arched an eyebrow. "You mean transferring your feelings for one person—deep love and gratitude in this case—onto somebody else who doesn't actually personify those qualities?"

I rolled my eyes. "Didn't know you were a psychologist, Detective."

"O'Hanlon raised her shoulders and shrugged. "I'm just a poor Georgia cop who's dealt with versions of sexual assault shit for about twenty years."

"Sorry to be snarky," I said. O'Hanlon didn't need to be the target of my anger. I took a deep breath and slowly let the air out. Yoga breathing could settle me down, at least a little.

She smiled over at me with sad eyes.

The air conditioner finally began to pump out coolness and leech the humidity from the air. I started to revive. "You know, Rio does have those qualities you mentioned, all of them, and add trustworthy. That's huge. And yes, I could be in love with him, but he's marrying someone else, and I probably don't really love him anyway. With two divorces behind me, my love-o-meter is seriously flawed. So, that said, let's leave the Rio Deakins topic alone. All I want is my baby back. That's all I care about right now."

O'Hanlon nodded her head and was silent. I felt a touch guilty at being such a pain in the ass, but not too much.

"Well, I know *I* can't go home and rest," she said.

"Me either," I agreed.

"I have an idea," O'Hanlon said. She eased the car out onto the highway. "Why don't we ride over to Watermelon Bluff and have something to eat at the Anglers Inn. We could poke around a little bit in town. Can't be more than, maybe, a hundred-and-fifty people who live there. Besides the Anglers, there's only the bait shop and that tiny marina for fuel and snacks. Maybe somebody will know something about Grandpa Trotter and his old fish camp. What do you think?"

"Let's go," I said, anxious to latch on to a purpose as well as some food. "Nothing to lose."

We drove the twenty minutes in silence, listening to the public radio station segment on low-country gardening. I loved to garden. It soothed me better than a good run or a hot bath—being in the moment, nurturing beautiful things. My roses in California were stunning and my aloe vera grew like a weed as did my bougainvillea. Too bad I couldn't garden my way out of this disaster.

The highway into Watermelon Bluff was thick with pine, oak, and dogwood trees. We passed a trailer park shaded by oaks that dripped with Spanish moss. Dirty, half-naked children, both black and white, played in a weedy stream too near the highway for safety. A mangy, gray, pit bull mix looked to be their only supervision. Maybe that was enough. A whole loving family on watch hadn't kept Jayden from getting killed or Dexter from being kidnapped.

The police radio crackled with random calls and

discussion. Nothing at all pertaining to our investigation, the one we were no longer supposed to be involved in.

In another mile, we turned onto a disintegrating blacktop road and headed into the little town. We passed run-down wood-frame cottages with peeling paint and sagging porches, many decorated with buckets of pretty red geraniums and other happy looking potted flowers. The crushed-shell main street was two blocks long, with an assortment of similar frame homes with better paint jobs than those on the back lanes. Out in front were long docks and stunning views of the river.

At the far end of the street sat the Anglers Inn and the marina. Only a few cars were parked in the lot next to the restaurant. An older couple dined inside the screened-in porch finishing what was probably a lunch of deep-fried shrimp, sweet potato fries, and slaw. My mouth began to water.

The restaurant was formerly a small, tin-roofed cottage, that now had an expanded front porch.

"We used to come out here for the Friday night fish fry when we were kids," I said, remembering the happy innocence of those times. "Hasn't changed much."

I looked up and down the sleepy main street. Two mutts ambled toward the docks, maybe about to beg for handouts at the back door of the marina where a bait shop employee was having a smoke and a sandwich. Just beyond the marina, two young boys struggled to pull a rowboat onto the rocky beach.

We parked the car and made our way up to the porch where we were met by a girl of about thirteen. She wore flip-flops and a cute summer dress, white with tiny blue anchors that I'd seen at Target. Mary and I preferred the languid circles of the overhead ceiling fans on the porch to the air conditioning inside.

Clouds were moving in and the temperature began to drop into a more comfortable range. The big oaks shook their gray, moss-clad branches in a fresh breeze and seagulls rode the rivers of cooler air over the bay. The intercoastal waterway merged with the Julienton, Little Mud, and Sapelo Rivers, barely a half mile out. The low country was a complicated web of swamps, creeks, rivers, and estuaries.

After we were seated and handed menus, I said to O'Hanlon, "I was thinking that if Ellery Trotter had a fish shack out in this area, he sure as hell would have been an Anglers Inn customer now and again. It's almost the only place people come, here, or the Wild Hog Barbeque Hut, just off the freeway. Could well be that folks know of him or the family."

"That's the kind of local thing we're looking for," she said.

Our friendly server returned with glasses and a pitcher of sweet tea.

"Does Miss Mimi still work here?" I remembered Mimi as the white version of my aunt Hattie—sassy and competent with a hidden heart of gold.

The girl stood up proud as she poured our beverages. "Sure does. Miss Mimi's my grandma. She owns the place. Took it all on herself when Grandpa died."

"Any chance we could talk with her when she gets a minute?" I asked. "I used to come here as a kid, would like to say hello."

"She's chopping up cabbage for coleslaw, but I'm sure she'll be happy to chat with y'all when she's done."

"Terrific," I said. "Give us a minute with the menu, and then we'll be ready to order."

"Take y'alls time." A couple of old fishermen trudged up the steps, so she put down the pitcher and hustled over to greet them.

"A very conscientious girl. She'll be the next owner," I predicted.

O'Hanlon smiled. "I'm going for the boiled shrimp, by the way. You?"

"Let's make it two, with a side of stone crab legs," I said, "with sweet corn and slaw." Oh yes, I definitely had a tendency for stress eating. My skinny jeans were killing me, and I'd only been in Georgia a few days.

The thought of comfort food brought a fresh wave of tears to my eyes. I dabbed at them with a red and white checked paper napkin. "I wonder if Dexter is eating anything. I want to save him some crab legs and slaw and order him a piece of sweet potato pie. I know it's ridiculous, but it makes me feel better."

O'Hanlon reached over and squeezed my hand.

Mimi Herbert shuffled through the door onto the porch, wiping her hands on her apron. She was eighty years old if she was a day. Although she didn't possess the physical breadth and girth of Aunt Hattie, she was still a substantial woman. Her short white hair was tucked under a dark blue Anglers Inn baseball cap. She wore ancient denim overalls and a faded Allman Brothers T-shirt. Wire-framed eyeglasses were spattered with what looked like mayonnaise. Not a shred of style but hang-dog eyes as warm as oven-baked bread.

"Well, my, oh my. You Flo's little girl? I know you don't belong to Hattie or Freddie May. Those gals are over here at least once a month for the fish fry."

"Yep, I'm Flo's." I beamed at her recognition.

"Come here," she opened her arms. "Let me see you, young lady."

I stood and embraced her. She gave me a damp, slaw-smelling hug, then let me go. "Yes, little Beatrice, all grown up. And how's your Ma doing? And your brother? He stops by now and then, usually for shrimp and grits. Once in a while to arrest somebody."

"Gotta keep him busy earning those big bucks," I smiled. "Momma's recovering from a heart attack but she's doing very well."

"Oh, Lordy. I'm so sorry. Glad to hear she's on the mend, though. Give her my best. I'll send some cranberry-pecan bread pudding for you to take to her."

"She would be thrilled," I said. *Perfect heart-health food.* "Miss Mimi, let me introduce my friend, Detective Mary O'Hanlon, from the Savannah-Chatham PD."

They shook hands. Mimi took both of Mary's in hers for a moment. "A pleasure, Detective O'Hanlon. You any relation to the O'Hanlon's from down the road in Darien?"

"Not that I know of, ma'am."

Miss Mimi started in on the local O'Hanlon genealogy. I knew this kind of discussion could go on forever and I wanted to ask her about the Trotters. In south Georgia, you have to chat and schmooze before you can ask the money question, but my patience was at the breaking point.

"Miss Mimi," I interrupted as graciously as I could. "Do you know of a family named Trotter who once may have had a fish camp not too far from here?"

"Well, sure, honey, I can tell ya all about 'em."

My heart leaped.

35

"Ol' Ellery Trotter was a real son of a bitch. Used to come into town and sell me crawfish for the Inn. Sometimes they was fresh and delicious, and then I started finding frozen crawfish, like from the grocery store, mixed in. And I was paying for premium." She took off her glasses and started cleaning them on her apron. "After that, we parted ways. Had a wife that disappeared early on, left him with about a half-dozen children that hung around. All as nasty as the old man, from what I can remember. Been years, though."

Miss Mimi's granddaughter spread newspaper on our table top, placed a bucket in the center for crab shells and corn cobs, then presented our plates. *Goodness me.*

"This is my grandchild, Tilda," Mimi said. "Best worker I got."

Tilda blushed and smiled. O'Hanlon and I added to

the girl's accolades. Then I immediately circled back to the information we were seeking.

"One of old Ellery's grandsons looks to be pretty much the opposite of your granddaughter, here," I said. "Name's Marcus—calls himself Muhammed now. He got himself into bad trouble. We're trying to track him down."

"We think it's possible he's holed up at Ellery's fish camp," O'Hanlon said. "You know anyone who might remember where it is?"

Miss Mimi folded her arms across her chest. A gust of cool wind blew down the street carrying the tangy smell of pluff mud and rotting seaweed. Big fat raindrops hit the tin roof of the porch with the wet sound of spit on a sidewalk.

Tilda poured fresh sweet tea, set out more napkins and flatware, nutcrackers for the crab legs, and a bowl of drawn butter. A low country culinary masterpiece was unfolding in front of us. I couldn't wait to bring Dexter and Alyssa here, Cornelia and her parents, too.

"Otis Suggs owns the Bluff Marina across the street," Mimi said. "He might know where ol' Ellery had his camp. Hard to imagine, but Suggs has been here even longer than I have. Ellery probably never really owned the camp, was the kind of man who'd move right in and call it his property, kill anybody who said different. Otis should be over there all afternoon. Usually is. Want me to call him and say y'all wanna to talk with him after your meal?"

"That would be wonderful, Miss Mimi. Thank you so much. " I didn't want to insult this old friend who had given us some great information, but we couldn't stay. "The food looks amazing. I don't mean to be disrespectful, but I think we'd better pack this to go and get over to the marina right away."

"No problem, honey. Sounds like a pretty intense situation. We'll wrap it up for ya; your mom's pudding, too."

"You are so kind."

O'Hanlon grabbed a couple bites of shrimp dripping with lemon butter while Tilda piled our food into to-go boxes and poured us fresh tea in paper commuter cups. We bid Miss Mimi and her granddaughter goodbye, left them an outstanding tip and ran across the road to the marina.

The rain was coming down fast now. The big lazy drops had turned to painful little bullets. A bolt of lightning split the sky out over the water, and thunder rumbled. The air crackled with the scent of ozone. Soon there was more lightning—much closer.

An old fishing boat was moving fast toward the dock. The pink-faced driver wore a yellow rain poncho, hood pulled tight around his face. He was met by an older black man who helped him maneuver the boat into its berth and tie up. The fisherman crawled out of the blue-and-white craft onto the pier with his catch. The two men laughed as they scurried toward the shelter of the overhang above the bait shop and snack bar. We arrived at the same moment they did, drenched. I pulled a tissue from my purse and mopped my face.

"Ladies," Otis Suggs said, a big smile on his wet, wrinkled face. He opened the screen door and beckoned us inside. Lean and weathered, Suggs had a youthful twinkle in his eyes. His hair was close-cropped and white—looked like hoarfrost melting on his brown plug of a head.

"You must be Miss Middleton, and you the detective from Savannah," he said. "Come on in, we're not afraid of a little water in here, are we Bo?" he said to the middle-aged, paunchy fellow he'd helped moor the boat.

"No, we ain't. Not at all. Gonna take this fish up to Miss Mimi. Got reds and trout. See if she'll fry 'em up for us later," he said. "Pleasure to meet you, ladies."

The screen door opened with a rusty groan then slammed shut. He splashed fishy water on the floor from the bucket containing his catch as he left the bait shop. My canvas shoes sucked it up.

"Nice place you got here, Mr. Suggs," I said. A giant stuffed swordfish was mounted on the wall behind him. Christmas lights were strung above the cash register and the soda machine. The walls were papered with yellowing photos of generations of south Georgia fishermen, women, and children with their prize catches.

"Thanks, Miss Middleton. Been my whole life here, can't think of a better way to spend it."

I nodded and smiled. "Mr. Suggs, Mimi said you might know something about a fish camp that once belonged to Ellery Trotter. Ring a bell at all?"

His sunny face went dark as the clouds outside. "Ellery Trotter," he said with a sigh. "Haven't heard that name in a long while. Passed away nigh unto twenty years ago, I reckon. Can I offer you a soda?" he asked. "Y'all can sit down if you'd like. Got a few chairs over there." He motioned to a couple of old rocking chairs next to the bait tank.

"Thank you, sir," O'Hanlon said. "Would be our

pleasure to join you another time. We're on a felony case right now. Need to track down one of Trotter's grandsons, fast. We think he might be at the camp."

Otis nodded. "I was out there once, maybe twenty-five years ago, with ol' Joe Samples. He passed on, too, last year. God rest his soul."

"So, you've actually been to the place?" An adrenaline rush accelerated my heartbeat.

"Yup. Old snake Trotter stole my outboard motor right off my boat. Was parked right here at the dock. I knew it was him but he denied it." Suggs turned to a detailed marine map on the wall and squinted his eyes, studying it. "Followed him out to the camp one day, and there it was. He shot at me, but I'd thought to bring my hunting rifle so I was able to grab that motor and hightail it out of there before he could wing me. The place is somewhere beyond Little Boy Creek."

"Think you could find it again?" I asked.

He left the map and moved to one of the rocking chairs, plunked down, suddenly appearing weary. He shook his head. "Doubtful, very doubtful. I got a good sense of direction, but the creeks and swamps change over all those years. Yes, they do. Roads are swallowed up. Landmark trees fall down and get covered with creeper."

"Would you be willing to *try?*" I asked, desperate for action. "You see, one of Trotter's boys kidnapped my son. He's holding him for ransom."

His eyes grew wide. "Well, that puts another light on it, don't it?" He rose from the rocker. "I will try, young lady, but I confess, I ain't hopeful, not at all. Been too long."

"When could you go?" O'Hanlon asked.

"Well, lemme call Bo and have him cover the marina for the rest of the day. If the rain keeps up, won't be much happening anyway."

"Thank you," I said, and wiped my eyes. "Thank you so much."

"Happy to give you a hand." He dialed the Inn, on an old beige plastic wall phone, circa 1970.

O'Hanlon and I returned to our car and called Luther. He told us that he and several of his deputies would meet us down the highway at the Wild Hog Barbeque Hut, and we'd all caravan with Otis Suggs. Shellman PD had a pretty good Toyota Land Cruiser for these types of deep in low country travels.

As we waited for Otis to take care of business, my phone sounded. I checked the caller—it was Kevin. I did not want to talk to Dexter's dad right now, so I let it go to voicemail. I had texted less than an hour ago with an update.

The phone buzzed again—this time a text from Kevin: *Call me immediately—emergency.*

"What the..." I tapped in his number. He picked up on the first ring.

"What's going on, Kevin?" I asked, feeling impatient. His sense of emergency was usually a lost pair of sneakers or a new dent to the Porsche.

"Bea. I got a call," he gasped. "They have Dexter, and they're demanding a ransom or they'll kill him. We have twenty-four hours."

36

I opened the car door and leaned out, losing my sweet tea on the crushed tabby we were parked on. The rain was still pouring down but not hard enough to wash away the vomit's bitter taste.

"What is it, Bea?" O'Hanlon asked, face stricken. "What's the matter?"

I sat back up and shut the car door. Motioned to O'Hanlon for quiet then put my phone on speaker.

"What do they want, Kev?" My voice cracked.

"They want ten million cash by tomorrow, or they'll kill him."

"Oh, my God," O'Hanlon whispered.

"What the hell am I supposed to do?" Kevin continued, voice high and panicky. "And he said no cops, or it's over. I can't get that kind of money in a day, or even a week. Who are these assholes? What's going on? Jesus, Bea, this is insane."

"What did the voice sound like?" I tried to stay calm, despite my terror. If I lost it, Kevin was a goner.

"It was electronically distorted. Definitely male, though. That's all I can tell you."

"He give you any instructions?"

"Said he'd call tomorrow at 9:00 p.m. Eastern time and tell me where to drop the money. Then he hung up before I could say a goddamned thing. I don't have any way to get in touch with him to negotiate. I can't get ten mil by then. This is fucked, man."

"Kevin, keep your voice down," I said, knowing that he was still a frequent target for paparazzi. They lurked everywhere. This couldn't turn into a tabloid circus.

O'Hanlon indicated that I should hang up and call him back. We had to talk.

"Okay, Kev, I'm going to consult with people who know what they're doing—"

"He said *no cops*. No, Bea, uh-uh."

"Kevin, we can't do this by ourselves."

"I'll call my agent," he said. "Sol will know what to do."

"Kevin, our son is not being recruited for the Lakers. We need my brother. I trust Luther and his people implicitly."

"What if they find out we talked to the cops?"

"They won't. Now sit tight and I'll be back with you within the hour, okay?"

"I'm boarding a plane to Montreal right now, then on to Atlanta tonight. I'll call you the minute I land in Canada," Kevin said, "four hours from now. Lord, Jesus, help us."

"Okay, four hours. We'll have a solid plan by then, or maybe we'll have Dexter." I was desperate to keep us both optimistic. It was too easy to fall the other way. "In the meantime, we have to stay calm. Do your meditations, okay? Or pray. I'm doing both." The man was cool steel on the basketball court—he needed to be the same right now.

I heard the loudspeaker announce boarding in the background. There was some mumbling about first class tickets. We said our anxious goodbyes.

Less than half of ransomed kidnap victims are returned alive. I read it on the internet last night. With that discouraging thought on my mind, I switched off my phone.

O'Hanlon waved to Otis Suggs. He waved back out the window of his old truck. We pulled from the lot and followed him toward the highway. Luther's voice came across a scratchy connection on her cop radio.

"Luther, go to your cell phone," O'Hanlon said. "I don't want this on dispatch."

"Ten-four," he said, then O'Hanlon's iPhone chirped.

She handed it to me. I put it on speaker again and struggled to keep my throat from closing up.

"Brother, somebody contacted Kevin and demanded ten million dollars, cash, by tomorrow night. Delivery's at a yet undisclosed location. Was a male voice, distorted electronically. Probably Marcus-fucking-Trotter. Said no cops or Dexter dies. That's all. Kevin is on his way to Atlanta in total meltdown. What the hell do we do?"

I grabbed onto an overhead handhold as we careened around a corner trying to keep up with Otis. The slow-talking old guy was a helluva fast mover behind the wheel. O'Hanlon pulled out around him and took the lead. She lit us up—lights flashed and sirens blared. Otis followed close in his old rust bucket. Evidently, there was something under the hood that had some juice.

There was silence on the end of the phone line for a long moment.

"Okay," Luther finally said, "I have a connection with the FBI in Atlanta. I'll see if he can meet Kevin at the airport. Agent Adam Kellogg—I trust him. He negotiated the kidnapping release of that Georgia Tech co-ed two years ago that was all over the news. Her dad was a Coca-Cola exec. Kellogg also worked with the military on a hostage release in Iraq. Knows all the right people in this realm. I can't think of anybody who could give us a better chance."

"I'll text you Kevin's contact info," I said.

"I'll call Kellogg. Get his feedback. Get a strategy going. What's your ETA? I'm in the Barbeque Hut parking lot, waiting."

"Ten minutes," O'Hanlon called into the speakerphone. She checked the rearview mirror. I glanced over my shoulder at the same time. Suggs was still with us and flashed his headlights, smiling. Not quite the quiet afternoon at the marina that he'd bargained for.

Ж

The parking lot was nearly empty at the Wild Hog Barbeque Hut. The name referred both to the 'que and the bikers that often frequented the place. It was after 3:00 p.m. and the rain had halted momentarily. The iconic local eatery was an old double-wide trailer with peeling paint the color of mustard and a walk-up window surrounded by a wide wooden deck containing a half-dozen red picnic tables. Only one table was occupied—three road construction workers in hard hats and orange reflective vests looked like they were taking a late lunch.

Luther was out on the deck standing by himself at the farthest table, talking on the phone. His shoulders hunched under a navy-blue Shellman County PD rain slicker. O'Hanlon pulled in next to the county Range Rover. Suggs slid his truck in right beside her. The construction workers looked toward us for a moment then returned to their Wild Hog Barbecue plates, Bud Lights, and probably fantasy football chatter.

O'Hanlon exited the car and popped the trunk, started rummaging around for equipment she'd be transferring to the Rover. I got out, grabbed the big bag of food from the Angler's Inn, and joined Otis Suggs. We leaned against the warm hood of his truck. His old khaki fishing hat was pinned with about twenty different fishing lures, mostly flies of various kinds and colors. The hooks looked ominous.

"Miss Middleton," Otis said. I realized that I wasn't correcting anyone who called me Middleton rather than Jackson or Strauss, my former married names. Was easier and felt right. Once I changed it back to Middleton, I would never change it again, married or not.

"Bea, please."

"Aw'ight, Miss Bea. I was thinking while we was on our way over here—there's some stuff coming back into my head 'bout all this. I recall there were two shacks out there: Trotter's place, and across, father down the creek, was one a lot bigger that belonged to an old gal named

Orpha Davis. She and Trotter was an item for a long time, both as nasty as a couple of cottonmouths. Some say they formed a business partnership, too, and ran meth outta there for years. Loaded fishing boats from her dock which is on a deep creek. Trotter's shack is on a shallow, swampy inlet. We should check her ol' place out, too, if we can find any of it."

A light bulb went off in my head. I pulled out my phone and dialed Aunt Hattie. I had moved her number to my favorites list after she had helped ID Doobius. It rang about a half-dozen times then switched to a recorded message: *This is Mode de Paree Salon in Shellman Corners. We are busy with beauty treatments right now so kindly leave your name and number and we'll call y'all back shortly.*

I left a message. "Aunt Hattie, it's Bea. What do you know about an Orpha Davis? Call me as soon as you can."

"Good idea to call your aunt," Suggs said. "Hattie knowed everybody 'round here. The intel that flows through that beauty shop of hers could probably make the CIA look like they git they information from a Dick Tracey watch. But you too young to know 'bout dat."

"I know about it—a decoder thing, right?"

"More like an early smartphone." He unzipped his raincoat, reached beneath the breast pocket and pulled out a handgun. "Here's another kind of smartphone."

My mouth opened and a little gasp escaped. He smiled at me and gave the firearm a quick, loving shine-up with a red bandana handkerchief.

"A Colt M1911, semi-auto, .45 caliber," he said, admiring the pistol, then he tucked it away. "No worries, got experience and a permit. He patted his chest. "I've had her nigh onto fifty years. I call her Marjorie."

"After a pistol-packin' mama you once knew?"

"Naw, after my favorite ol' coonhound. Best gal I ever had." His face was serious as a funeral.

"You military, Mr. Suggs?" I asked.

"Korea," he replied. His lips pressed into a thin line.

Then O'Hanlon came around the truck holding a rifle along with her Glock in a shoulder holster.

I suddenly felt way underprepared for this. "I want a gun," I said. Damned if I'd be holding the bag of shrimp and cornbread while they were shooting it out with Trotter and his gangsters. Guess I shouldn't have left my birthday Glock back in Santa Monica.

"You're a civilian, my sister," Luther said, also gunned up. A hunting knife in a sheath was strapped to his thigh in addition to his ballistics.

I glanced at the Land Rover—two rifles were in a rack in the rear window. I wanted to be the one to put an end to Marcus-fucking-Trotter, once and for all. My fingers itched.

"Don't even think about it," Luther said. "Let's go. Everyone in the Rover. Otis, thanks for your help with this. Front seat for you, wing man."

"My pleasure, Sheriff, but like I tol' the ladies, it's been decades since I been to this place. Things change fast in the swamps an' marshes."

I swallowed hard. I knew I was putting too much faith in Otis's ability to find the fish camp. He was sharp but he was also a very old man. And he was correct about the low country—it was malleable and shifty as quicksand.

"We'll do the best we can. We're running short on

options," Luther said. "We'll have a chopper following us from a distance, so as not to alert these assholes. The Coast Guard is on standby in case we need them. Time's a wastin'. It'll be dark in a couple hours, so let's move."

We headed down County A-56, then after a few miles, turned off onto what appeared to be the entrance to a sandy, scrub-pine and palmetto-choked utility road, no wider than a lane. It was barely discernible from the highway. A wild boar scampered in front of us. It shrieked and snorted before cutting into the underbrush.

"I think this is it," Otis said. He got out of the vehicle and stomped around in the weeds, swatting at insects, until he found a crumbling gatepost. "Yeah, this used to be gated but looks like the termites had other ideas."

He got back into the car and picked burrs off his trousers, tossed them out the door. Palmettos scraped the Land Rover like fingernails as Luther pulled into the woods. We rolled our windows up to avoid getting smacked by their rough fronds and to avoid encounters with any creepy creatures that might call them home.

"If we're on the right track, should be the remains of an old tin-roof juke joint maybe a mile down from here," Otis said, scratching his head.

The little bit of sunshine that had peeked through for the last hour was extinguished by a new front of heaving, cinder-gray clouds. I clicked on my weather app—severe thunderstorm warnings coming our way.

My phone rang—it was Aunt Hattie.

"Auntie, thanks for calling right back." Aretha Franklin's "Respect" was playing on the radio at the beauty shop. "Anything on Orpha Davis in your network? We hear she had a fish camp near Trotter's."

the tables turn. It could happen here, to us. Never, never give up. It's one of the best things I learned from my dad. That, and no matter how much cash you have, without people who really love you, for *you*, it's nothing."

Cornelia licked her cracked lips, which were moist and shiny red only a day ago. "I'm stuck in this van with Mother Teresa of the basketball court."

Dexter smiled, then grimaced with pain.

"I'm sorry, I'm being a jerk," she said. "I won't wimp out. I get pretty bitchy sometimes—low blood sugar or something. How about you? You okay?"

Dexter nodded. He was nowhere near okay.

She sat up straighter and shook the hair out of her face. She was as beautiful as ever. He would kill anyone who tried to hurt her. He glanced over at Meat Locker, all three hundred nasty pounds of him, and knew it was a hollow promise.

Pretty soon the van turned off onto a road that was slow and potholed. There were no sounds of other traffic, just the rain, the drone of a sports talk show on the radio up front, and snoring.

"There's the big guy and the driver," Dexter whispered. He squirmed, trying to find a nonexistent comfortable position. "Looks like they're taking us somewhere out in the major boonies. Maybe we can make a break for it when they try to move us outta here. Run like hell into the forest. I doubt the big dog can move too fast."

"It doesn't matter how fast or slow these assholes can move cuz they both have guns, Dexter." Her eyes were locked on a candy bar that was half eaten, still in the big guy's huge paw. "I'm so hungry. That candy's all

---

"Well, honey, I don't know 'bout no fish camp. I went to school with her but she dropped out in about 7th or 8th grade. Got pregnant and drafted into the family meth business, or so I heard. Her daddy was murdered somewhere around then, too."

The brutality of life squeezed at my gut. It was unbelievable what we people endured on this earth. I pressed my thumb to the pressure point between my eyebrows—the third eye, the site of extra perception.

"Never heard much 'bout Orpha after that," Aunt Hattie continued. "I do know that she passed, supposedly an overdose, probably ten years ago. Her people may have moved on to Florida, but they pretty much disappeared from 'round here a long time ago."

"Okay, thanks, Auntie," I said, more disappointed than I should have been. Time was ticking and even a Dick Tracy watch couldn't save us.

37

He was a ginormous dude, like a pro football defenseman—somebody they'd call "Meat Locker" or "Chuck Roast," or something similar in Farsi. His pale gray eyes were small and dim. Not a lot in there, Dexter thought. All stupid power with a brain that had only two functions—to cause hurt, or to graze mindlessly on junk food and video games. Right now, Sadam was in phase two and fading fast. The man could, however, change up at the flip of his cranial switch. Dexter had accidently flipped the switch when he told the asshole to stop drooling all down his ugly face over Cornelia.

When Dexter came to, his eye was swollen shut and his head felt like a sloshing tub of water. His ribs ached and his energy level had flatlined.

Now asleep in one of the two back seats of the rusty, fishy-smelling panel van, Meat Locker snored

like a chainsaw as his two hostages were being bounced around by all the ruts in the road. Dexter recalled that it was the same vehicle they had been in before when they were first abducted. A dude he didn't recognize was at the wheel.

Cornelia's YouTube tutorial on escaping from duct tape hadn't worked. Her wrists were bloody from trying. Dexter looked over at her. She had stopped crying a while ago. Her face was closed and distant.

"Cor?" he whispered.

She didn't respond. She was somewhere else.

"Cornelia, look at me."

Slowly, she turned her head toward Dexter.

"You cannot lose faith, girl. People will come for us, I know they will. Hear me?"

She sighed, her shoulders slumped. "Tell yourself what you need to believe, Dexter," she said softly.

"My dad's gonna pay the ransom and then they'll l[et] us go. It'll be soon."

"Oh, my God, you are such a child. They'll take [the] money and then they'll shoot us both in the head, [like] they did Jayden, if we're lucky. If we're not lucky, th[ey] take it slow—cut off our fingers one by one and [send] them to our parents."

Dexter tried to twist his bruised, lanky body t[oward] her.

"Cornelia, you can't go there." He was alr[eady in] that dark place but refused to be pulled down[.] "We gotta stay positive, gotta plan. I've seen [ ] basketball games when we've been down tons [ ] with seconds to go. Somebody sinks a thre[e,] somebody else fouls, a steal, another three-p[oint]

I can think about. That, and death."

Dexter sighed. They rode quietly for another forty-five minutes and then the van pulled to a stop. Meat Locker woke up and immediately finished the candy bar. Cornelia looked like she had been kicked.

There was a loud pounding on the side of the vehicle. Meat Locker flashed a twelve-inch hunting knife.

"No," Cornelia screamed.

Dexter kicked out with his legs and landed a hard shin shot. It barely registered. Fighting Meat Locker was like trying to take down a redwood with a nail file. Hopeless.

The man grabbed Cornelia by the hair, then he sliced off her restraints. Did the same with Dexter.

The doors to the van flew open.

Satan was waiting.

Muhammed wore tight jeans, military-grade rubberized hiking boots and a camo T-shirt that displayed his chiseled chest and arms. A pistol, the dull gray color of a sand shark, was secured in his black nylon shoulder holster. Diamonds still sparkled in his ears. He smiled, hungry-like, as Dexter was dumped from the van onto the ground at his feet.

Then he watched Cornelia climb out on her own, the top of her hot pink thong undies peeking over the rear of her black tights.

"Gonna tap China girl hard, uh-huh," Muhammed said to no one in particular.

No doubt that Cornelia had a sweet little ass. Who wouldn't admire it? But Dexter could sense horrible dark thoughts fleeting like noxious sylphs behind Muhammed's ball-bearing eyes. His malevolence was palpable and cold as a dead body.

Meat Locker simply had the look of a child who wanted another piece of candy.

Dexter cursed his own helplessness. His world spun like a pinwheel as he struggled to his feet.

"What'd ya do to the boy, big man?" Muhammed chuckled.

"Just slap heem aroun' a leetle. Got a mouth on heem, as dey say." He turned and lumbered up toward a pole barn on the edge of a river where workers loaded plastic-wrapped packages into a fishing boat. Food was laid out on a picnic table.

"Can we have something to eat?" Cornelia asked, voice small and apologetic. She couldn't help but scope out the spread from KFC.

Muhammed dug in his pocket then handed her a piece of gum. "Split it with your friend," he said and herded them toward a rubber inflatable Zodiac boat that rested on the bank of the creek. A cloud of gnats hovered at the shoreline.

Cornelia stuck the gum in her pocket. As she swatted her way through the insect swarm, a gust of wind blew her long hair across her face, shrouding a look of hatred.

The two teens followed Muhammed's instructions and climbed into the rubber boat. Their hands and feet were no longer secured but running would clearly be a joke. They'd be dead in a second.

The rain had turned to a heavy mist and the wet muddy ground smelled faintly of sulfur. Into the watery forest of cypresses, they rode with the devil at the helm of the small black boat.

"Y'all heard of the river Styx?" Muhammed asked.

He lit up a joint. Made a gesture of offering to Cornelia.

Cornelia shook her head and inched closer to Dexter.

"Yeah, I know about it," Dexter said. "I'm in AP Greek history. It's the mythological river between the living and the dead."

"Smart little fucker, ain't you?" Muhammed steered them deeper into the darkening swamp. "Your bitch mama's gonna cry when your empty skull washes up on the shore where she tried to take me down. Oh, yeah, she'll cry." He licked his lips and shook with glee.

38

Farouk lit up a fresh cigarette and watched his son review delivery and accounting information on an iPad. Their dark brown eyes met for a nanosecond. The resentment and suspicion between them was a poisonous pain that never left Emad's gut, no matter how much weed he smoked. He would see this last deal through then disappear.

An open-topped fishing trawler pulled up to a long dock that jutted into the deepest part of what was called Black Issue Creek. They were less than two or three miles in from the much more navigable Julienton River that hooked up with the intercoastal waterway. Emad noted that the boat's registration decal was current and much-used nets and related equipment filled the deck. Couldn't look more nondescript for these waters. He checked his watch and smiled. On time. There would be near to twenty similar craft, one after another, loading up here and then heading for Florida.

The two Al Alequi men acknowledged the grizzled old navigator of the trawler, and within minutes, the door to the fish hold was open and workers began to lade bricks of heroin. They were brought down to the dock in wheelbarrows from a fish shack and pole barn atop a shallow rise. Within forty-five minutes the boat was stuffed like a Thanksgiving turkey. With a wave from the pilot, the craft disappeared back down the oak and cypress-shrouded creek, only to be replaced by a shrimper of similar size and vintage. The gentle lap of its wake rocked the dock as it pulled in.

"Think we'll be done by midnight?" Farouk asked his son. He squinted his eyes and tried to follow the notes Emad was taking on his tablet, but the angle of the sun on the screen made viewing it from the side impossible.

"We'll be done earlier than that," Emad said. "Eleven at the latest. No snags, as they say."

Farouk nodded, took a long pull from the cigarette. "We'll all be home in the cool, dry mountains soon. I hate this humidity."

Emad felt his body go taut. He breathed deeply to relax but couldn't stop the heat that rose up his neck. He made no reply and closed the tablet case with a snap. He'd soon be in the mountains too. The Santa Monica Mountains, thousands of miles from Afghanistan. He had work to do before then, and it had little to do with the drug deal going down now.

"Where the hell is Muhammed?" Emad demanded. "That asshole is up to something. The fucker's a major liability. You and Grandfather don't believe me. I hope you're both right."

"I think he's with the detainees down the creek at his grandfather's cabin."

"Detainees? Ha. You mean the kids—the children, Dexter and Cornelia?"

"Yes, them," Farouk said. "He has them secured as Grandfather Parsa had asked." He tossed his half-finished cigarette into the creek. It extinguished with a quick sizzle. Minnows darted as it sunk into the dark water.

"If they're so secure," Emad said, "he doesn't need to spend hours over there. We agreed that he would leave them alone and that he'd stay completely focused on making this deal move smoothly."

Father shrugged his shoulders. "Why don't you row over and check on him, if you're so concerned?"

"I am concerned. I think he may be trying to make his own deal on the boy. Muhammed's a greedy bastard. This job should give him as much money as anybody could need. Messing around with kidnapping is beyond reckless."

"He wouldn't be that stupid," Farouk said. "He's a complete professional."

Emad scowled and watched the workers—three short, stocky young Mexicans, a white guy with full-sleeve tattoos of Bible quotations, and a dim-witted black man who was supposedly Muhammed's second or third cousin-in-law. The bricks began to pile up in the shrimper's hold.

The sun had emerged and turned the day hot and sultry again. Soon they were drenched in sweat. Biting insects tamped down by the rain were now back in full force. Both men swatted at mosquitoes and yellow flies. Farouk pulled a container of insect repellant from his back pocket and sprayed himself, then handed it to Emad who did the same.

Emad gazed down the creek toward the Trotter fish camp. "I'm going over there," he said and handed the tablet to his father. "He should be up here helping us, not diddling with those two brats."

"I'll call him, tell him you're coming." Farouk lit up another cig.

"No, don't do that. I want to surprise him."

Farouk shrugged again then squinted at the tablet's screen. He pulled out wire-rimmed reading glasses and put them on.

Emad walked down to the dock and untied a weathered rowboat from a pylon. About an inch or two of water filled the bottom. Mosquito larvae wriggled in the tea-colored liquid. He didn't bother with the oars. One oarlock was broken anyway. He squeezed the gas bulb then pulled the starter rope on an old fifteen-horsepower motor. After a few tries it sputtered to life with a cough of blue smoke. He would find out what Muhammed was really up to.

39

Two long, slow miles down the road but no sign of an old juke joint. Luther, Bea, and O'Hanlon had bet on Otis Sugg's sketchy memory—it was a hand that wasn't looking like a winner.

"Naw, this ain't it," Suggs said. He took off his fishing hat and scratched his sparsely tufted head.

My heart dropped. Thirty minutes into this and we're back to square one, again. Time was ticking and we didn't know where the hell we were going. The low country included hundreds of square miles of labyrinthine waterways. How would we ever find Dexter and Cornelia?

My phone rang. It was CNN again. They would fire me before they even offered me the job. I let it go to voicemail. Down to two bars, I hoped we wouldn't lose our cell signals. I glanced at the time. Kevin would be landing in Montreal in an hour. How was that all going to go down? I prayed that Luther's faith in Agent Kellogg was fully warranted.

"Okay, we're heading back out to the highway. We'll try again," Luther said, calm and reasonable, or at least sounding that way. "Nobody said finding the camp was going to be easy."

It had started raining once again and the wind was kicking up. A murder of crows blew across the sky overhead, buffeted by erratic gusts. Luther reported back to headquarters on his radio to update his people.

"I'm hoping between all our phones, we should be able to keep coms up," Luther said to us. "I've been asking for a decent radio system since I got here. Dispatch gets a little iffy once we're beyond thirty miles. So, from there on, it could be a whole lot iffy." He shook his head, disgusted.

"I'm on two bars right now," I said.

"I got nothing," O'Hanlon said.

"I'm two bars, too," Otis said. He squinted at his phone. "Or maybe that's one bar. Old peepers ain't what they used to be."

Another couple miles down the highway, Otis saw something familiar.

"That's it." He bounced a little in his seat. "That's the old gate. Used to be painted green. See—the paint's about gone, but it's still kinda greenish. And that big old live oak—hasn't changed a bit." He pointed an arthritic finger at the tree. "No trespassing sign has a few more holes in it. The board nailed up there with Starlight Lounge on it's gone, but I'm purty dang sure this is it."

"Okay," Luther said, "let's check this one out."

I prayed hard.

Luther veered off the road and made a sharp turn on another old rutted path into the swamp. The Range Rover fishtailed in the loose sand. I grabbed onto the overhead handhold.

"The ol' Starlight come up during prohibition and closed down in the early fifties after WWII," Otis explained. "Heard it was quite the place. Lots of great blues played in that joint, lots of great Q and 'shine served up. Lotsa rockin' and a rollin'. Sorry I missed it."

Quite a slice of history—I was sorry I had missed it too. I hoped that this path was where it all went down; then we'd have some hope that we're going in the right direction. I took a deep breath, and peered into the woods, looking for the remnants of the Starlight Lounge.

The rain was spitting hard. Luther turned on the windshield wipers. They slapped intermittently back and forth. The day was bleeding away as we plunged into the low country wilderness once again. The incoming storm would make our trek increasingly difficult. I checked my weather app. It would be another couple of hours before things got really bad. The swamp would become a giant sponge, sucking at our every step and obscuring any landmarks in a confusing, dark puzzle.

Then, Otis let out a whoop.

The sagging roof of the Starlight Lounge loomed at two o'clock. It looked like a gray hammock strung across old bones of a cabin that had collapsed under the weight of time and decay. A rusted-out oil-drum barbeque lay on its side next to an equally disintegrated vehicle of some unknown variety. Ferns grew up from inside the car windows. Vegetation had overtaken much of the building as well, but the place was unmistakable.

Hope began to rekindle in my heart but was tempered with grim reality. As twenty-four hours had come and gone, the odds of finding my boy alive began to fade.

Ж

We'd driven a bit more than two miles beyond the juke joint when the path dead-ended at an ancient fallen oak tree. Its great prostrate body created a home for a fecund forest of ferns, lichen, and insect nests. The swamp stretched out on both sides of us now. A packed-sand path raised several feet above the waterline but had washed out in quite a few places.

"Looks like we're footin' it from here on," Luther said. He put the car in park and turned off the ignition. "Y'all ready for this?"

"I'd guess it's another three or four miles down this path," Otis said. He scratched his head again. "I think it's straight on 'til we get to Little Boy Creek. Used to be this log bridge. They done a pretty good job makin' it. If we're lucky, it might still be there. Mebbe a couple miles more beyond that to Trotters. Mebbe less. Gonna be tough once it gets real dark."

"We have no choice. Let's move." My skin literally crawled with frustration. I took a series of short Lamaze breaths, the kind that help you get through childbirth. "The kids could be dead by morning if we wait." O'Hanlon glanced at me and Luther looked away.

They could be dead now, remained unsaid.

We climbed out of the car and donned our individual versions of rain parkas and boots. My footwear was a pair of running shoes. We stuffed energy bars, flashlights, water bottles, and our cell phones into our pockets. Everyone but me had a gun and ammo. Luther had a full backpack of who-knows-what. He locked the car and spoke into his radio informing HQ that we were now on foot.

"Got something new for you, Sheriff," the dispatcher reported. His voice was staticky.

"S'up, Murf?" my brother asked.

"From our helicopter, we spotted a damn parade of fishing boats and shrimpers headed up the intercoastal. They turned off into the Julienton River, went up Chimney Creek and then disappeared. An hour later, some of the same boats were backtracking. Could be nothing. Could be the Afghanis."

"We know they're working out there somewhere nearby. Shit."

"We can't keep an eye on 'em anymore today—storm's getting too rough. Baker had to bring the chopper down."

"Ten-four," Luther acknowledged. "Thanks for your good work. Be sure to give the Coast Guard a heads-up on everything."

"Done, sir."

"Good work, Murph. Likely we're heading out of range but keep listening hard. Over and out."

Luther exhaled a long breath. "Let's check our coms again." He pulled out his smartphone and shook his head. "Anybody got anything?"

"Two bars here," O'Hanlon said. She tucked the phone back into the pocket of her bright yellow Savannah-Chatham Metro PD slicker.

"Nothin' here," Otis said.

"I'm not getting anything either." I pulled the hood up on my raincoat. My skin was clammy and uncomfortable inside the unbreathable waterproof material. I bounced on the balls of my feet to keep myself from running, shrieking, into the woods demanding from the universe that Dexter come back to me. Immediately.

"Okay, let's move out before we lose any more light." Luther zipped up his backpack and pulled it over his shoulders.

One by one we crawled over the big old tree, getting dirty and wet in the process. It was probably ten feet around its spongy trunk. Once past this roadblock, the path narrowed. We walked single file among sandpaper-surfaced palmettos and wiregrass. The smell of decaying organic material intensified.

It was almost dusk when we finally reached the log bridge. We stopped for a moment, encouraged by the find. We congratulated Otis on getting us this far. We'd been walking for over an hour. Each step had tried to claim our shoes, each footprint quickly filling up with water as we moved on. It had not been an easy hike so far.

"So, who wants to try it first?" Luther asked with a smirk. "I'm the heaviest—don't want to break it and make the rest of y'all swim."

The stream was about fifteen feet across and appeared to be four or five feet deep in the center channel. Most of the tidal creeks were shallow and thick with mud at the bottom. The mud could run as deep as the water.

"I'll try it," I volunteered. I was probably heavier than Otis or O'Hanlon, but they didn't argue. I could see that neither was looking forward to balance-beaming across the splintering logs.

Otis held my hand as I mounted the slippery bridge. It immediately moaned and sagged under my weight. I moved gingerly, clenching my teeth. My running shoes offered pretty good traction.

"Come on folks, if I fall what's the worst that can happen—a little water? No biggie, right?" I was trying to brighten the group's flagging spirits.

"Hypothermia," Otis said, refusing to be brightened. "And leeches."

Inching my way over the bridge, I finally leaped to safety on the far bank of the creek.

O'Hanlon clapped and volunteered to go next, not to be outdone by my daring.

Her rubber boots turned out to offer less stability than my light shoes. She lost her balance. At the same moment she plunged into the creek, I noticed that the long gray sticks that had fallen from a low-hanging branch above the water weren't sticks.

They were moving fast toward her.

"Shit. Get *out*."

She screamed and started to splash and scramble to the shore.

It was too late.

The water moccasins' fangs connected with her flesh.

40

Luther managed to smash one of the snake's sleek, arrow-shaped head with a rock. Two more of its cousins slithered away farther down the creek in retreat.

We pulled O'Hanlon out of the water and propped her up against a wide cypress knee on a hummock at the far end of the bridge. We were all soaking wet. Her face was ashen and she gasped for breath between clenched teeth.

Luther ripped through his backpack. "Got a snakebite kit in here, but no antivenin. Lay her down."

I held O'Hanlon's freezing hand. I knew that when people go into shock their extremities become cold. All the blood rushes to protect the vital organs. O'Hanlon was going into shock.

"Where did it get you?" I asked.

"On my thigh, first. Feels like a red-hot ice pick."

Then she held up her opposite arm and revealed a swelling red wound on her wrist with two piercings in the middle.

"The damn things nailed her twice," I said.

"Makes a wasp sting feel like a kiss on the cheek." O'Hanlon started to rock back and forth to help cope with the pain.

"Let's look at the leg wound," I said.

We struggled together to get the wet, sticky pants below her knees. Luther finally pulled his knife and cut them off. The bite on her thigh was swelling faster than the one on her wrist.

Jesus H. Christ, this woman had to get to a hospital, immediately.

"Where's your cell phone, Mary?" I asked. Using her first name seemed more appropriate right now. "You had the most bars up when we started."

"In my jacket." Her lips were turning whitish.

I searched through her pockets. The phone was gone.

"Coms? Check again, everybody." I demanded. "Anything?"

Luther and Otis both shook their heads. We were on our own.

"Move back, Bea. Give me a little room," Luther said. He kneeled on the ground next to Mary and began the rough procedure of slitting the skin with a scalpel between the fang marks and then pumping out the venom with an ineffective-looking suction device. It was her only chance. It didn't look like a good one.

O'Hanlon flinched as the instrument slit her tender, swollen skin. Sweat beaded on her face and she shivered violently. It was all done in minutes. I bandaged the injuries with gauze from the backpack.

"She can't walk, it'll make the poison spread even faster," Luther said. "I'll carry her back to the Rover. We had cell transmission there. I'll call for an ambo and get some assistance organized. I'll jog back here as soon as she's on her way outta here."

"Okay, what do you want us to do?" I knew I wasn't going to be able to wait for him to get back and he knew it, too.

"You two keep moving ahead, carefully, take your time. Don't approach the camp on your own. Hear me? Mark your way with this so I can find you. Breadcrumbs—okay?"

I nodded and he handed me a can of neon-pink, glow-in-the-dark spray paint.

"I'm bringing SWAT. Something feels really bad out here." He gently lifted O'Hanlon into his arms.

I had the same sense of foreboding.

"I want Mary's gun," I said. She tried to oppose my insistence with a moan, but I ignored her. "I'm sure as hell not going to be out here with unarmed."

"You'll be okay," Luther said. "If you sense anything, and I mean *anything*, you'll stand back and wait quietly till I show up with the posse. Is that clear?"

Clear as mud. "Luther, that's bullshit. I want a goddamned weapon."

I slipped the Glock out of O'Hanlon's holster and stuck it in my waistband. It was like the one Luther sent me for my birthday, the one I should have traveled with after all.

)X(

Just beyond the fish shack with its ancient tin roof and moldering wood siding, Marcus Muhammed Trotter sat on an old tree stump overlooking a long, narrow sandbar. Gran'pappy Trotter's beach had been the evil playground of Muhammed's youth. Where a freshwater spring dripped onto the mossy edge of the tidal creek, thirty alligators piled together in the warmth of the fading sun, some on top of each other like stacked logs. They ranged in length from a baseball bat to a double kayak.

Muhammed reached into a crumpled brown paper bag and grabbed a struggling rat by the tail. He'd found it nested in some old blankets up at the camp. He tossed the stunned critter into the water in front of the gators.

Splashes and grunts ensued.

Lethal tails roiled and smacked the wet sand. They sounded like gunshots.

In seconds, the rat had been swallowed whole by Old Tom, a ten-foot gator with a nasty scar running across his back from when Gran'pappy tried to kill him with a machete years ago in a drunken binge. Gran'pap was dead; Old Tom was still alive and looked kick-ass fast and powerful.

Gran'pap's favorite sport, besides beating up his five young grandsons and raping his only granddaughter, was throwing living things to the gators after getting hammered on homemade moonshine.

Muhammed could barely remember his mother. He was only five when she died. There were various stories about how she came to meet her maker. Nobody really knew who all their fathers were. There was no one to take them but Gran'pappy. And take them he did, along with his nasty whore, Orpha. The kids called her "Orifice." Eventually, the ones who survived their tag-team abuse, ran away to live in the Savannah and Atlanta projects.

Muhammed's oldest brother, Maurice, got them the hell out of that back creek the week after their sister died. Maurice was about eighteen at the time. Muhammed, newly twelve, was the only one at the shack when his fourteen-year-old sister, Arletta, slit her wrists after Gran'pap and a couple of the brothers had their way with her. It had been going on for years and she was pregnant. Again. Pappy'd made the first baby disappear.

Muhammed sat with her and held her hand as she bled out. He knew she'd be better off dead.

That was the last time he had felt anything other than rage or numbness. For a time, torturing animals became an outlet for the pressure cooker that was his brain. He came to enjoy their look of panic and betrayal as he tied them to a rope and dangled them in front of the gators from a fishing pole or from the overhead tree branches. Eventually, that wasn't enough.

Old Tom would like Bea's brat and the China girl. Maybe Doobius, too. What a stupid-ass name—Doobius. Emad Al Alequi was just another entitled prick. Farouk and Grandfather Parsa would be relieved to lose the worthless fucker.

And then there was Beatrice Middleton. Ah, Beatrice. She had been a perfect target for his rage. From a good home, smug, pretty—she had never suffered a day in her privileged life. People needed to suffer and Bea's education in pain and loss had yet to be completed. He was the teacher.

※

Emad's leaking dinghy puttered up to the half-submerged dock which led to the old Trotter fish camp. The woods surrounding the cabin included a privy and what looked like an old smokehouse. They were all eerily quiet. The place felt abandoned and smelled faintly of burned wood.

He tied the boat up and clambered onto the dock. It sunk beneath his weight. Termites had made this place their home; every board looked rotten and precarious. His running shoes were soaked in no time. They squished as he walked up the rise to the front porch.

"Muhammed. Where the hell are you?" he yelled. Carefully, he mounted the steps amid frightening creaks and moans. He pushed open the front door.

He was right—the shack was empty. The single room contained a small table and two chairs, a rusty metal bed with a chewed-up feather mattress and a chipped ceramic sink with a hand pump. A couple of ancient, empty cans of tomato soup and a pile of broken Jack Daniels bottles were strewn across the small counter. A black-and-yellow spider the size of a softball had woven its home into the threadbare and moldy kitchen curtains.

Emad shivered as he took another step into the dim cabin. A pile of disintegrating porn magazines spilled out from under the bed. Rat droppings were everywhere. A cold whisper of anxiety ran down his spine. Where were the kids? And where was Muhammed? He called out once again to no response.

Rain began to ping on the metal roof. Emad returned to the porch and peered across the creek. Insect-seeking fish broke the surface as the raindrops splashed like pebbles. He descended the steps and headed toward the privy. An old half-moon was carved in the gaping door. He peered into the shit hole with help from a dying flashlight, afraid of what could be there. Mushrooms grew in the darkness, but nothing else. He had this vision that he'd be looking into Dexter and Cornelia's dead eyes. Muhammed was planning something bad, he knew it. He should've brought a gun with him.

The only other place they could be was the smokehouse; at least it looked like one—square and sooty, with a chimney. Or it could be a still or a meth lab. Or maybe Muhammed had secured the kids off in the woods someplace. The asshole seemed to know this godforsaken swamp like the back of his hand. Emad shook his head. Trotter was scum—too bad the family couldn't, or wouldn't, see that.

The quiet of the camp exploded. Blood-curdling grunting and trumpeting, sounding like an elephant herd in frenzy, stopped Emad in his tracks. Gators? Jesus. Reverberation from the commotion carried through the air from maybe a quarter mile farther down the creek. Nearby, a thin cry of distress rose from the smokehouse. Emad ran to the outbuilding and pulled up a crossbeam lock. He wrenched open the door.

Two sets of dark, frightened eyes met his own. He had to make a fast decision: take them and run, or be the good son his father prayed for, and leave the kids to die.

41

I squinted down the sight line of the Glock. Otis was not happy to be abandoned by police officers and stuck with a lowly civilian who didn't even have a Georgia carry permit.

"Want me to give you a quick lesson on how to use a pistol?" he asked. "Got the magazine in right? Know how to use the slide?"

"Uh-huh, I do." I settled, aimed, and pulled the trigger. The plastic suction device we'd used on O'Hanlon's snakebites popped into the air. It had barely worked to begin with, now it was toast.

"Well dang." Otis removed his hat and scratched his head, as I found was his habit. "That looked purty good to me."

I smiled. "I'm not law enforcement or military, but I had the occasion to take a couple shooting classes."

Actually, I'd completed a certification program in Los Angeles and kept it current.

"Okay, then. Let's go, Miz Annie Oakley." He took off down the path toward Trotter's fish camp, and God willing, my son. I followed along quietly and strained to sense any threat. Thunder rumbled in the distance and the air took on a greenish hue.

I hit landmarks with a big dot of orange spray paint as we hiked deeper into the swamp. The path was now more like a narrow game trail. I noticed coyote scat full of rabbit fur. Faint deer tracks were pressed into the damp mud. No evidence that indicated anything human, but I figured we had a few miles to go before we were in range of the Trotter fish camp.

A blood-curdling series of roars and bellows erupted from somewhere nearby. The little hairs on the back of my neck stood up on end. Had I not known that lions didn't live in Georgia swamps, I would swear that was what I was hearing.

"Otis, what the..."

"Bull gator at ten o'clock," he said. "Keep moving. They can outrun a horse at a short distance."

We walked fast and tried to stay calm. Didn't want to communicate that we were potential fleeing prey to the big reptile. I was *not* in the mood to be anyone's meal.

After a quarter mile of terrified speed-walking, we collapsed together onto a downed tree trunk and guzzled our water. I took off my rain parka and wrapped it around my waist. My body dripped with sweat. I was so over-heated I thought I would faint. Otis looked even worse than I felt. Despite the urgency of our mission, I knew we had to slow down.

264 | SUE HINKIN

"We gotta go back and mark the way," Otis said. "Can't have Luther get lost tryin' to find us."

He was right, we hightailed beyond the potential gator encounter so fast we'd forgot to leave breadcrumbs.

"You sit here and get your breath, Otis. I'll backtrack. Very carefully, I promise."

He raised a minor protest but I could tell, at more than twice my age, he needed the break.

Discouraged by the slowness of our progress, I trudged cautiously back the way I thought we'd come, making marks as I went, looking for where I had left off. Every rustle in the undergrowth made my anxiety spike. Snakes, gators, blood-sucking insects, wild boar, swamp panthers—oh—fuckin'—my.

Seemed like an hour before I finally found the location where I'd made the last hot orange dot. I leaned against the tree, grateful that I hadn't gotten lost. There had been confusing forks in the trail, but my marking system held up.

I rested for a moment then turned again toward Otis and pursuit of the Trotter fish camp. Bone-tired, I knew the worst was still before us.

X

After several miles of carrying O'Hanlon, who was shivering violently, Luther stopped and carefully put her down on the sandy track to catch his breath. His shoulders were on fire. The adrenaline that had initially kept him going was beginning to wear thin. He pulled his iPhone out again to check for reception.

Praise the Lord—a bar appeared. His sweaty fingers made dialing mistakes. Hell, he only had to hit two digits for the speed dial. Finally, he got it right.

"Sheriff Middleton?"

"Murph. Thank God. I need an ambulance and backup ASAP. I'm on the trail, heading for the Land Rover. Detective O'Hanlon has been bitten by water moccasins and is in shock. Pulse is sketchy, BP probably low—we need help here, now."

"Got it, Sheriff. I wrote down that you turned onto an old fire road at the 14.5-mile mark from the highway."

"Right. You'll go in 2.3 miles and then there should be an old juke joint on your right. The Rover's beyond that. I'll try to meet you at the turnoff from the highway if I can."

"Luther?" O'Hanlon said. She tried to sit up. "I'm so thirsty."

"I need an ambo, Murph. Stat."

"On its way, sir."

"Over and out."

Luther pulled a water bottle from his pocket and held it to O'Hanlon's lips so she could drink. Most of it ran down her chin. He stripped off his backpack and began unbuttoning his shirt.

"What are you doing, Luther?" she asked, eyes barely open. Her lids were pale and bloodless. Her fingers tried to clutch at the sand. "I wouldn't mind you being the last thing I see in this life. But my daughter, I can't leave my daughter."

"I'm gonna get this wet shit off of you and wrap you in something dry. You're losing too much heat. And baby, I'm not gonna be the last thing you see. Not this decade, anyway."

He peeled off her parka and blouse, the pants were

already long gone and wrapped her in his navy-blue XXL Shellman County Sherriff's polo. He discovered some dry athletic socks in the pack and was able to put them on her and pull them all the way up to her knees. Then he picked her up, pressed her against his warm chest, and hit the trail again.

He would not let this woman die. No way in hell was she going to leave him.

"If you live, will you marry me? And I'll care for your daughter like she was my own," he whispered in her ear but she'd lost consciousness.

42

Emad stared at the two teenagers. They stared back at him like the proverbial deer in headlights. He had seen them as they crawled into the van at the warehouse, but somehow now they looked so much worse than when he had talked to them only this morning. Dexter especially looked bad. He'd had the crap beaten out of him. Between Muhammed and big Sadam as their minders, it was no wonder. Emad knew that if he didn't step in to help, these kids were never gonna make it. He owed Jayden. Jayden was murdered because of him. He had to make it right.

"Come on, come with me, quickly." He had no idea what he was going to do with them or where they would go.

"Doobius? Are you here to save us, or—?" Cornelia's eyes were wide and distrustful. Dexter's were swollen to slits.

"I'm gonna get us the fuck outta here," he said and offered them both a hand.

Slowly, they tottered out of the smokehouse, dehydrated and confused. Emad paused and made them both drink Gatorade from his water bottle and split a half-eaten Cliff bar that had been in his pocket for at least a week, maybe a month. They wolfed it down, making little mewling noises.

Then Emad heard a metallic sound. A bullet chambering? Shit. He froze, then whirled around, almost losing his balance.

"What the hell do you think you're doing, asshole?" Muhammed had a pistol aimed at Emad's head.

"Oh, no," Cornelia cried.

Emad felt his bowels loosen but he knew he had to match Muhammed's intensity and confidence. The man was a bully, attracted to weakness like a heat-seeking missile toward a warm beating heart.

"I'm making sure the kids don't starve to death. You're really shitty at this stuff. I'm taking over. Father and Grandfather want you at the dock to help supervise. They hired you to be the security partner, not fuck around with your little hostages. Go, get out of here. And put that damn gun down."

The standoff seemed to last for an eternity.

Muhammed de-cocked the gun and started to holster it, then abruptly changed his mind. He aimed his weapon again at Emad.

"In the smokehouse, all of you," he said, voice dark and dead.

"No fucking way. My father—"

A fast, brutal chop—Muhammed hit Emad in the jaw with the butt of his gun. Bone cracked like a dry stick. Emad fell to his knees and spit out part of his tongue. Blood streamed down his shirt. His eyes rolled up in his head and he passed out.

Muhammed waved the gun at Dexter. "Boy, get Emad in the smokehouse. China bitch, I'll be back to take you for a ride real soon."

They hurried to obey.

Once they were all inside the smokehouse, Muhammed dropped the crossbeam back into place which securely locked the door on all three.

Then he took off to make a phone call. Ten mil wasn't gonna to be enough.

Dexter watched him through a tiny knothole as he disappeared into the forest.

X

It was almost closing time and the last client of the day still languished in her chair. Almost done. Hattie gazed out the window of her gold-and-leopard-print wallpapered salon, *Mode de Paree*. It sat on Main Street in Shellman Corners, a town three blocks long, frozen in time, circa 1953. She couldn't help but worry and wonder about Bea and Luther dashing off into the swamps to confront who-knows-what crazy group of maniacs. The whole situation was completely surreal.

As she rubbed product into Mabel Atherton's newly-dyed black hair with mahogany highlights, Hattie was grateful for her always interesting, but relatively danger-free life in Shellman Corners. She knew all the shop owners and the workers in the business district. She'd enjoyed butting heads with them at the Downtown Economic Development meetings for over forty years. Nothing much ever developed, but they made sure the streets were clean, walls were graffiti-free, and that there were always big pots of geraniums and sweet potato vines hanging from the lamp posts during the summertime.

With a pick and a hairdryer, Hattie began coaxing Mabel's short hair into a spiky explosion.

"Couldn't help but overhear you while I was waiting." Mabel, seventy-five years old trying for thirty, stared at herself in the gilt-edged mirror, and then took a swig of Orange Fanta. "I knew Orpha Davis's little sister, Dolphine, a long time ago."

"You did?" Hattie's interest was piqued. She turned off the hairdryer and continued to primp Mabel's hair with her fingers. She had to find out more about this, fast. It could prove helpful to Bea and Luther.

"I actually went to their family fish camp with her for the Fourth of July once," Mabel continued. "Nice little spot, but Dolphine and I hitched back into town after about two hours of trying to evade Orpha. Gal was seriously crazy—on a meth bender most likely. We got the heck outta there. Told my mom about it and ol' Dolphine was crossed off my friend list fast as you could say 'firecracker.' I also got grounded for a month for hitchhiking."

"You remember anything about where the camp was located? Like how far from the highway?" Hattie asked. "My nephew—"

"The sheriff?"

"Yup, he's trying to track down some nasty criminals

out that way. Having a hard time finding the place."

"He's a good lookin' man, ain't he?"

"Luther? He is for sure, smart too."

"Gotta find me one like that, my, my." She brushed a stray hair off her animal-print cover-up. "Looks a little like Idris Elba, don't he? I loved *The Wire* but I'll never forgive them for killing off his character, Stringer Bell. A bad boy with a redeeming heart. Stopped watching it after Idris was put down. Same with *Game of Thrones.* Once Ned Stark was beheaded, was over for me."

"Who?"

"Ned Stark, whose house sigil is the dire wolf, and uncle of the hot bastard love child, Jon Snow."

"I guess I'll have to watch more TV 'cause I don't know what the mercy you're talking about." Frustrated, Hattie primped Mabel's hair a little too hard and evoked a wince. "Oh, sorry. But dear, let's get back to the fish camp."

"You can rent all the seasons on Netflix."

"Uh-huh, I'll be sure to do that, but about the fish camp." She squeezed some moisturizing sheen gel into her hand and garnished Mabel's hedgehog-esque do. The woman seemed to speak ten times slower than usual. Mabel had to get her to cut to the chase.

"Yes, well, hum, Trotter's camp. Tell that cute nephew that we came into the place by boat. Can't recall anything much 'bout that. Those backwaters all look the same to me. But when we hitchhiked to town, we walked for a couple miles and passed an old warehouse. I think it might have once been part of a shrimp-processing outfit. Looked completely abandoned but outta nowhere one of the Trotter boys came running at us, screaming and waving a gun. He chased us for about a half mile. Dolphine and I were both on the junior high cross-county team so we outpaced 'im. Lost our rubber flip-flops in the process, though. Mine had big yellow daisies on 'em and I was really upset."

"Shame about the flip-flops," Hattie said, trying to keep Mabel's memory flowing.

"After we recovered from the fright, we had another mile or so to the highway. I'd have no idea where to find that road now. Zero."

"Mind if I tell my nephew whatcha told me?"

"No problem, and I'd be more than willing to have Luther interrogate me any time."

Hattie rolled her eyes. "I'm sure you would, darling. Now, look at that pretty style on you. I think we're done, time to close up shop. In a bit of a hurry today, honey."

As soon as Mabel slowly collected her belongings, paid, droned on a few more minutes about TV shows then finally left, Hattie tried to call Luther. No response. She left a tense voicemail.

"Call me, nephew, I may have a lead on another way into Trotter's."

She disconnected then noticed that she had received a voice message herself. She didn't recognize the number. Probably an insurance scam or a politician. She pushed "Listen."

There was a sound like crunching paper and Hattie almost hung up, but then a voice spoke that put her nerves on edge.

"Long time, Hattie, you bitch."

Hattie drew in a quick, hard breath. *Who in the world?*

"It's Orpha. Stay away from my business, or more people you care about are gon' die. Feel me, old woman?"

"You're dead. Ten years ago."

"Not yet, bitch, not crafty ol' Orpha Davis, Trotter."

"Trotter?" Hattie dropped the phone and slumped into a salon chair.

43

Dexter, Cornelia, and now Emad, hunched against the sooty wall of the smokehouse, practically on top of each other. Overhead, beams supported a variety of rusty, blood-stained hooks where the owners of this dump, whoever they were, hung whatever they were smoking above the central stove. Dexter guessed the swampers might've eaten anything—from coon to fish, maybe even rattlesnake. Was crazy Muhammed going to hang and smoke them? The thought made him shudder. He cursed the vivid imagination on which he had once prided himself. Right now, he wished he was dumb as a rock and knew nothing, felt nothing.

Cornelia nestled up closer. The warmth of her body was welcome in the chill from the burst of wind and rain that had begun. Her closeness aroused him a little, which was kind of nuts, given their situation. Her brown eyes looked up at him, then closed. Her face was pale and streaked with a line of soot, like a thin dark cloud moving across the moon.

Emad sat across from them, head in his hands. His light-gray designer sweatsuit was torn and bloody. *Imagine* was tattooed on right hand.

"So, you're Doobius?" Dexter asked, curious to find out more about their new partner in misery. The guy's lank hair hung to his shoulders and curtained his face. He smelled lightly of weed.

Emad took a deep breath and grimaced. "My head feels like it's gonna explode."

"He gotcha good, the prick," Dexter said. "Any ideas on how to get outta here?"

"We're pretty much fucked. This place is far enough away that my father won't see or hear anything, and he's not gonna get in a boat and look for us. Father and Grandfather don't swim. They actually hate the water. Both get seasick at the smell of the ocean. I'm surprised they went for this boats-and-creeks shit." He grimaced.

"What do you mean?" Dexter sensed what was going down but wanted to hear more from Doobius.

"They're drug dealers, they fucking run heroin production in Afghanistan." His eyes and his voice filled with tears. "I can't talk, my jaw's killing me. And I'm so dizzy."

"Probably a concussion or something. I think I got one too." Dexter watched Emad throw up in the stove. Had it been only a day ago that he and Cornelia had puked in the dog cage? Seemed like eons.

For a while, they were all quiet, listening to the soothing sound of the rain beating on the roof of their little shack and the occasional call of a bird or a bullfrog deep in the forest.

"Your cousin, Jayden, was amazing," Emad said, perhaps feeling a bit better after vomiting. "I wanted to help him share his talent with the world, that's all I wanted to do. Just shine a light, you know? Shine a fucking light, as Elton John would say."

They remained in their own thoughts until they heard someone humming a tune beneath the sound of the rain. *Bad Boys, bad boys, whatcha gonna do?* It came closer.

Cornelia looked at Dexter, confused. "Sounds like an old woman."

"What the fuck?" Emad touched his jaw and groaned.

The bar across the outside door scraped as it was lifted and dislodged. Cornelia glued herself against Dexter. The door to the smokehouse flew open. Muhammed stood on the narrow porch, a coil of thick rope draped across his shoulders like a prayer shawl. On his head, he wore a long gray wig of matted hair.

"Fuckin'A. What's with the witch hair, Muhammed?" The effort to speak seemed excruciating for Emad. He broke out in a sweat.

"Come, Emad Al Alequi," Muhammed the voodoo witch chick said, his voice high, feminine, and sing-songy. "*Allahu Akbar.*"

"*Allahu Akbar,*" Emad returned, barely able to utter the words.

Emad glanced back, eyes forlorn as he stepped from the smokehouse. Dexter stood and tried to follow but Muhammed shoved him back into the building. He bounced off the stove and fell to the charred stone floor next to Cornelia. She shivered violently.

The two sat huddled together, tense and hypervigilant. Eventually, the sound of a boat motor receded in the distance. Had Muhammed left? They looked at each other and breathed a tentative sigh of relief. Did he take Doobius with him?

And then the screaming began.

※

A Shellman County squad car drove into sight beyond the huge downed oak tree, at last. Sweat dripped down Luther's face and into his eyes, nearly blinding him. Beyond the tree, the ambulance rumbled toward them, going as fast as anything could possibly go on this overgrown, backwoods fire road. Sand and mud flew up from its tires. Luther wanted to burst out in tears. Some help, some hope. He was losing Mary fast and there was nothing he could do about it.

"Here. Over here," he shouted. He laid her on the sand and waved his arms, leaped onto the tree trunk, signaling the EMS. They spotted him right away and pulled up to the far side of the fallen oak.

In no time they had O'Hanlon over the tree trunk and onto a gurney, hooking her up to an IV to administer the antivenin.

"Will she be okay? What do you think?" he demanded from the paramedics.

"Depends on how she reacts to this stuff. Gotta get her to the ER. Like now. We'll be in touch."

No place to turn around, they quickly backed down the road toward the highway. At this point, all Luther could do was pray. It was in His hands.

He let out a long, shaky sigh and shook his head in frustration. He glanced at his iPhone and noticed a call from Aunt Hattie. He'd return it later.

Luther's radio crackled to life. It was Murph the dispatcher.

"Sheriff, just heard that the bus arrived. Savannah Memorial is waiting for O'Hanlon. Over."

"They just pulled out. How 'bout my backup? What's the ETA?"

"We have two radio cars about ten minutes out from your location, but we had a 911 from your, uh, called herself Aunt Hattie May, and she said before we did anything you had to check her voicemail. She was highly insistent—said something about an Orpha—"

"Orpha Davis. Owned a fish camp near Trotter's back in the day. Supposedly did some meth trafficking. Dead a long time."

"Well evidently, the dead woman called your aunt."

"What the hell?" Luther scrubbed the damp stubble of his beard. "Not possible."

"Dunno. Sounded like she might have something that you should hear."

"Okay, Murph. Back with you soon. Over."

Luther's heart raced as the ambulance siren sounded from the highway. It receded fast, heading for Savannah. Please, God, be merciful and let her live. He wiped his eyes with the back of his hand and then dialed Aunt Hattie on his cell.

It took ten rings before she finally came on the line.

"Auntie?"

"Luther. Thank heavens. Mabel Atkinson left and said she had been at the Trotter place years ago. It was a couple miles beyond an old shrimp-processing plant out in the woods. Not much but maybe that can help." Hattie reported Mabel's description of how she and Dolphine got out to the highway from Trotters.

"Thank you, Auntie. This could be a break."

"There's more."

"About Orpha Davis? Fill me in. My dispatcher said they thought Orpha called you, but we know she's been dead for years." Luther tugged on the light blue scrubs the EMS tech had lent him.

"Do we know that?" Anxiety edged her voice. "I got a call about twenty minutes ago from someone who said she was Orpha Davis—Orpha Davis Trotter. *Trotter*. Maybe she married the old loon. But she threatened me and the family. Said she'd kill us if we didn't back off."

Luther's brain began to spin. If Orpha was still alive and linked up with what would be her stepson Marcus, then he had an accomplice as insane as he was. Was she living out in the swamp somewhere like the undead? Was she tied into the kidnapping scam somehow?

"Auntie, I want you to pack up and head over to Momma's as soon as you can. Rufus, too. Let's not mess around with this threat. I'll have a radio car stay close in the neighborhood until we catch these assholes. Excuse the language, Auntie."

"They're total assholes, dear," she said. "I'll round up everybody and we'll be on our way. Please, nephew, be very, very careful"

"Will do. Get moving now. And thank you."

He depressed the button on his phone to disconnect. Then went to dispatch.

"Murph?"

"Yes, sir."

You have any video from your flight yesterday?"

"We do."

"Good. Review it ASAP for anything that looks like an old warehouse or pole barn due south of my current GPS coordinates, twenty-mile radius. I'm going back down the trail to find my sister and Otis Suggs. Will probably lose coms shortly. According to my aunt, the old Trotter fish camp is likely about two miles north from the warehouse building. Her source says it was a defunct shrimp-processing facility. Might be good to get a hold of some of the old shrimpers in the area, see if they remember the place."

"Yes, sir." Murph's voice crackled and shorted off and on.

"My guess is the Afghanis are at Orpha's camp beyond there, loading their heroin into boats that turn around and make their way out into the intercoastal toward Florida and the Gulf. Let the Coast Guard know to pick up anything at all that looks even remotely suspicious." Luther paced back and forth in front of the fallen tree and slapped at biting insects.

"Will do, and a couple cruisers should be arriving in minutes."

"Thanks, they're here now." Two squad cars emerged from the palmettos and drove slowly toward Luther and the downed tree. Luther motioned them forward.

"Murph, call me right away if you see this warehouse-type structure on the tape. If you can locate it, I'll send these guys over there with the SWAT team. If not, they'll follow me into the swamp on foot." Luther watched the officers get out of their cars. They were intense and purposeful; ready to roll.

"Trouble is, Murph, we're not sure where we're going to end up. Could be at the Trotter camp, or maybe our old guy doesn't remember right. Don't wanna waste anyone's time wild-goosing it."

"Yeah, got it. Too bad we lose communication in there."

"This is the last time that's gonna happen. Council does not close session this year until we have funding for an upgraded coms system in place. I'll hold them at gunpoint if I have to."

"Copy that. Ten-four, Sherriff, over and out."

Luther greeted his backup officers and instructed them to wait until they heard from HQ. If Murph and crew found a warehouse, the officers would turn around and meet up with SWAT. They'd need maximum firepower for a possible confrontation with the Afghanis. If the warehouse was a ghost, they'd follow the breadcrumbs and be backup for Luther at Trotter's camp.

With fresh bug spray, more water, and snacks from the Rover in his pack, Luther took off back down the trail at a brisk jog.

44

Thunder crackled nearby. Farouk looked up and scowled. The sky was a bowl of dirty rinse water about to spill forth. The heavens were opening and the rain started again with force, as Muhammed guided the dinghy to the dock and tied up.

"Finally. Where have you been? And where's Emad?" Farouk demanded, seriously pissed off. "We need some help here. This is not a vacation, we are not relaxing at Sharm el Sheikh, scuba diving and sipping tea."

"He's going to stay over there for a while, supervise things," Muhammed said. He stretched his back and plucked a long, gray hair from his shirt.

"What do you mean, 'supervise things'? What's to supervise? Lock them up and leave them." Farouk started to pace.

"Your son's a bleeding heart, in case you never

noticed."

Farouk shook his head, a look of disgust on his face. "Damn storm is supposed to hit within the hour and we have eight more boats to load. If we don't make it out of here tonight we're in big trouble."

"We'll move the worker bees along. Sweeten the pot with a few more bucks. We'll be fine, Farouk. You always freak, man."

"I'm concerned, and for good reason. You need to be more concerned, much more concerned."

Muhammed ignored him. He was more interested in an aging white trawler that pulled up to the dock, piloted by two women.

"That'll help get the worker's blood up," Muhammed said. He smiled at the two brunettes. Neither were particularly attractive except for the fact that they were female and both wore short cut-off jeans. The rain had made their wet T-shirts cling provocatively to their otherwise unimpressive breasts.

Farouk opened an umbrella and stood under it, trying to light a damp Marlboro in the blustery rain. His phone rang. He dug it out of his pocket and squinted to see the call number.

"Yes?" he asked, then listened quietly. "Okay, we're closing shop."

"What?" Muhammed asked. Farouk's body language pulled him immediately away from the women.

"Our spotters out on the highway report a sheriff's van and black-and-whites coming our way. Let's close the fuck up. Tell those girls to get the hell outta here and we'll be in touch. I'll radio the rest of the boats to scatter."

Farouk turned and ran up toward the pole barn screaming orders. Sheets of rain now fell and billowed like glassy curtains obscuring the pole barn and the frenetic workers. The women pushed off from the dock and disappeared down dark watery veins amid the cypress forest.

※

Although we were soaked through and through, Otis and I put our rain parkas back on for insulation and protection. Rain streamed down his old fishing hat and I pulled my hood up as the storm finally began to unleash the promised monsoon. Not quite a tropical storm, but still intense and dangerous. We always got more than our share of severe weather warnings in Savannah that never materialized, but this one was not a false alarm. We didn't have rain like this in California, even during *el Niño* season.

As we continued down the narrow trail, the ground became increasingly spongy and hard to navigate. Otis tripped on a root that skulked across the path and took a hard tumble. Fortunately, he's a tough old guy and the ground was reasonably soft. We stopped again for a break on the edge of a cypress hummock and found ourselves near an old campfire clearing.

"Looks like a slave camp from way back when." Otis rubbed the shoulder he'd fallen on. "Plenty of that during the Civil War. My people was out hereabouts 'fore the proclamation was signed."

"Lotta stories to tell, difficult ones," I said, imagining having to live, fearing for your life, in this bug-infested hell. Some loved the swamps, were drawn to them like a bear to honey, but I couldn't see it.

As we silently contemplated our shared history here in Georgia, our thoughts were interrupted by a far-off screaming. It was faint but so horrible and blood-curdling that I had to swallow down the panic that began to crush my chest like a heart attack.

Otis froze, then reached for his gun. His hand rested on the damp metal for reassurance. "I'd say we'd better get going, Miz Bea. Things're gettin' bad out here. No time to waste."

I followed him as we continued down the trail with a renewed sense of urgency. The screaming became louder and more tortured. It seemed to go on forever, then mercifully, began to wane. We were heading straight for it. It was definitely human but was not Dexter or Cornelia—of that I was pretty sure. Maybe Dexter and Cornelia had already screamed themselves to death. I stopped myself from going there.

Soon, it was quiet once more except for the rumble of thunder and the sound of the falling rain. The swampy forest was barely lit. In a dark, ominous twilight, ghostlike mist began to gather amid the underbrush. We had flashlights, but to avoid detection, we didn't turn them on. Our eyes glued to the narrow band of sandy trail before us, we crept forward.

After another slow, soggy half mile we stopped again for a break, exhausted as much from the emotional journey as the physical one. I could tell that Otis, especially, was losing steam. The storm was getting worse and the thunder and lightning were frighteningly close. I had also run out of spray paint. No more breadcrumbs.

A bolt of electricity ripped the sky. I could feel

electrons dancing on my skin. I touched my hair to be sure it wasn't starting to stand on end. I'd read that happens before you get struck.

Another bolt flashed nearby. As I looked up, above me hung a man. I felt like I'd been tased, paralyzed, my skin vibrating. His arms and legs were gone; only his upper torso and head remained.

What was left of the victim, below his ribcage, was skin that appeared ragged and chewed off. Blood dripped from the corpse like pink rain onto the vacant stretch of beach. Lightning came again and the image of the ravaged man embedded itself on my retina like a photograph on film. I gasped and pressed my hand over my mouth to keep myself from screaming out.

Otis and I backtracked fast down the trail and held onto each other to keep from collapsing.

"Ol' Pappy Trotter's beach," he said, breathless. "Gators congregate there—he used to feed them. All sorts of stuff. Animals, some said even people. Good Lor,' who do ya think the guy is?"

"I think it may be my nephew's band manager. Calls himself Evan Doobius but his real name is Emad Al Alequi. As much as I can tell, the face looks like his picture."

"He the one they think shot Jayden?"

"I don't think so. He seems to have been Jayden's friend. But his father and grandfather are likely leaders of a drug cartel who've set up out here. A nice remote place with relatively easy access to the intercoastal. Luther's after them."

"Why'd they kill this boy? Their son, grandson?"

"I have a sick feeling that Emad may have been

murdered for trying to help the kids. One thing I do know for sure is that Marcus Trotter is working for these drug assholes and he is one helluva vicious psychopath."

"Looks like a Trotter kind of murder to me," Otis said. "Didn't know the gran'kids but ol' Emory Trotter was one sick piece of shit. 'Scuse my language, ma'am."

"Only if you'll 'scuse mine."

He nodded with a flicker of a smile that died in an instant. "The main camp is mebbe a quarter mile down the path here."

"I think we need to go in and check the place right away." I was insanely anxious to see if Dexter and Cornelia were there.

"No, Miz Bea. We need to wait for the sheriff. Can't be far behind us by now. He move fast, was a football star, weren't he?"

"Yes, but it could be too late if we wait."

"No use all of us dyin', Miz Bea. He said to wait. We wait."

I knew he was absolutely right, but the waiting was too much. I began to move forward. Otis drew good ol' Marjorie from his holster and aimed her my way.

"This is for your own good, Miz Bea. You'll thank me later."

My mouth opened in shock.

"You wouldn't shoot me Otis."

"I'd wing ya to stop ya from gettin' all us killed. Those Trotters are smart, sneaky lizards. Mebbe just waiting for us right now. I know a mother's love for her son is a powerful thing but doesn't always make for strategic thinkin'. I'm an ol' man and you're a young lady who can shoot something sittin' on a log real good, but Trotter, the boy—I heard the sheriff say he Special Ops. Please, Miz Bea, wait for your brother to help us out. We'll have a much better chance at being successful all 'round."

Otis was right. When I hunkered down in the rain next to him, he returned ol' Marjorie back to her holster. I bided my time waiting for Luther by scheming about how I would destroy Marcus Trotter.

45

"He fed Doobie to the alligators, didn't he?" Cornelia knew the answer.

Dexter couldn't meet her eyes. He looked around the smokehouse again, seeking a way out, but it offered nothing. It was a place built to last. He realized that he and Cornelia weren't the first hostages to be locked in here. He noticed initials scratched roughly into the wood. Cypress was hard stuff, not like oak, but pretty dense. He wondered if the other prisoners had used their fingernails to carve out proof that they existed.

"We may have only a few hours before we die. Could be a horrible death," Cornelia said with little emotion.

Dexter groaned in frustration. There had to be hope somehow. He had come up with a last-ditch plan. Probably worthless, but at this point, something was better than nothing. He turned to Cornelia.

"Listen, Cor, we have to take action, even if it turns out bad. It's our only option. When we hear the devil coming, we'll fly through the door the instant he starts to open it. It'll give us a couple seconds 'cause he won't expect us to do anything except be victims. Then we'll run like hell, away from the gator sounds and we'll split up so he won't get both of us. Run for all we're worth, run our brains out, okay, girl? Whoever makes it will do a movie on YouTube about the other one, to, you know, let people know that we lived, even though we're young."

Cornelia tugged on her hair and contemplated the Hail Mary plan. "Okay, Dexter, I like that idea. We sure as hell have nothing to lose."

"Agreed." He smudged dark streaks of soot beneath their eyes like NFL players or warriors in *Call of Duty*. He murmured, "We'll be empowered by the elements of long-dead swamp creatures hung from hooks."

"Possums and muskrats?"

"No, foxes and wolves and coyotes."

"Smart, survivors. How would you do a video about me if I don't make it out of here?" Cornelia asked.

Dexter paused for a moment. "I dunno, like collect pictures, interview people, play your favorite music—Jayden's music maybe."

"How would you do mine?" he asked as he lightly rubbed his swollen chin.

"Like this." Her eyes caught his and said it all.

Cornelia ran her long, thin, piano-player fingers up Dexter's thigh and explored with gentle determination. His aching, bruised face soon became inconsequential as he kissed her, deeply. It was a man and woman kiss, edged with desperation and ruined innocence.

"Let's not die virgins, okay?" She placed his hand on her breast.

Making love to Cornelia in their filthy rawness was the best thing that ever happened to him. They wanted life and were not going to let it escape easily.

Then the sound of the boat engine returned.

X

Otis and I rested against the trunk of a fallen pine. I heard Luther before I saw him. He was a big man, not capable of creeping cat-like though dense, coarse underbrush. Moved more like the Taurus he was.

"Luther, here, brother," I called softly. He emerged from the woods, dark as wet cypress bark, looking like a crazed Othello. We filled him in on what lay ahead.

Luther and I followed Otis to the strip of beach. For now, the gators had abandoned their gathering place. Luther did a quick flashlight scan of the area then extinguished the light. Half a man hung from an ancient live oak that expanded out over the creek. Tendons and shreds of bloody flesh swung eerily as he twisted in the wind like a Halloween specter. His eyes were open and his mouth was set in a scream. At least twenty empty ropes dangled from the branches above him like dark streamers. The Trotters had done this before.

A metallic stench from the blood pool beneath his corpse was pungent and made me gag. Even the rains couldn't wash all the body fluids and entrails away. Gnats and flies swarmed. A torn running shoe bobbed near the waterline along with what appeared to be a coil of small intestines.

"Doobius," Luther whispered.

"Gators, tons of them usually on this strip," Otis glanced about furtively. "Used to being fed here. This place has bad juju, really bad."

Luther scanned the shallows for any hint of gator. "Why would they do this to their own kid?"

"Maybe someone else did it. Someone pure evil, pure Marcus Trotter." My eyes met my brother's, connecting despite the darkness.

Luther nodded and rubbed his whiskered chin. "Is this area part of the fish camp?"

"Yessir. Straight on ahead's the cabin. This here's the edge of what Ellery claimed was his." The old man shivered, his face looked tired and drawn. "That grandkid of his, this Marcus—probably watchin' us right now. Trotters was a group that skittered around like goddamn spiders—then suddenly, your boat motor was missing or your bucket of shrimp disappeared." He squeezed my hand. "Or your son."

I took a deep, painful breath and peered into the murky wilderness. It surrounded us, pressing toward us like gray-green pincers. The pain was becoming unbearable.

"Otis," Luther said, breaking the numbing spell, "you've been amazing, we owe you so much. But I want you to stand down and stay right here for now. Let me check it out, see what's going on up ahead. You okay with that?"

"Whatever you say, Sheriff, but don't think that your sister here's gonna do the same. Had to pull ol' Marjorie on her to keep her from runnin' right on into God-only-knows-what."

Luther eyed me and frowned.

Shrugging, I conceded guilt.

"I realized that Otis was right and I settled down. Behaved myself, didn't I, Otis?" I had to stay settled down and controlled for the duration. I almost made a terrible mistake in planning to tear in there by myself and single-handedly murder Marcus Trotter. Wouldn't help Dexter to have his mother dead.

"Good job, Otis." Luther looked over at me. "I asked him to do whatever it took to keep you here until I showed up."

He winked at the old man.

I gave them both a disparaging look, but Otis might actually have saved my life.

Luther pretended to ignore me. "Otis, if backup shows from HQ, direct them toward the camp, okay?" He handed the old man a fresh bottle of water and a mini pecan pie wrapped in plastic. "Take some sustenance, too."

"You betcha, Sheriff." Otis gratefully accepted the food and drink.

"How is Mary?" I asked, almost afraid to hear the answer.

"Not sure. An ambo took her back to Savannah Memorial. She was in shock and passed out but they had the antivenin line going. All that's left is prayer."

It was clear he didn't want to talk about it further. I understood.

We left Otis on the trail, slowly opening the pie, hands slightly trembling. He was an inspiration but I knew that the awful situation and challenging hike had taken a hard toll.

X

I followed Luther in a long arc around the fish camp. We took our time and progressed with maximum stealth. He stopped when the three-building compound came into view. No lights were on. It appeared completely abandoned, had that feeling of desolation. My heart sank. All this hopefulness and anticipation—for nothing?

Luther could tell I was profoundly disappointed.

"Beazy," he whispered, "we're gonna stay put right here for a couple minutes, wait and watch. We're just getting started, okay? We'll find the sonofabitch."

I nodded in acknowledgment, anger growing hot in my belly. *Where the hell was my baby boy?* I bounced on my toes, unable to still myself, about to explode in every direction. It was an old habit from when I was a runner, waiting for the starting gun.

Luther put his hand on my shoulder, warning me to chill. "My SWAT team's heading into what we think's the Orpha Davis camp on the far side of the back river, about a half mile from here. The Afghans are likely working from her place. Has better access to the intercoastal."

"I'll bet Trotter pulled the logistics together for them."

"I think you're right. And, this is so bizarre—a woman, or someone with a woman's voice, called Hattie an hour or so ago and threatened her life for getting involved."

"What?" I stopped short, stunned.

"We've got a death certificate on Orpha from a decade ago, so we think it may be Marcus, or Muhammed, whatever he calls himself now."

"Like he might be having a psychotic break?"

"That, or maybe he's playin' us. Who knows," Luther

rubbed his eyes.

The adrenaline I'd been relying on to confront Trotter with was gone. I felt grim. "So, what do we do now?"

Darkness had completely enveloped the swamp. The only light was a pale-green, Luna-moth-like luminescence coming from the creek. A dinghy bobbed at the end of a crumbling dock. It was like we were in a scene from a horror movie, except this was real.

The heavy rain had abated for the moment. I mopped my eyes with a disintegrating tissue then stuffed it back into my pocket.

"Let's approach the cabin," Luther said. "You ready?"

I nodded and checked my Glock—O'Hanlon's Glock. "Show yourself Trotter, you piece of shit," I hissed. All I needed was one shot.

Suddenly, from behind us, a loud scream tore through the heavy, saturated air. I grabbed Luther's arm and froze.

"Came from over by Doobius. God, no," I said, in a desperate croaking whisper. "Sounds like it could be the girl."

"Shit, come on." Luther pulled his gun from its holster and held it close. I put a death grip on my weapon and followed right behind him.

When we got to the beach, Otis hung from a tree above the edge of the creek. Body limp, he appeared unconscious. Bright alligator eyes shone in the light of a dim camping lantern left in the sand.

Beyond Otis, Cornelia and Dexter hung from ropes tied beneath their armpits, their mouths were taped shut. Both twisted in panic, struggling to keep their feet high above the hungry, vice-like jaws. The movement brought the gators toward the activity like sharks to blood in the water.

I screamed, consumed with horror. My heart felt like it would rip from my chest.

The sound of a boat motor roared to life from near the Trotter cabin and droned off down the creek. Strains of a woman's voice sang "Moon River." Or was I imagining it? Was Trotter splitting into his alter ego, Orpha? Was that possible? All I knew was that he was escaping. God, how I wanted to tear after him and put a bullet through his skull.

A big gator bellowed and its neck shown dark and gold in the lantern light as its gullet undulated. Luther aimed at the rope above Dexter's head and took a shot. The gators scattered. The bullet hit the rope and cut it through. My baby boy dropped to the ground.

We rushed forward and dragged Dexter away from the creek. The gunshot had caused the gators to move back into the water, but not disappear. Eyes glowed like embers on the raindrop-pitted surface, waiting for another opportunity.

I ripped the tape from Dexter's bloody mouth and held onto him like I was dying. His body felt like stone.

"Get Cornelia down, now." His voice was weak and hardly discernible. "Please, get her down."

I could not let go but had to. I left my son on the low bluff above the sandy spit of alligator beach and turned to help the others. Luther and I were able to untangle Cornelia from the ropes. The girl sobbed when I embraced her. Her face was black with soot.

"You're going to be okay, honey. We're all going to be

okay. We'll call your parents as soon as we can."

She was crying too hard to speak. I helped her up the bank and sat her next to Dexter. She plunked down beside him oblivious to the mud and rain. They held and comforted each other in a way that right now, I couldn't.

I turned back to the beach. Shiny eyes blinked from the shallows. Otis was the toughest to get loose. Luther sawed at the rope with his knife. Unconscious, Otis was dead weight. Only a few hours ago he was safe at his marina, planning for a great meal of freshly caught trout and redfish. Now, because he'd agreed to help us, he tenuously clung to life. I tried to support the old man's weight until he finally came free of the ropes.

We carried Otis up near Cornelia and Dexter. He was barely breathing.

"Looks like a nasty blow to the head knocked him out," Luther said. He ran his finger along the deep gash then looked up at me with a worried frown.

"We have to get Doobius down from there. Now," Dexter said, insistent. His voice sounded much older than it had a few days ago.

"I'm sorry, Dexter," Luther said. He patted the boy's arm. "But he's evidence. We'll have to wait for the medical examiner."

"Then I'll wait with him." My son stood and walked stiffly toward the ruined body that twisted in the wind.

46

Flashlight beams probed the rainy forest. Swaths of illuminated plant life disappeared into blackness and reappeared again closer. I did not hear conversation only the squish-squish of boots navigating the soggy undergrowth toward us.

"Your backup?" I whispered to Luther, "or Trotter's thugs?"

He stood and drew his weapon, crouched down a few yards along the path. "Police. Who's there?" He demanded in his most authoritative voice.

"Sherriff Middleton?"

"Affirmative."

"Savannah-Chatham Metro, sir. Detective O'Hanlon sent us. Thought you might need reinforcements."

Luther slowly stood up. "She thought right."

Four men and a woman tramped into the clearing,

all wearing police rain ponchos. The woman was the SCMPD medical examiner who had processed Emad's duplex, Annabelle Borchard.

Only when I sighed with relief did I realize that I had been holding my breath.

"Sergeant Phil Sanderson," the leader said.

He was tall and thin with a beak-like nose.

"Sanderson, glad to see you and your team." Luther holstered his weapon.

Cursory introductions were made all around.

"So, how's O'Hanlon's doing?" Luther feigned only a professional interest.

"All swollen up like a goddamn water balloon, sir, but strong enough to tell us to get our sorry asses out here to help all y'all take care of business. Said your SWAT is full-out after a heroin cartel down the creek. And there're two kids that need to be found real fast."

I could see Luther's shoulders relax at the news of Mary, but that only lasted for a moment. "We have the kids," Luther said, motioning to Dexter and Cornelia.

Yes, we have them. "Thank you, Lord, thank you," I said softly with every fiber of humility and gratitude that I possessed.

"We also have a badly wounded older gentleman, Otis Suggs."

Annabelle moved quickly toward the victims, shrugged her backpack onto the path and began digging through the contents. She pulled out reflective emergency blankets and wrapped them around Dexter, Cornelia, and Otis, who was starting to revive. Immediately, she took their vitals and checked them over. I was so happy to see her.

"Don't get to work on live ones too often anymore," she said and smiled at us. Her fine dark face reminded me a bit of Momma's.

I bit my lip to hold off the tears. Live ones they were, thank heavens, live ones. I went over and rested my hands on Dexter and Cornelia's wet heads for a quick moment, to make sure they were real and not figments of my frantic imagination.

"Gotta get all these folks to an ambo. We'll take 'em by boat over to where Shellman SWAT's coming in." The ME squinted at her watch. She pulled a satellite phone from beneath her poncho and called headquarters back in Savannah. They were clearly a better-equipped department than their Shellman County cousins.

I moved closer to my son and Cornelia again. I wanted to throw my arms around them but they needed space. Dexter's hand in mine was like a small, feral animal. I trusted he would do what he needed to do to cope right now. I wouldn't push.

The rain, which had let up for maybe ten minutes, began again in a great gasping deluge. An eye-frying bolt of lightning hit a towering live oak tree across the creek. It exploded in a fiery display like a transformer erupting. A huge branch ripped off the main tree and crashed to the ground. The smell of combustion and electricity washed around us in hot waves. Raindrops sizzled and evaporated in puffs of steam.

"Holy Moses," Sanderson said. He was not looking at the split tree. "What the hell?"

"Evan Doobius, aka Emad Al Alequi," Luther said. "Gators chewed him up good."

"Sweet Jesus, that is gruesome," Annabelle said.

"And I've seen a lot of bad, bad stuff. Looks like you got yourselves a major crime scene here."

I stood up and began to pace. "We gotta find the piece of shit who did this. Murder, kidnapping, the attempted murder of these two kids and the old man, not to mention drug running."

"Any ID on the perp?" Sanderson asked, unable to tear his eyes from Doobius's gently swaying corpse.

Luther paused and then nodded, face flushed with anger. "Name's Marcus Trotter, also know recently as Muhammed Al-Sadr. He's a local but has decades with military and paramilitary groups. Knows his nasty real well."

I shuddered, then bent down to help the medical examiner with her heavy pack. "Let's get the tarp raised so Annabelle can keep Otis and the kids out of the rain."

"We'll clear the fish camp once more, then find this son of a bitch," Luther said.

The Savannah officers went to work. They set up lights, an equipment tent, and strung the tarp across several stout trees on the rise above the alligator beach, out of their lethal reach. Doobius was cut down. It was a grisly task. Afterward, one cop excused himself into the bushes and wretched. Freed, Doobius was placed into a body bag.

Cornelia touched his forehead, and left dots of soot, like ashes on Palm Sunday, before Annabelle zipped him up. Seemed like a holy anointment of sweetness after his brutal ending. The two youngsters huddled beneath the tarp with Otis and what was left of the young man who'd so respected Jayden, his music, and rising talent.

I paced, furiously. Jayden and Doobius—both

dead, Otis wounded, perhaps fatally, and the kids were probably harmed in ways I couldn't yet know. Marcus Trotter was responsible.

My hand went to my Glock. I found comfort in the ice-cold touch of the trigger.

※

When Muhammed puttered up to the dock at Orpha Davis's fish camp, he saw that Farouk, Grandfather Parsa, Sadam, and Sama were loading themselves into a fast-as-hell cigarette boat that could outrun anything, especially on a crap night like this one. Would be bumpy as shit, but that'd be half the fun. These water demons were harder than hell to detect by radar except on flat calm seas or at close range. It would be impossible for the Coasties to intercept the flyin' Afghanis.

Al Alequi's grunt workers had chugged off down Black Issue Creek in a rusting shrimp boat. Muhammed pulled his troller alongside the white-and-black Orca-esque power vessel. Farouk leaned over the side, the heavy features of his face trembling with anxiety.

"Come on. Get in. They're gonna be here any second. And where's Emad? We can't leave him."

"He left *you,* man." Muhammed sneered. "He and his little bitches have stepped out on their own. Get goin' now or you're gonna spend your life bein' water-boarded up the ass in a federal pen."

Trotter turned his dinghy away from the sleek vessel and headed up the creek.

"No. Muhammed," Farouk called out, voice barely audible beneath the storm, "What are you doing? Get in. Where are you going?"

"I have shit to take care of. We'll hook up later. Assalam Alaikum."

"But my son, Emad."

"Let him go, Farouk. You'll see him in goddamned heaven along with the seventy-two cock-sucking virgins. Go on, you motherfucker, go."

Sama at the wheel, the engines roared to life and the powerboat flew out of the swamp toward the Julienton River, the intercoastal waterway, and the Atlantic.

After the Afghans disappeared, Muhammed continued up the creek about a half mile until he came to another beach. Small, narrow, and hard to spot from the channel, it was like Gran'pappy's, but without the gator convention. He landed the old boat on the shore then crawled out onto the crunchy shell tabby. His boots were soaked. With a hard pull, the boat came across the sand and shells, then was docked, obscured in the underbrush, several yards from the shoreline.

He grabbed a black plastic garbage bag and threw it over his shoulder like a crazy black Santa Claus loaded with contraband for the good little girls and boys. He always put a little candy away in case a deal got all got fucked up. Never come to a party empty-handed, and he was going to party tonight, despite no China girl. Another time. For sure. Tonight was all for Bea and Orpha.

47

I kissed Dexter, gave Cornelia's shoulder a squeeze, then followed Luther, Sanderson, and the Metro PD uniforms toward the Trotter fish camp. My spirits, while high moments ago, now crashed precipitously again. Trotter had disappeared, but that man would not walk free. No way in holy hell.

Annabelle handed off the SAT phone to Luther. He called his team down river where they'd arrived at Orpha's, and ordered a Zodiac to pick up Dex, Cornelia, Otis, and me. After dropping us off, it would return for the others. News was that Orpha Davis's decrepit pole barn was empty, except for a poorly hidden cache of Heroine and fentanyl. To leave that much behind, they must have fled in a bat-shit hurry.

The black rubber boat finally pulled up to Trotter's dock. Luther and the uniforms helped us load our wounded, the first batch to be transported. Annabelle would continue working the crime scene with help from her Savannah colleagues. The craft held almost a foot of water as we headed down Trotter's shallow tidal waterway toward the broader and deeper Black Issue Creek. Rain was heavy again, and the wind gusted. Spanish moss danced like banshees, grabbed at our hair, and plied us with wet, weedy fingers as we passed beneath the skeletal cypress trees.

We huddled together for the ten-minute trip to Orpha Davis's fish camp. Klieg lights had been set up at the dock and further up at the dilapidated pole barn above the landing. At least a dozen of Luther's officers appeared to be moving about the area. Most wore slickers labeled SWAT in reflective yellow lettering. Several men came down to the dock to help us tie up, disembark, and find shelter in the barn. Inside the building, piles of heroin bricks were being pulled out of a subfloor storage space and loaded onto pallets.

Luther went to check in with his operatives.

Otis lay on a tarp on the dirt floor of the pole barn. I tried to help him sit up but he pushed me away and started to crawl toward the door.

"Otis, come on, stay put so you can rest. You've had a bad hit on the noggin," I tried to keep my voice friendly and light so as not to upset him further.

"Who the hell are you?" asked me. He looked around in a panic. He tried to stand up but was too dizzy to even make it to his knees.

"We're all friends here, Otis. I'm going to get you a cup of coffee to warm you up. That'll make you feel better." He looked at me, eyes almost closed, then collapsed back down onto the tarp, his energy spent. Cornelia knelt down next to him.

"We're all going to be okay now, Mr. Suggs," she said. Tears slowly dripped down her cheeks and streaked the soot on her face like the scratch marks I'd once left on Trotter's.

I trembled with cold and horrible recollections. I commanded myself to compartmentalize, immediately.

Otis and the kids each received a hot cup of caffeine. Somebody handed me a bag of hush puppies which I passed around. Dexter's jaw was too swollen to eat but he slowly sipped coffee, closed his eyes and seemed to savor the warm liquid. Otis refused food and started to nod off. I tried to keep him awake but he was out again.

Ten minutes later, the ambulance arrived along with a blue sedan.

"FBI," one of the SWAT team members said to his partner as they stacked the plastic-wrapped parcels of contraband at the far end of the barn. Cornelia, Dexter, and I sat across from the open sub-basement on a scarred wooden bench. I had never felt so utterly drained.

Two men in dark pants and nylon parkas emerged from the car and headed toward the dock. The paramedics unloaded a gurney and were pointed in our direction. A young woman in her early thirties, slender with several ear piercings and hair in a swingy brown ponytail, led the way along with her partner, a Hispanic man in his fifties with a short jar-head style haircut.

"Hi, I'm Ellis, and this is my partner, Cruz. Let's take a look at everyone and see how we're doing." Her eyes skimmed across the obvious patients.

I nodded. "I'm Bea, and this is Otis Suggs," I said.

"He's at least eighty years old, got hit on the head. Regained consciousness for about fifteen minutes, and now he's out again. My son, Dexter, seems to have been beaten up pretty badly and Cornelia—"

"Okay, we'll take it from here," Ellis said, cutting me off. I knew that my voice was rising and I was getting too upset for the comfort of the patients.

Cruz commenced working on Otis, and Ellis checked out the kids. She talked quietly with Dexter and Cornelia and they answered her questions in vivid detail, their voices detached and void of emotion.

I walked away for a moment, not able to handle what I was hearing. I counted the ways I could make Trotter suffer for all of this.

Cruz recruited one of the SWAT team members to help load Otis onto the gurney. As they strapped him in, the old man began to wake up again and struggle with his restraints. I came over, rested my hand on his arm and tried to talk to him. He calmed down a bit.

Ellis followed and laid her blue-gloved fingers against his cheek. "It's gonna to be okay, Mr. Suggs. I'll be with you all the way. That aw'right, sir? Gonna take good care of y'all."

Though her voice was sugary, I could recognize a steel magnolia when I saw one.

Otis nodded his head toward Ellis then seemed to lose consciousness again. The SWAT officer, a bulky guy who looked like an ex-Marine, along with EMS Cruz, carried the gurney over the soupy parking area and loaded Otis into the back of the ambulance. They returned with a backboard and helped Dexter onto it. My boy seemed to be getting worse in the half-hour since we'd left the fish camp. His face continued to swell, his eyes disappeared into deep purple bruises and his body was feverish. My heart had become a feverish, deep purple bruise as well.

Ellis hung back with Cornelia. "Miss Cornelia," I overheard her say quietly. She casually returned a stethoscope to her pocket. "Were you sexually assaulted?"

My throat tightened and tears began to well. Cornelia looked at me, and I could sense her discomfort. I stepped back but not out of hearing range.

She moved closer to Ellis. "The devil guy threatened it all the time, but he never did it. I had this weird feeling, you know, like maybe he couldn't really get it up."

He hadn't raped her. I sagged against the barn wall with relief. But it also hit me as a strange comment, given Trotter's former propensity for extreme sexual violence—that he might now be impotent. It had been two decades since I'd known the asshole.

I followed the SWAT guy and Cruz as they lifted my son's stretcher into the ambo. I hated letting go of Dexter's hand. Ellis followed with Cornelia. She held her arm and helped her navigate the deep puddles. After Cornelia and Ellis climbed into the back, the narrow bus was loaded almost to capacity.

"Are they all going to be okay?" I asked Ellis. My voice caught in my throat.

"Mr. Suggs is the worst." She seated Cornelia on the bench near Dexter and hooked her up to an IV.

"A concussion?"

"I'd say a probable skull fracture. Miss Cornelia's suffering from exposure and dehydration. Your son likely has several facial bones broken and damaged ribs but he's young and strong."

Cruz called for them to hurry up.

"You'd better jump in the front if you're going to come with us." Ellis slammed the back door of the ambo shut.

My cell phone buzzed. It was Kevin, surely desperate for news of our son.

I answered. "Kevin?" His voice was garbled.

"Wait a second," I called to Ellis. "I'm coming with you. It's Dexter's dad and my reception's breaking up."

I ran the few yards over to the pole barn where I had been able to raise two bars.

"Bea?"

"Kevin. We have him, he's okay."

He started to bawl hysterically.

"Ma'am, we need to be on our way," Cruz yelled and revved the engine.

"One sec, just one sec," I demanded. "Kevin, gotta go, we're heading to the hospital, I'll call you from there. He's safe now."

"Can I talk to him?" Kevin begged. I could hear him blow his nose. "This is all my fault."

I held my tongue. Blame served no purpose. "Kevin, you can talk to him soon. I gotta go..."

I turned back toward the ambulance. It was taking off without me.

Fishtailing in the unstable sand, grit flew into my face from beneath its wheels. I screamed for Cruz to stop. The thought of being parted from Dexter again was excruciating. I ran after the ambo but couldn't keep up.

I needed transpo immediately. I started to ransack anything with wheels. The radio cars were locked tight. I pulled open the door of the FBI's dark-blue Crown Vic, but no keys. I'd seen vehicles hotwired but I had no idea how to do it.

I dashed over to the two SWAT team members who'd returned to organizing the drug parcels. The Marine guy had disappeared. With little enthusiasm, a dark-haired officer with a soul patch and thinning hair said he'd find me a ride—if he could.

He *had* to. And where was Luther?

For fifteen miserable minutes that felt like hours, I sat in the cold barn with no sign of anyone who was willing to take me into Savannah. Rationally, I knew that processing a million-dollar haul of narcotics was going to take precedence over a worried mother's need for a ride back into town. I called my own mom and asked her to let the family, and the Changs, know that we had the kids safe. When I told them they were being transported by ambulance to the hospital, Momma and Honey were out the door and on their way over to Savannah Memorial before I could finish my report. I also asked her to call the Angler's Inn and let that community know about Otis.

Kevin called again asking for reassurance. He was finally in Atlanta waiting for the storm to clear so he could get a flight into Savannah Hilton Head Airport.

"He's on his way to Savannah Memorial, Kev. Momma and Aunt Honey will meet him there."

"I can't believe you're not with him—"

"Later, Kevin, we'll talk soon." I hung up. I had no patience for explanations.

Where the hell had my brother disappeared to? Highly agitated, I jogged back down to the creek's edge.

Despite the wind and rain, the Klieg lights held. I

could pretty much see where I was going. As I approached the landing, the Zodiac boat and a small Boston Whaler floated at the end of the dock. Luther was onboard along with the rest of the SWAT team and the two FBI agents.

"Where're you going?" I walked quickly onto the swaying pier and pulled my hood tight over my head. The rain beat down on my shoulders like nails pouring from a jar.

Luther leaned over the side of the Zodiac toward me. The Whaler had cast off and was heading down the creek away from the Orpha Davis fish camp.

"Trotter's boat's gone. The Afghanis got away, but he may still be in the area. We're gonna look for his boat. "And no, you can't come. This is police work. You stay dry in the barn until we can spring somebody to get you into Savannah. Patience, Bea."

"Fuck patience, Luther. I'm part of this, dammit."

"You're too vulnerable right now, Bea. Let us handle this. It's what we do." He looked away and nodded toward the driver.

"Are you playing the hysterical mother card with me? I can't believe you're leaving me. You're disgusting."

I was furious. He knew it and pushed off, refusing to argue. Both boats disappeared into the misty darkness. I stood on the end of the dock and watched my own long, dim shadow undulate in their wakes.

Seething, I returned to the barn and downed another cup of coffee and several hush puppies that had been rolled in cinnamon and sugar. What I wouldn't give for a few shots of good whiskey, or even crap whiskey. I could be sitting here for hours while Marcus Trotter eluded the cops and the Fibbies.

A text came in from a phone that indicated Cruz the paramedic was the caller.

Was Dexter's condition deteriorating? I tried not to panic.

"It's Bea," I said.

"Mom?" His voice sounded far away.

"Dex? Are you—?"

"I'm okay. We had to leave, couldn't wait for you. Mr. Suggs is crashing."

"Oh, my God." He should be snug in his rocking chair at the marina instead of battling for his life. I wiped away tears.

"Listen, Mom—"

"Oh, please, God, save Otis. And Gran and Aunt Honey will meet y'all at the hospital. They're on their way."

"Mom, listen to me." His voice was strident. I snapped out of my teary moment. "The evil guy, Muhammed—he said he was going to kill every Middleton until he got to you. He's gonna do it too. Tell Uncle Luther, right away, please."

My head spun. I had to refocus, immediately.

"Okay, baby, I'll let him know. See you real soon. Dex—" He clicked off before I could tell him I was praying hard for everyone. Well, almost everyone.

Marcus Trotter was somewhere close by. And he wanted me.

I could feel his demonic energy drawing me toward him like matter into a black hole. My patience was gone. I couldn't sit still or passively stand by any longer. Luther could cruise up and down the creeks, but Trotter would only stop with me. *I* was what he wanted. It was between *us*.

I made my way to the landing again. The rain had finally stopped. Roiling cumulus clouds began to break up. The sound of swamp creatures began to overtake the silence in the moments after the rain ended. Cries of night birds, croaks, screeches, and the incessant buzzing of cicadas rose. They made the treetops sing with the energy of high tension wires.

Then I saw it. Upside down in the darkness beyond the dock was a kayak labeled Shellman County Fast Water Rescue. I'd sea-kayaked in Baja, Mexico, and around the Channel Islands off of Ventura County plenty of times. A small kayak like this was highly maneuverable and quiet as a drop of rain. I could check out the shoreline, get in closer than Luther's rig could—look for signs the others could not see, and then report back.

I texted Luther: *I'm taking the kayak. Will let you know if I see anything—will be careful. Can't sit any longer*.

Immediately a one-word response came back. *No*.

I typed in *YES*, hit Send then turned off the ringtone. Stuffed the phone in my pocket. I could see the face light up but I ignored it.

Mist rose from the water like white smoke. I turned the craft over and slid it into the creek.

48

"Are you expecting her soon, sonny?" Orpha asked, in her sing-song voice.

Marcus ignored her. He had removed his wet clothing and rubbed his body with pig fat he'd bought from the Wild Hog. Gran'pap always did the lard before a big hunt, said it was warrior tradition in Africa. It was one of the few things 'pap had ever told him that he thought might be true.

The tattoos etched onto the skin of Marcus's muscular chest and arms glowed in the light of a kerosene lantern. Amid a tangle of red-eyed gators, Old Tom crawled down his spine, a bloody arm clenched in his teeth. The tats had been created by a true artist. The reptiles seemed to slither and writhe as he moved.

Glass votives with pictures of Jesus and Mary illuminated an assortment of animal hides that lay across the old table his mother had brought into the summer house all those years ago. This round, bug-infested gazebo-like place with rotting screens was still Marcus's favorite hiding place. When Gran'pappy was really loaded, he'd pass out before he got this far. Orpha, however, could always find him. This was her favorite hidey-hole, too.

The old woman stood across from her stepson. Long gray hair, still pretty, was like the Spanish moss on the live oak that grew over Gran'pappy's beach. She'd been nailed to the wall with crucifixion-like spikes. Her skin had long ago moldered away and her skeletal head smiled with the same sick, gap-toothed, meth-addled smile of her youth. Her eyeballs, brown and yellowed, along with her privates, were still in the bottle of formaldehyde on the window sill.

"Come here, sonny. Wanna touch this? You always liked to."

"Shut the fuck up, Orpha," Marcus said. He pulled on a pair of dry camo pants and slipped his feet into moccasins. His arms and chest remained naked, a long gray wig covered his close-cropped hair and an Afghani tribal scarf wrapped around his neck. "You ain't got nothin' I wanna touch anymore. I'm waiting for her."

"For *her?* You waitin' for the bitch who done fucked you up?"

"You da bitch tha' done fucked me up. But yeah, she the one, ol' lady. Should be here real soon." Marcus opened a shiny aluminum travel case containing a matte-black Colt .45 and a selection of hunting and combat knives lined up in a lethal row on a custom-molded foam insert.

Personal and face-to-face, his favorite weapons were knives. The Indonesian karambit, with its sexy curved blade, was hot as shit. He also had a lovely French Nimravus fixed blade, a utilitarian Blackhawk combat folder, and many others. Orpha had enjoyed the Indonesian piece. Sliced like a scalpel, ripped like tissue paper. Perhaps Beatrice would like this instrument as well. So many choices—where would he begin?

For their first meeting, Marcus decided to exchange his scarf for a jade-handled neck knife. He'd seen her brother and his troops pull away. She'd be smart enough to notice the kayak and angry enough to think she could stalk him when so many others failed. His ass was so tight under their noses that he felt aroused.

"Sonny, bring wine and flowers, won'tcha?" Orpha called to him. "Funeral flowers, sonny, and blood wine, oh yes, indeed."

Marcus pulled a small plastic container of coke from the black garbage bag and slit the top with one deft flick of steel. He paused for a moment to admire the jade handle, then scooped powder onto the blade and studied it, mesmerized. He held it beneath his nose. With a hard sniff, the shit disappeared up his flared nostrils.

Marcus gasped and shook his head violently. His eyes bugged open, and he stretched his neck. Vertebrae popped and crackled, and his skin began to buzz. On his way out of the screenless screen door, Orpha called to him.

"Blood wine, baby, lip-smackin' fine."

He moved through the dripping undergrowth toward the summer camp beach—that's what his brothers had always called it. He could hear the faint dip and pull, dip and pull of her paddle moving the kayak along the placid creek. She'd be looking hard; would be sure to see the marks where he pulled up his boat. She'd follow.

Marcus smiled and thought about the only nursery rhyme he'd ever known. It was Orpha's favorite.

Will you walk into my parlor? said the Spider to the Fly,
　'Tis the prettiest little parlor that ever you did spy;
　Dip, pull, drip, drip, dip, pull—stop. Ah yes, at last.
　She'd spotted the parlor. Come, little fly.

𝕏

I drifted silently as a leaf toward the narrow strip of beach a quarter mile or so down from the pole barn dock. The surface was smooth and pristine from the rain, except for a deep groove where it appeared a boat had been pulled across the sand. Footprints scuffed the ground. Luther would never have spotted this from the Zodiac or the Whaler.

The tide was coming in toward me, filling the creek. The spit of land would be underwater in ten minutes. My shoulders burned from hard paddling against the current. I made my way to the edge of the beach and dug my paddle into the sand to keep from being pushed back downstream. I pulled out my camera and snapped a photo which I texted to Luther.

I listened intently and concentrated my senses but heard only the sound of shells grating gently beneath my little craft, and the lapping of water against the molded plastic hull. With a careful movement, I crawled out of the kayak and lugged it onto the ribbon of beach.

Mosquitoes descended and began to bite. They tried to drive me back onto the river. I swatted them away but it was a losing battle. I followed the groove and drag marks in the sand up to the edge of a low embankment. I parted the coarse salt grass—would his boat be there?

Bingo.

My heart hammered in my chest.

I peered carefully around—no sign of life. I took out my phone to snap another image for Luther, then hit send.

At that same moment, I noticed that not only were there footprints disappearing into the woods, but also prints returning to the beach toward the live oak trees that sat along the creek like a congregation of ghostly Druids.

Before I could react, Trotter dropped onto me from above. Like a great wolf spider, pouncing and preparing to drag me off to his burrow, his hand was over my mouth before I could scream.

I flashed on the bodies falling from the ropes at the alligator beach. A cold blast of terror pounded through my veins. Knocking me off my feet with a vicious kick, he pushed my face down deep into the razor-edged vegetation. His weight on my back was crushing. I couldn't see him behind me, but I felt a blade against my neck—then a stinging slice and the first warm, coppery scent of blood.

My mind reeled back to when he did this to me as a teenager. Wild panic almost paralyzed me. There would be no Rio Deakins to rescue me. However this played out, I decided I would *not* be a victim this time.

"Nice job, sonny, got this one on the hook. Just like

ol' times—dancin' and a prancin' tonight, yessiree."

I was stunned by the bizarre, high-pitched voice. Sounded like a woman, but I knew it was him. Marcus pressed his rock-hard body against mine and secured me around the chest with one arm and pricked my throat again with the knife.

"One sound, and it'll be your last."

I knew Trotter had no intention of taking me easily with the slice of a blade. He had other plans.

I could feel his hot, oily skin and smell the stench of putrid meat. I flashed again on the afternoon he raped and tried to kill me at Fugitive Point. I felt the horror, and then the fury. I seized the fury and focused. It was my only chance.

He yanked the Glock from my waistband and tucked it away. Next, he took my cell phone and tossed it into the creek. Then he pushed me down again, my neck twisted at an agonizing angle. My skull was ready to snap off at its stem.

"Move, and it'll only hurt worse, Beatrice." He drove my head into a pile of sharp shells again and ground his boot heel against my ear as if crushing an insect. My face was being de-skinned by a cheese grater of jagged mollusk remains.

I didn't move. My mouth was full of grit, my eyes squeezed shut and my face burned. He stepped away and pulled my kayak into the woods.

"Get the fuck up," he growled, in his own voice.

Trotter pulled me to my feet. I scrambled, spitting sand, and wiped my eyes with my sleeve. The scratch marks I must have made on his chin so many years ago shone subtle silver. He touched the spot as if remembering. Then he smiled with an evil, tooth-gritting leer.

"Beatrice fucking Middleton. I've waited for you all my life."

I couldn't show him the terror I was feeling. "Hello, Marcus. It's been a while." That calm acknowledgment spoke volumes. Beneath my carefully dispassionate voice, I was ready to stab him through the heart.

He frowned and shoved me again, this time away from the creek. Awkwardly, I stumbled forward into the blackness. He continued to punch and kick me along an almost nonexistent path to wherever we were going.

In minutes we came upon a crumbling screen house. The soft light from inside seemed cruelly hospitable.

With my gun in his hand, Marcus held the door open and motioned for me to enter. "Welcome to summer camp," he said, sounding like the parody of a friendly counselor.

Counselor from hell.

His affect was a sick mix of courtesy and murderous intent. I stepped into the room and assessed it, scanning for tools I could use against him. After all, I was a reporter with an eye for detail. The details might save me.

Pushed against a wall was a battered wooden dining table with two chairs. On the table was a pile of small animal skins, like from otters and swamp rats. An old-fashioned crystal kerosene lamp sat on a moldy lace doily. Glowering, religious-type votive candles flickered dimly, and then there was a Styrofoam Wild Hog Barbeque to-go box filled with nasty-smelling pinkish glop. Next to it rested a high-tech aluminum case. Only God and Marcus knew what was inside. Something very professional, and very lethal. I stemmed an involuntary shudder.

White powder from a baggie spilled onto the floor. Several bricks of heroin were stacked on a chair. Beneath the table, I spotted an array of ropes and wires and two hammers. A baggie filled with long nails sat next to a red five-gallon gasoline can. That was all I could see in the shadows, but it was more than enough to massively amp up my fear-meter. My knees went watery. What you could do to a person with that simple shit was something I didn't want to let myself think about.

"How long do I have to wait to be introduced to this lovely young thing?" Marcus's high-pitched voice asked.

I turned and finally got a look at him. His eyes gleamed; his oily dark face was partly shrouded by a wig of long gray hair that hung to his waist. His body was ripped, covered with alligator tats and Cyrillic lettering. He looked the complete measure of Special Ops training, mercenary ruthlessness, and stone-cold insanity.

"This ho the one that's gonna pay?" the woman's voice asked.

I followed Marcus's wild gaze to the dark, far corner of the room, and there she was. Right then I knew it was Orpha Davis—skeletal, horrible, and nailed to the wall. Her hand bones lay on the floor; the fingers were loaded with rings. One for every conquest? I gagged. Orpha laughed again. His, or her cackle, was terrifying—part shriek, part hysteria, all crazy.

I had to keep talking, to slow him down. He twitched and picked at himself like he was under attack from red ants.

"So, this here is Orpha Davis? Your stepmother?

Your lover?"

"You gonna be next to her soon," Marcus said. He pushed me against a center pole that held up the roof then leaned over to grab a chair and bindings. I was not going to allow myself to be helpless, not this time. *Not ever again.*

With that mantra, I turned and bolted for the door—hit it so hard it wrenched off its hinges. I ran as fast as my former basketball-player legs would take me. I visualized the kayak ready to float me away. I could see a lightness begin to emerge ahead as the beach clearing and the creek drew closer. Please God, almost there. Just ten more yards.

Then, the earth pulled out from under me and I was flat on my face, again. Nose half buried in the ground, I gasped to breathe and sucked in the taste of sulfurous pluff mud and salt.

Marcus grabbed me by the hair, yanked me to my feet and dragged me, stumbling and falling, back down the path to the summer camp from hell. I screamed as loud as I could until he hit me in the mouth. Then I choked on my own blood. The pain was dizzying but I would not give in.

I managed to twist away from him, half of my hair still in his fist. I was no match for him, physically, but I got off a good kick to the groin. I crawled away toward the beach, struggling to stand up and run. He got me by the foot. I shrugged out of my shoe, but he grabbed my ankle then thrust himself onto my back.

"Lively little bitch, ain't she, sonny?" the Orpha voice said. "Ol' Pappy Ellery would've had a ball with this one."

"I'll have a ball for all of us," Marcus whispered in

what almost sounded like a third voice. Gran'pappy? Sweet Jesus.

Marcus was practically choking me to death as he pulled me by the back of my sweatshirt along the path. Then threw me into the gazebo, as if tossing a Frisbee. I crashed to the floor and slid under the table. Landing on the ropes and wires and knocking over the gas can, I grabbed it, wrenched open the top, and threw the can at Marcus. The contents splashed over him and soaked his face and long, gray Orpha hair. Gas fumes filled the air.

I scrambled to the table top and snatched the kerosene lamp. He let out a fierce howl and lunged at me—a coal black panther with piercing yellow-green eyes. I hurled it at him with everything I had. Flames ignited with a terrible whoosh.

Trotter was on fire. He rolled on the floor and struggled to rip the gray wig off his head. My Glock skittered across the floor and I flew on top of it. As Trotter came after me, the wig caught around his neck and caught fire.

Kerosene splashed and the rotting termite-infested frame of the screen house ignited. I managed to hold onto the Glock and pulled the trigger, aiming the best I could. The smoke was dense and I couldn't tell if I'd hit him or not.

I didn't see the chair coming at me until it was too late. The universe shattered. As I shook my head and tried to clear my vision, Trotter ran out the door and toward the creek. I crawled after him. The rafters were beginning to fall around me. That sonofabitch, I would not let him jump into the creek and float away to freedom. I picked myself up and bolted for the door.

I could hear him thrashing down the trail in front of me. Fire flickered, and I saw Trotter rolling on the ground, attempting to put out the flames that had burned through his pants. Whatever he'd lathered on his skin appeared to be sizzling. He saw me coming and ran toward the water. "I'll be back for you, bitch," he screamed.

I fired again but he didn't slow down. My head reeled from being hit by the chair, and I could barely tell up from down, but I would not stop.

49

"What's that?" Luther demanded. He tilted an ear downriver from where they'd launched toward Orpha's fish camp. His brows drew together in concentration. The crew went quiet. There it was again. A scream? Or a bird call?

Luther checked his beeping cell and saw the photo Bea had sent of the sandy inlet with the pull marks and boot prints.

"We're turning around." He made a circular motion with his finger and then signaled over at the Whaler with a flashlight. The boats both reversed course. They reduced their speed to a slow troll and listened. They didn't hear the sound again.

"Came from this side of the creek." Luther peered into the darkness along the edge of the water.

They swept the shore with strong flashlight beams.

The tide was coming in fast, and Black Issue Creek was filling up. Overhanging branches and downed trees, dense cordgrass, sandbars, and shell colonies shown in the probing light. Imprints on the sand would soon disappear. Evidence would be washed away.

The Zodiac glided as close to the creek's edge as it could without hanging up. With the rain clearing, currents of cooler air freshened the atmosphere, soft edges sharpened. "What's that?" Luther's voice was low. He aimed his light onto the shore. "Look at that beach—I see some disruption. Those footprints?"

"Maybe animal tracks?" Sanderson squinted. He shook his Maglite. The batteries were fading. It brightened for a moment then dimmed again.

Luther pointed. "What's that?" Agitation tightened his chest. A kayak paddle bobbed at the shoreline. "She took the Fast Water Rescue kayak. Oh, shit."

Quietly, the Zodiac pulled up to the shore. Luther climbed out and examined the prints in the sand. The Whaler stopped midstream and held its position against the tide.

"Definitely footprints. Recent," he said. "Looks like the photo she sent."

The others climbed out to assist. The Whaler would stand by.

"Sheriff," one of the men called. "There's a dinghy and our kayak over there in the brush."

Luther followed the pull marks in the sand up to the two boats. His throat tightened.

Sanderson sniffed the wind. "I smell something burning. Wood, and maybe, I dunno, something nasty."

Fifty yards down from where they were standing, a

man careened out of the darkness glowing like a nearly burned out Fourth of July sparkler. He threw himself into the creek. Sparks followed him into the water and extinguished.

Luther directed the spotlight in his direction. "Fucking Trotter?" He ran along the narrow waterline then stopped dead. An ominous groan sounded, like the trumpeting of an elephant. Sanderson, right behind Lucas, shined his dimming light toward the center of the channel. Half-dollar-sized eyes reflected back at him. Sanderson aimed his shotgun, but in the chaos of flailing limbs and roiling water, man could not be distinguished from beast. Then all was quiet. Old Tom and Marcus Trotter disappeared.

"Luther," Bea screamed from somewhere back in the darkness.

The scent of fire became stronger and soon the flames danced in the distance, painting the swamp with eerie licks of bloody light. The sound of crackling and collapsing timbers grew louder.

"Beatrice."

Luther started to run.

The small screened-in cabin was engulfed. The roof groaned and dropped several feet, about to give way completely. A shower of sparks rose into the air. The men surrounded the structure and peered inside, trying to see through the smoke, looking for movement.

Nothing.

Luther blasted through the open door. Heat singed his face and his eyebrows sizzled. On the wall, a laughing skull looked down on it him.

"Bea's here, she's alive," Sanderson yelled from

outside. "Get the hell outta there."

Luther turned and ran; the screen house imploding in his wake.

50

A week later, we sat around Momma's dining room table. It smelled of lemon polish and delicious food, not fire, blood, and salt marsh. Sometimes I think I'll never get that stench out of my mind, or that final image of Trotter's boot bobbing in the stream, still attached to part of his leg.

Holding hands in prayer, we thanked God for being alive. It was truly a miracle that we were all here, all together around this table. Dexter, Aunts Freddie May, Hattie, and Honey, Skinny Rufus, Mary O'Hanlon, Luther, Otis Suggs, Rio and his fiancée, Lindsay, and my ex, Kevin, a head taller than anyone else. Otis sat adoringly next to him. We'd invited Cornelia and the Changs, but they had their own family time going at their restaurant on Tybee.

Luther reported the disappointing news that the

Afghans had escaped. Only three of the probably twenty fishing and shrimp boats packed with drugs had been apprehended by the Coast Guard. None of the crew members knew a thing besides their own itinerary. Information had been kept close by the Afghanis.

Talk of crime and trauma was bringing us all down. As the blueberry cornbread came around, I decided it was a good time to tell the family about my new job. We needed to keep our eyes looking forward.

"Hey everyone, I have an announcement. I finally got a chance to talk with CNN yesterday."

"And?" Momma asked.

Bright, questioning eyes all turned my way. Kevin was the only one who wouldn't give up focusing on the collard greens and sweet potato fries.

"And, I've accepted their job offer. I'll be doing special West Coast reports for CNN. I start in ten days. Working out of the Hollywood office, and from home when I want to."

"Congratulations, Bea," Lindsay said. "I knew we'd be colleagues again. It's a nice bunch out there."

"Way to go, Sis," Luther said.

All joined in the congratulations and well wishes.

"I'm so excited, and relieved to be employed." I was actually all that, plus pretty nervous. There was a piece of me that wanted to move on to something different, but to where or what, I had no clue yet.

"What do you think of that, young man?" Aunt Hattie passed the fried chicken to Dexter. He'd been very quiet.

"That's great, mom," he said. "CNN's cool."

"Cool" was a pretty tepid remark from him. I thought he'd be happy, but he sounded something else. Something else not good. He'd barely strung two sentences together since his police deposition. Stayed in his room playing on his iPad and texting Cornelia.

"But I've been thinking," he said. He randomly picked at the food on his plate, not eating any of it. "I don't know if I want to go back to southern California."

I dropped my fork with a clatter. "What do you mean?"

"I thought maybe I'd stay with Gran and Aunt Honey and go to Arts Academy High School like Jayden did. They have a good film program."

"Santa Monica High has a great film program," I said, trying not to panic. I addressed the family with urgent enthusiasm. "My friend and colleague, Lucy Vega, teaches in it. She's amazing." Then back to Dexter. "You always say how much you've learned from her, Dex."

He nodded and poked at his food.

Two minutes ago, I'd sensed such a tight family bond, now I felt like it was falling apart. "You'll be fine once you get home, Dexter, back with all your friends. You love SaMo High School. And you'll miss your sister."

"And what about me?" Kevin said, never one to tolerate long being left out of the spotlight. "You'll miss me, too."

"I love Alyssa, and I love you Mom, and Dad—you are both amazing. But I'm not the same person anymore."

Tears sprung to my eyes and I pushed my plate away. "Okay, we'll talk about this later." I wished that Trotter could burn a thousand excruciating deaths. One sure as hell was not enough. He was responsible for this whole web of pain. He was dead but he'd never let go. Honey's son was gone, my daughter Alyssa, and traumatized

Dexter were both leaving me, my mother could have another heart attack and die, Rio was marrying another woman. I couldn't stand it.

Feebly, I excused myself and ran from the dinner table. Up in the guest room, I threw myself on the bed and sobbed.

A half hour passed and I heard footsteps on the stairs. Rio stuck his head into the room. As if I didn't need another layer of confusion and frustration to parade through the door. I was already feeling guilty and ashamed enough for leaving a dinner table full of friends and relatives.

"Go away. I don't need you trying to rescue me again or save me from myself. Please, Rio, leave me alone."

"Listen, Bea—Lindsay and I are heading back to Atlanta tonight."

"Have a real good trip." I pulled a pillow over my head. How mature.

"Hey, I thought I'd ask if we could bring Dexter along with us for a couple days. He seems open to it. I have a PTSD group meeting tomorrow night that he might find interesting. And it would give him a chance to see Emory. He might want to think about it for his college list."

"PTSD," was all I heard.

Of course, why hadn't it been apparent to me? Maybe Rio could help guide Dexter. I certainly didn't seem to be able to touch him. As a mom, I was in over my head, and too emotionally enmeshed to know how to proceed. I took a deep breath. I had to let go and trust the universe to lead me. But all I really wanted to do was hold my baby boy in my arms and keep him safe from everything. Unfortunately, it was too late for that. The more I wanted my son to be the same old Dexter, the farther he pulled away.

"Yes, okay, that might be a good idea, if he wants to go."

I sat up on the edge of my bed and wiped my face with the pillowcase. Rio sat down next to me, but not too close.

"I think he does want to come with us. It would be good, give him space to think things through a little more before he makes any big decisions."

I nodded.

"Pecan pie's being served. Why don't you come back down? You didn't want the healthy dinner stuff anyway now, did ya?"

I didn't respond. We don't have healthy dinner stuff in south Georgia.

"Hey, we're alive, Bea. This will all work out. What matters is that we're upright and breathing and back in the fray, right? All the rest will unfold."

I looked up at him, pressed my hands to my forehead and tried to soothe my aching brain. "I'm sorry. You are completely right."

"Nothing to be sorry about," he said. "You'll get through this. We've all been lost in the wilderness, Beazley."

I stood up and wiped my eyes again, blew my runny nose. "You know how much I hate it when you call me that?"

He smiled.

I followed him down the stairs and was met by Dexter who greeted me with a big hug, the first one since we'd found him. And the rest of the family, still in their seats, passed around pecan pie with big dollops of ice cream.

The Burn Patient

1

Sister Catherine Lucia Ruiz was a healer. As the only curandera in a remote corner of the central Mexican highlands of Guerrero, it was a challenging place for a woman of integrity and faith to ply her trade. She chose not to question but to trust in Him. All were God's children and deserving of compassion. And every day there was an opportunity to bring a sinner back to the Father. She trusted that the Lord had placed her in the center of the world's black tar heroin production region for this reason.

Tall and slim, she was strong and sinewy with thick silver hair woven into a braid that hung down her back. Sister's hands were as elegant as a ballerina's despite being well used, and her face held a mature beauty that had only been enhanced by age and experience. Such finely chiseled features and intelligent brown eyes would turn heads even now as she closed in on seventy.

She stirred a fragrant eucalyptus-tinged brew on her wood stove, then removed the pot from the fire and placed it next to her pump sink to cool. As she did often, Catherine Lucia leaned back against the counter and smiled. She never tired of admiring her home and medical clinic, it was a dream come true. In exchange for her services, men from the village and surrounding area had helped her build this clínica many years ago. The thick, white-washed stucco walls kept her cool in the summer and warm in the winter. Floor to ceiling built-in shelving overflowed with periodicals and books on science, medicine, herbology, religion, and she loved fiction. A Dorothy Sayers novel lay open on the kitchen table next to an empty coffee mug.

Sister Catherine Lucia also had a small outbuilding where she boarded her horse and kept goats and chickens. Completely self-sufficient, she had a well for water, a forest of wood for her stove, and a propane generator fueling the small refrigerator that preserved her medicinal preparations. She spent much of her time on the big porch that overlooked her garden. In the rafters above hung drying flowers and herbs that were the source of many remedies. Big clay pots of aloe vera sat on either side of the steps. A privy hid behind century plants that sprouted 10-foot stalks blazing like pale yellow torches in the January sun. The chickens liked to roost beneath the plant's spiny fronds, safe from predators.

Tired from overseeing three challenging childbirths in less than a week, she pushed strands of lanky hair from her face. And then there was the young man who had been bitten by rattlesnakes and almost died, and then there was the chance discovery that Lucy Ruiz, a newswoman from Los Angeles working on a documentary team in a nearby village, was likely her niece. Sister's heart reached out to Lucy, but she'd made a decision many decades ago to be a ghost. She'd carved out a life, a rewarding one. Placid at times, frenetic at others. She was shaken by this chance discovery. Or was the Lord opening a door on another path?

Her head began to ache. She must get back to the work. There, she was confident and at peace.

Sister was grinding dried herbs with a mortar and pestle when she heard approaching footsteps crunch through the leaves and gravel on her path. The hens clucked and the horse nickered at the approach. Two gray tabby cats, curled on the rug near her feet, raised their heads and twitched their ears like tiny satellite dishes.

She stepped down from the porch and wiped her hands with a linen towel as four officers from the Policía Agricultura de Guerrera Alta, known as PAGA, carried a man on a canvas stretcher up the steep trail. Her home-clinic was over two miles from anything that could be called a road.

Now it appeared that Luis Alvarez and his drug cartel had another disaster for her to heal. Why couldn't they transport their casualties to the hospital in Tingo Tia? She would refuse no one, but these men were clearly not doing God's work. She would always, however, try to bring them to the Lord while they were in her purview. Crossing herself, Sister Catherine Lucia closed her eyes for a moment and prayed for God's support and blessing upon her efforts.

"Buenos días, Captain Alonzo. What challenge do you bring me today?" Sister stuffed the cloth she was holding into one of the big pockets in her apron. The men hauled the stretcher up the steps.

"Good day to you, Sister," Alonzo said, panting. He was in his mid-twenties and serious-looking, with a wispy goatee. "We have a burn victim. Male, mid-thirties, healthy, until this happened." The men bent down like pall bearers and placed the stretcher on the porch.

One of Alonzo's team pulled out a cigarette. Sister shot him an intimidating look of disapproval. She would not have nicotine smoke contaminating her herbs. He returned it to his pocket and mumbled an apology.

The Burn Patient is available April 1, 2020

About the Author

Sue Hinkin is a former college administrator, television news photographer, and NBC-TV art department staffer. With a B.A. from St. Olaf College, she completed graduate work at the University of Michigan and was a Cinematography Fellow at the American Film Institute. A long-time L.A. resident, she now lives with her family in Littleton, Colorado.

Her first novel in the Vega & Middleton mystery series is *Deadly Focus*. *Low Country Blood* is her second novel. *The Burn Patient* is forthcoming in 2020.